TIME'S REACH

TIME'S REACH

A NOVEL

by

Rachel Wyatt

OOLICHAN BOOKS

LANTZVILLE, BRITISH COLUMBIA, CANADA

2003

National Library of Canada Cataloguing in Publication Data

Wyatt, Rachel, 1929-

Time's reach / Rachel Wyatt.

ISBN 0-88982-205-0

I. Title.

PS8595.Y3T45 2003 C813'.54 C2003-906753-X

The Canada Council | Le Conseil des Arts
for the Arts | du Canada

We gratefully acknowledge the support of the Canada Council for the Arts for our publishing program.

BRITISH
COLUMBIA
ARTS COUNCIL
Supported by the Province of British Columbia

Grateful acknowledgement is also made to the BC Ministry of Tourism, Small Business and Culture for their financial support.

We acknowledge the financial support of the Government of Canada through the Book Publishing Industry Development Program for our publishing activities.

Cover photograph by Linda Martin.

Published by
Oolichan Books
P.O. Box 10, Lantzville
British Columbia, Canada
V0R 2H0
Printed in Canada

For Alan

and

In memory of my father, K.J.R.Arnold (1900 - 1981)

ACKNOWLEDGEMENTS

I am very grateful indeed to all the people at Oolichan Books, Ron Smith, Hiro Boga, Linda Martin and Jay Connolly, for their encouragement, careful editing and attention to detail.

My thanks too to Louise Young who kept insisting that I write this story.

PART 1

Time Difference

For he was always glad to mow the grass,
Pour liquids from large bottles into small,
Or look at clouds through bits of coloured glass.

"The Hero," W.H. Auden

He was an old man walking along a railway platform humming to himself. He was a young man strolling in an alpine valley singing, *Röslein, Röslein, Röslein Red, Let me climb into your bed.* Fragments of songs, patched with words of his own, skittered through his mind all the time these days. Complete lyrics he'd known for years and years had deserted and left him with a dustbin full of odd lines that made no sense. Only the tunes remained clear. *Röslein, Röslein rot.*

'Herr Rosenbaum isn't with us any more.' That was the 1933 trip. Or was it '34? At any rate it was when the whispering had begun and with it a sinister pantomime sense of look-behind-you. And it was forty years ago. Now he was an old man limping along a railway platform and if he kept on singing to himself people would assume he was crazy. Not that there was a soul about. The lamps were flickering as though they weren't sure whether it was dark enough to justify light and there was a rope round the benches outside the waiting room to show they were newly painted. There was no comfort here. He leaned against the grimy brick wall for support. She'd been after him to get a new raincoat. Perhaps he'd buy one next week to look smart when they went out with Maggie. There'd be the usual argument. *Why does it always have to be beige?* Because I like it! *Get something to last, Bob.* Why?

The café was closed but the smell of baking and stale coffee hung in the air like a threat. Not much had changed in a hundred years except that the lamps had been converted from gas to electricity. Dirt from the days of steam still blackened the stone walls and he felt like an old man. Trains still ran to the coast, through Hellifield and Bell Busk, to the bright lights and loud music and crowds of Morecambe. Magic names for the kids years ago. They'd stand by the carriage window to see who could catch the first sight of the snaking metal loops of the roller coaster. Maggie chewing her fingers, David jiggling up and down and laughing, both of them eager for the thrill of being scared half to death. And the thrill of scaring their parents half to death. Ice cream, the sea air, the tide going out almost out of sight and leaving that expanse of sand, all shifted in his memory. Can we go on the pier, Dad? Can we ride on the donkeys? The Cyclone, little cars speeding up and down what looked like railway tracks thrown up by an earthquake—perhaps the inventor had seen such a thing—was left till last. And then in a crowded carriage on ordinary straight tracks, the journey home. Darkness, sleepy children, Ovaltine, bed.

Maggie could have caught an earlier train and arrived in daylight but had chosen not to, so here he was in this dim light alone, a prey for hooligans. He took a tighter grip on his stick. On his way out of the house, the woman next door, misnamed Valerie—Valerie was a name for a delicate, fine sort of lass—shouted, "Tha'll be early for t'train, Bob." She was a damn know-all, standing in her doorway for no good reason except that she didn't want to miss anything. She could have spoken perfectly well if she'd wanted and did when she sang in the town choir. That affected accent should've gone out with the Brontes but there were those who liked to be quaint, harking back to the dark ages of tribal warfare and Vikings or if not as far back as that, at least to the time when the 'Satanic' mills still throbbed with the sound of machinery and there were demands to be met, orders to fill, and a man had places to go. It had been exciting then. Life had purpose when there were commercial reasons for going into town every day and for going abroad once or twice a year. *Dear One, I arrived in Budapest this morning and sold 14,000 lbs to Veider yesterday. Hope to be home on Sunday. Love, Bob*

While he was still in the house putting his shoes on, Frieda had said, "I don't know why you have to go and meet her. She can manage." Was she trying to save him from going out in the dark or was she jealous of his being the first to greet their child? Did she think he might whisper something subversive, *Your mother's not what she was*, in their daughter's ear? There was nothing to stop her coming with him except that she wanted to remove any specks of dust that might light on the furniture in the next half-hour. And he was glad to be on his own.

He heard a sound behind him and turned as quickly as he could but it was only a late pigeon hopping about looking for crumbs. He could have taken the taxi down but he didn't want to be picked up and have to sit talking to the driver while they waited for the train. Besides, it would have cost more. It was a silly bit of economy. Old habits from his travels long ago died hard. Every time he came back tired out from making his way from Verviers to Berlin and half way round Europe by the cheapest ways he could find, Frieda would say, you can be sure Mr. Nick and Mr. Hermann don't stint themselves when they go abroad. But they were the bosses, the sons of old Kleeman, and he was an employee and had to prove that he was diligent and careful with the firm's money. Or at least he'd thought so then.

The train was late and he was a young man walking along a railway platform on a dark evening at the border between Serbia and Austria. Men in uniform were moving up and down the train, slamming doors and staring into the passengers' faces. The voice on the loudspeaker said, *Der Zug nach Wien*, and he was a hungry young man who only wanted to go to the café and buy a sausage and a cup of coffee. But his path was blocked by two soldiers. *Kommen Sie mit uns, mein Herr.* When he tried to remember their faces afterwards he could only see a blur of healthy skin. He'd known enough not to ask questions. He had gone back to the carriage for his luggage as he was told and then like a lamb carried the two heavy suitcases to the shed, one soldier behind and one in front. Open! one of them said in English. He'd had to watch while they rifled through his wool samples and then his carefully folded clothes, getting shreds of wool all over his best suit, crumpling his starched shirt. They didn't care that he had to meet Herr Rosenbaum as soon as he got to Vienna next morning. Herr Rosenbaum was a smartly dressed man who set a lot of store by appearances. The soldiers' uniforms, the polished brass, the guns, all shouted power: No compromise allowed here.

He'd wondered briefly as he stood there in that cold shed, whether Frieda, suspecting him of treachery, had called some bureaucrat in Berlin and caused this to happen. But she was not a linguist and if she'd wanted to, she could have telephoned the office and prevented him from setting out on that trip at all. He set her up as a culprit because he didn't want to believe that these German soldiers knew his secret.

Das ist alles? The train was panting and snorting and he was to be left here and would never get to his meeting and would end up in one of Hitler's prisons to languish and die forgotten. Herr Rosenbaum would mark him down as inefficient and would never deal with the firm again. Alf Kindle would get his job and there would be less money coming in for Frieda who was expecting and wanted the little bedroom wall-papered and . . . . He still, now and then, had the old nightmare which ended every time with Frieda weeping alone against bare plaster walls.

He had managed to say *Ja* to the soldiers. He hadn't known what other answer to give. All he wanted was to get away from them and be on time for his appointment next day. Would a brave man have stood up to them and shouted, 'Leave my things alone!' or *'Ich bin Engländer.'* For months afterwards, he'd wondered what would've happened to that hero. At any rate, he didn't take the risk, he just walked away giving his interrogators a polite nod before he returned to the train. And the next morning . . .

The signal down the line raised its arm. The loud speaker said: "The train from Leeds is now approaching the station. Stand clear please." There was a chugging, rattling sound as the engine pulled its three carriages alongside the platform and stopped. He moved forward too quickly, half expecting to see Gerda, in her brown skirt and jacket and that mannish hat she used to wear, leap off the train and rush to embrace him. Just when the train seemed about to move on without releasing a single traveler, he saw Maggie stepping down from the second carriage.

She embraced him and he felt small with her arms round his shoulders. I'm very, very glad to see you, Love, he wanted to say but he only said, "Here, let me carry that."

"No, Dad. It's all right."

She was wearing a long reddish coat that drooped round her calves, and a bright scarf he hoped he'd given her one Christmas. There were bags under her eyes and a twist to her mouth as if, since last summer, she'd suffered a blow she hadn't told them about. The brown suitcase she was carrying weighed her down but he knew that if he wrested it from her, it would likely tip him over.

"You're alone then?" Wrong question. He didn't know why he'd asked it. He knew she was on her own.

"It's all right."

"Your mother booked a taxi. She didn't want you to be getting into one of the Paki ones."

Maggie's mouth tightened again. He was sorry he'd said that too. He could have left it alone. Just mentioned the taxi. He was glad that his children had enlightened views but it made a gulf, a place they couldn't always walk across. And he himself had no objection to the Pakistani immigrants. He felt sorry for them, coming to this much colder place, expecting better jobs, hoping to be comfortable, and then being let down when the industry failed. But Frieda saw them as being responsible for the troubles in the wool trade, for unemployment, his own lack of a pension, the poor bus service, and the crowds in the doctor's waiting room as well as every outbreak of flu. He'd given up arguing with her. But here with Maggie, there were other things to talk about.

"The weather's been awful. We've been waiting for you. The sun always comes out when you're here."

"I bring sunshine!"

"We'll go to Bolton Abbey. You always liked that."

The old ruins hadn't meant much to the kids when they were little but they liked hiding in the grass and picking bluebells. They used to run on ahead of him pulling up the flowers so the sticky white stems showed. *What can we wrap them in?* He'd find a few dock leaves for them to make bouquets. Then they'd go off and hide under the stone arches of the aqueduct. *Come and find us, Dad.* But of course, the aqueduct wasn't there, it was in Nab Wood. Maps had become jigsaw puzzles. Now places got confused in his mind except the one that was branded on his brain as indelibly as the mark on a cow's arse.

Come and find us, Dad. When they were young they thought he was always present in their games and didn't guess that his mind was often in a quite different place. Well, he would give his whole attention to this child now. "Are you hungry?"

"I had something on the other train."

"Your mother's been baking."

Maggie laughed.

"Before we get there . . . "

"What's wrong?"

"Don't mention David. She'll get into one of her states."

"I'll have to some time."

"Not tonight. I wish you'd come in daylight." In spite of himself, he was spoiling it again.

"There was something I had to do in London."

Something *she* had to do in London! That was his phrase! His life! For ten years and more it had been his reason for coming home a day late from one of his trips abroad. With those few words, he'd implied a day at the Wool Exchange. Important business on behalf of Kleeman and Sons. Buying Australian merino. Bidding for lots of the best raw wool and sometimes the worst. All of that was true. But it was the other business that delayed him longer, the transactions he couldn't mention. At the beginning, they'd given him a document to sign threatening all kinds of trouble if he revealed one single word, name, address or hint. And he'd signed willingly, barely reading the document that put him in thrall to new masters. At the time he'd seen it as a simple exchange: truth for adventure. But what had this child to do in London that was more important than coming north to see him and her mother? What could she possibly . . . ?

The taxi was waiting outside the front entrance of the station and the driver, a big fellow with a solid Yorkshire look about him, took Maggie's suitcase from her.

"You're back then, Maggie," he said.

"For a couple of weeks."

There was recognition between them, something else he didn't know. Was this fellow a schoolmate? Someone she'd met before? Or was he himself now so far out of it that he recognized no one?

"Need a hand, Mr. Parkes?"

"No, thank you."

He put one foot into the taxi, his stick slipped, and his knee gave way. He fell back into the driver's arms. Damndamndamn-damn, he muttered, cursing more under his breath. This was not right. Not the way he wanted to greet his daughter. Why did he need to seem sprightly?

The driver and Maggie helped him up and set him on the front seat.

"There was a loose stone," he said.

"They should clear the place up," the driver said. "It's a right mess."

He wished they'd let him fall onto the cold cement. It would have been a rehearsal for the day that would come before long when he was laid out on a slab prior to cremation. He pictured it in the night sometimes and in that picture he was naked, holding a long-stemmed lily, pain free and at peace.

He turned and said, "No need to tell your mother that I fell."

His knee was hurting as if imps with knives and hammers were inside the joint stabbing and striking to destruction. After the second accident, Frieda had sold the car for a good deal less than it was worth. And now this man who knew Maggie and who treated him with deference was at the wheel, going slowly as if it was a funeral.

"It's quicker the other way," he said. If it hadn't been dark he would've pointed out the hills and told her the names of them although he knew he'd told her on every visit. When did children become visitors? How did that happen? It was too long ago to remember.

Visitors. Strangers. Someone to be accommodated, catered for. That was the trouble. Frieda had spent the last few days tidying, cleaning, fussing as if it was the Queen who was coming to spend a fortnight in the back bedroom not 'our Maggie.'

She'll not want instant coffee, go into town and get a tin of Blue Mountain. Are there decent coat hangers in that wardrobe? I'll put a hot water bottle in the bed to air the mattress. The new duvet, thick as a pillow, had cost fifty pounds. *Well they're used to luxury over there.*

Maggie tapped him on the shoulder. "Dad, are you all right?"

"I'm all right."

While she was here this time, he was going to show her the photographs. He'd intended to do so on her last trip and the one before but hadn't got up the courage. When she did finally look at them, her face would change and she'd turn to him and see him as a stranger, a different kind of dad from the man she thought him to be, whatever that was. He surely wasn't, in her eyes, a hero, a man of substance. He'd been to all three of them, his wife and children, a man who managed, a man perhaps who might have done better. A man they loved all the same. Over time, he'd come to resent that 'all the same' because he knew that he was more than an all-the-same man. There'd been days when he wanted to climb up Harston Fell and shout from the top, "I am not ordinary!" But that was when he could still climb.

And she was saying, "There was a bomb scare at Kings Cross."

"Bloody IRA," the driver said, over his shoulder to her. "They get a lot of money from your part the world."

"That's in the States," she said. "A lot of Irish immigrants there in Boston and New York."

Robert shuddered. Belfast, his childhood home, his school, old Mr. Fraser and the dream poem, football on Fridays, good times, were all lost in a mist of violence. His accent, rubbed smooth over time, still marked him as a son of Erin and people occasionally turned away from him in crowded places as though at his age he was capable of making explosive devices in the cellar and sticking them on the underside of cars. *Bloody IRA!*

They pulled up by the house and Maggie got out of the car and said, "Thanks, Ron."

She'd taken money out of her handbag before he could reach into his pocket for the ten pound note he'd put in there specially. It hurt more than his knee, that she'd paid and that this burly man who seemed to know them saw him as helpless, hopeless, old and not well off, a man who fell easily and must be paid for.

I would like you to know, he began to say to her under his breath, what I did in the war. Well one of these days, tomorrow, or Sunday, he would surprise her by saying it aloud.

"We'll go to a concert while I'm here, Dad," Maggie said as they walked up the little path to the door.

They wouldn't, he knew, but he was glad she'd said it. He'd

taken her to her first real concert at Eastbrook Hall in Bradford. She'd've been about fourteen and the pianist had played Beethoven sonatas and finished with Liszt. Restless at first, she'd watched the musicians and then, slowly, listened to the sound and become entranced. He wanted to remind her of it but there was Frieda in the doorway, overwhelming, embracing, drawing them into the house on a wave of cooking smells.

Love. You look tired. Did you have a good flight? I'm fine. Well, you'll be able to rest now. You've been busy, Mum. That's a nice coat. The women went on cooing at each other while he limped past them unnoticed and dragged the heavy bag up the stairs. Had she brought rocks from Canada?

He lay down on the bed for a moment. When she was little, they used to put a packed stocking at the foot of the beds late on Christmas Eve, her bed and David's, with the house smelling richly as it did now, of cake and pastry and eggs and butter. But those were smaller beds in the other house, the house where the telephone was in the dining room. One Christmas Eve he'd spent hours setting up the toy train for David, arranging the tracks, the tiny passengers, trees, and the boy had looked it over and said, 'There's no clock on the station.'

She'd been ten when he returned from 'Ireland' that time. David must have been fourteen. Frieda was still putting in long hours at the canteen. All of them were too busy with their own affairs to notice that he was in a bad way. What if they had noticed? What if they'd said to him, You look awful, Dad. Tell us what's wrong? He could only have lied to them and said, It was a sandwich I ate on the train.

A few weeks later, when the war ended, when the celebrations had died down, it wasn't over for him or for thousands, millions of others. And the refrain in his head when he went into the warehouse, or to 'Change, or to the mills in Hebden Bridge or Halifax, ran 'If they knew, if they knew.' Driving over the Pennines, looking out at that stark and wondrous scenery he could try to drive out the demonic pictures by singing as he drove over the winding roads: "When Irish Eyes are Smiling" and "Kitty of Coleraine." But however loudly he sang, his mind always came back to the large office panelled with rich wood and the silent person who entered on soft feet and set a tray with tea and biscuits down on the shiny desk and withdrew leaving him alone with a man who waited for the door to close before he began to talk. He had a plummy accent, that man, and he spoke with great assurance and all the weight of government and royalty behind him.

A young idiot then, Robert had run up the stairs in that monumental building, thrilled to be part of Kipling's Great Game. But when the Game grew intense, vital, dangerous, he was old enough to know that it was beyond fun.

Well Mr. Parkes, you did have an adventure. That was after the event at the station. They always knew. That was the fearful thing. Not that there was anything for them not to know because he had never betrayed them. But he did wonder whether there was a line of them, each one following the man in front, stretching across the continent, the last one standing in the station shadows on that dark evening. And would they have rescued him if the soldiers had marched him off towards some jail or camp? He'd never had any illusions about that. They would disown him. A British businessman, travelling in Germany disappeared today. He was last seen boarding a train . . . .

What have you got to tell us?

And that was when he betrayed the others, the ones he'd talked to on his journey. The men who trusted him to sell them good quality wool and who invited him to their homes to meet their families and friends. They shared their thoughts with him, held nothing back. Even the Van den Kerkes weren't safe from his deception. *This man Hitler, he has good ideas. He's not a man to be despised. My son has been called up. A hush-hush job.*

It was the overheard conversations the men in London were

really interested in. Some of our agents have a way of making things up, Mr. Parkes. He was never Robert, never even just Parkes, always the respectful Mr. Parkes, although he knew very well that to them he was a simple, expendable, commercial traveler who could speak a couple of languages. A fairly useful man. A disposable, momentary man, a pair of ears. If he had disappeared, he would have been an all-the-same man to them too.

The soldiers had taken his bags back to the train that day and tossed them into the carriage leaving him to jump in as the train moved off. He fell into the corridor and struggled back to his seat. The two women in the corner drew themselves together. One of them even pulled on her gloves as if to protect herself from contamination, stroking each finger into place with hostile deliberation. The man beside him murmured a comradely word but he didn't respond. He heaved his luggage back onto the rack and took up his book. From then on he was the simple salesman from Yorkshire. Let them flatter him. Let women murmur to him about his *treuen, blauen Augen*. Let them offer him sweetmeats and Riesling and naked dancing girls with tambourines. He had nothing on his mind but making sales. Nothing to disclose but wool. He would be all ears and no voice. The usual very polite English businessman: Herr Parkes to the clients. Robert to the Van den Kerkes. *Liebchen* to Gerda.

He was in the Brieters' living room when a stranger came in and said, "I was told to meet you here," and the comfort in the old house drained away and the chair on which he sat gripped him with its wooden arms till he could hardly breathe.

"I never could get your father into a cave. Except the once."

They were coming up the stairs, the two women. Frieda was talking about going to Ingleborough. She'd always been fascinated by stalactites. He tried to get off the bed quickly but fell onto the floor dragging the new duvet with him. He pulled himself up clenching his teeth to hold in the cry of pain that desperately wanted to escape and pushed the duvet back into place.

"I'd have carried the case up, Dad."

"He likes to move around. It's good for him."

"Well, thank you," Maggie said, as if they were hotel staff and she might tip them later if they treated her well.

He threw out that unworthy thought. She loved them. They loved her. But their love was stretched across a growing chasm of unshared experience. And his was the least known of all. Your father the stranger, your husband the spy. Frieda who might have guessed his mystery, had lost her intuition over time, buried it in a heap of details, or perhaps like bones, that part of a woman's mind lost strength as she aged. He felt irritated some days that she had never once looked at him in a serious way and said, So tell me what you were really doing over there.

As for Maggie, he only wanted to believe that in the main she was happy and that the man she loved, loved her, and that in the mornings they talked to each other in a nice way, decently. He also wished, and he wished it hard till it was like a prayer to God, that she would one day have a real adventure and be as scared and exhilarated as she and David had been when they rode on The Cyclone in Morecambe. Or as he himself had been over there on the Continent at times, leaving out that last terrible trip.

She was looking out of the window now at the hill behind the house and he and Frieda were standing like statues as if they'd all three been caught in a shared daydream.

"We'll leave you to it," Frieda said.

Yes. That was right. Let the child unpack. Let her come down to them when she was ready. His knee was so stiff that he wasn't sure he could make it down the stairs or even out of the room. Frieda had her back to him and Maggie was lifting her suitcase onto the bed. He held onto the chest of drawers and then the wall and followed his wife. If he fell downstairs, he would land on her and she would cushion his fall. Then lying on top of her soft body which he hadn't done for some time, he'd whisper, *I'm not the man you think I am.*

My parents are getting old. Such was the self-sacrificing statement Maggie had made to her friends and to Theo before she set off on this journey, awarding herself a touch of unearned nobility. And now that she was here, she was overwhelmed by their love, their need for her. She opened the case and took out her dress to hang it in the wardrobe, then, overcome with sudden weariness, she pushed the case to one side and lay down beside it. The duvet had been thrown roughly onto the bed in a careless gesture, as if, mixed with delight, there was a sense of why has she come to disturb our little aging life. No need to tell them that she had run away. Run away from the last scene played out in the living room, run away from the room itself which had in that moment of shouting and dismay looked like a room furnished by strangers.

The scene wouldn't go away. There it was again replaying itself, on automatic rewind in her head, as it had done on the plane, the train, even on the short drive from the station while she was worrying about Dad's fall: Theo standing with his back to the fake fireplace. Theo looking away as she held out the newspaper with the article in it. Theo in his jeans and turtleneck, slim and earnest, and preaching doom as usual.

I'm talking about the future, Maggie. I worked my ass off for this company, Theo. You still appeared to have one last night. Don't be coarse. I should think, I just think you should see that they're polluting the environment. What kind of a word is 'environment?' It means the world we live in. The air that surrounds us. And I don't need that rich American coming up here and telling us what to do. We need all the help we can get. It says here, the first of a series by Theo Krause. That's my name.

After that he became reasonable, condescending. Maggie darling, we can get over this. Let's go about it rationally. Come and sit here with me. We are both right, partly.

She was aware of how she looked. She knew he wanted to take her to bed even though their bedroom still reeked of last night's sex. He wanted to persuade her that it was something they could overcome and pour them both a glass of wine and look at her as if this was the beginning of their life together.

And that was when she shouted words that were likely unforgivable. You think you're so damn right. But you pander to the left. It's never what you really think. You do it because Griffiths pays you to stir things up. You're a goddam phony and that beard is ridiculous.

He'd turned away. Their longstanding compromise was broken: She'd admired his writing although she disagreed with much of what he wrote. He respected the work she did but saw the product as damaging to the future of the planet. Their life together had been a deception held together by threads of love and laughter. He agreed to live with her even though he was offended by what he referred to as 'your product.' He sat at his desk every day and wrote against everything she did and she went to work every day for a company that produced and exported materials he considered harmful to the atmosphere.

Yesterday he'd driven her to the airport and moved to kiss her as they waited by the security gate and she had stepped away, lifting her flight bag and moving on, not even looking back.

She hoped to clear her mind in all this space, this cleaner air. He probably hoped she would return cleansed, purified, a new woman ready to see his point of view.

She projected the other scene, the fantasy he probably ran daily through his mind: She says, Darling, I'm pregnant. I'm thirty-nine and pregnant. I'll stay at home and you will write and we will rearrange our lives. He replies, Oh my beloved one. We'll be a family and I will make sure you have everything you want and our child will be a genius.

The drama would be quite different if she returned and cleared her things out of the house and returned to her single, independent life.

At the office there had been curiosity. Why had she chosen to go away, take two weeks off, at a time when the office was short staffed and the hearing date had been set for September sixteenth? My parents need me. I have to make curries for them because I read that turmeric wards off Alzheimer's disease—something that must surely be on their minds every time they forget what day it is or wonder why they've gone into the kitchen.

Yes, she had come all this way to see what state they were in. She had come to give them a good time. She had come to enjoy herself and that's what she would do. She went downstairs humming a line of the song her father used to sing while he was drying dishes. "'She was just the sort of girl, my boys, I'd have you all to know . . . '" And she'd come to find out the rest of the words.

Her father was sitting in his stiff-backed wing chair. Every five years it had to be re-upholstered and always in the same linen hunting print. His leg was resting on a low stool. Her father with his limp, his eyes now red-rimmed, and his teeth browned with smoking three cigarettes a day since he was twelve, watched her come into the room.

Maggie looked around till she caught sight of the photograph, herself at nineteen, in a silver frame, as if she only ever came back in order to make sure that she had a place here. The large picture of the three of them in uniform, David the cadet, Dad the warden and herself in her Girl Guide outfit, stood in its usual place, on the bookcase. The light oak table was in the window as it had been on her last visit. The four chairs were neatly pushed in. The standard lamp in the corner still needed a new shade. Above the fireplace was the picture of two monks at prayer. Across from them on the other wall, a series of prints of cathedrals, all that was left of religion in the house. On the hearth was her grandmother's old toasting fork as if it was possible to toast crumpets over the ornamental flames, captive behind their glass shield.

He watched her looking round and said softly, "Your mother never thinks much about her surroundings."

Had he spent time in better appointed houses? Or did he think that with another mate, he might have lived in a *Home and Garden* fantasy? Perhaps he wished for his daughter a different setting, imagining her home to be a perfect palace. She smiled at him and said, "It's comfortable."

The TV dominated the room like a third person. The silver cup she'd won for hockey stood on a little red mat on top of the set. On the table, the white cloth, three cups and saucers, milk, sugar, the old brown teapot. Her mother, Frieda the warrior, came in carrying a plate with biscuits on it. She too looked at the photograph as if to confirm her daughter's identity.

"You haven't changed much, Maggie."

"Oh but I have. She was naïve, that girl. Downright stupid."

"You were in love."

"It was a mirage."

More of a joke! Trekking off to Germany hand in hand with a boy she'd known for three months. And wearing an outfit in that odd indefinite colour, mixed in what vat. What had she been looking for then but ruins perhaps, signs of desolation? At any rate she'd returned home in three weeks, depressed, bereft and sure that she would never find another love.

Her mother poured out the tea, remembering that she took a little milk and no sugar.

"I was stupid, Ma."

"You were young," her mother responded and did not add, and

25

lucky not to be abducted, killed, left by the highway for vultures, human and otherwise, or worse still, pregnant.

"I'd like to go back there," Maggie said, "to Germany." It came to her then, in that very moment, a need to travel to Europe. She was drawn by more than the wish to visit rebuilt monuments and restored cities. The urge pricked at her mind, as if by going back to Germany now she would find the key to a mystery, solve her problems and learn how to lead a better life. Some people sought these answers in Indian ashrams or Tibetan monasteries. She was drawn to Berlin, the Black Forest, Dresden.

"And how's young Greg?" her mother asked.

"He's grown since that was taken."

They were looking at a picture of David's son. Standing beside a car in front of a motel staring down an empty road, half in shadow, he was a forlorn boy looking towards his future. A handsome, fair-haired, straight featured, no ear-ring, no facial fuzz, clear-eyed, un-drugged kid. There were two ways this could go. Her mother would either say, *Our only grandchild*, and make her feel guilty for not having three children or she would mention the forbidden name and excuses would have to made for the delinquent David.

Maggie quickly said, "I've brought you something."

"You shouldn't always be bringing us things."

"I know you like this," she said and handed her mother the nicely wrapped bottle of Arpége. To her father, she gave a book about the building of the CP railway. On his one visit to Canada, the train ride through the Rockies and in particular the trip through the Spiral Tunnels had fascinated him.

Her mother had never learnt to say a simple thank you, this is just what I wanted, but she was stroking the bottle and in a moment unscrewed the top and sprayed a little onto the back of her hand. She offered it to Maggie to smell.

"Don't keep it just for special occasions," Maggie said. "It loses its scent over time."

Her father looked at his gift quickly, flicked through a few pages, and then set it down as if there was something toxic about it.

"Dad?"

"I'll look at it tomorrow in daylight, love. I'll really enjoy it. I've never forgotten that day going through the mountains. What a feat of engineering." But he was distant as though there were other mountains, other railways on his mind.

Her mother managed not to refer to her daughter's childless state and none of them mentioned David. It was desultory, late evening family chat. Much was known between them but little said as though they had all the time in the world to exchange their views on God and truth and literature and third world poverty. Instead they revived dead relatives and repeated old tales of misadventure.

Her father turned over the pages of the evening paper and showed her pictures of a flood in India, people and belongings stranded on the edge of the river, water over rooftops, dead animals floating towards the ocean.

Maggie kissed her parents and said it had been a long day.

As she got undressed, she heard laughter from downstairs. Her father had turned on the telly to watch his favourite program about three old men behaving like Huck Finn and Tom Sawyer and Jim in a nearby moorland village.

Your system is obsolete. Did you call me obsolete? Obsolete, obstructive, obsessive!

Get out Parkes. I've had enough of you and your games. David couldn't stop the words running round in his head even while he was trying to imagine Maggie over there in Kelthorpe talking to their parents. They would enquire about her journey and then speak of old holidays, the quirks of their relatives, the day the cat got stuck in a tree. And underneath all that, unspoken, *When is David coming?*

I'll come if I have to walk there, Mum. His fear of flying covered that other fear, a dread of being pulled back into a cozy sort of life, a repetitive Sunday-dinner-with-the-family existence, and into the morass of his mother's never expressed sadness. This was something he kept to himself. When he called home these days, the conversation was short as if she always had something else to do. Sometimes when he dialed the number and the phone kept on ringing, he felt that she was there but knew it was him and wouldn't pick up the receiver.

He was lying on a chaise longue in the O'Briens' garden. John and his father were arguing beside the barbecue. Linda and Diane were in the kitchen making salad. It should have been a peaceful moment but his thoughts wouldn't stop chasing each other round in his head. *Obsolete. Obstinate.* He still wasn't sure whether Baker had simply meant for him to get out of his office or to leave the building for good. At any rate he had taken the latter route out onto Bay Street and home, free. He slapped the mosquito on his knee and squashed it before it could suck his blood. The smoke from the barbecue should have killed any insect within a hundred yard radius; the smoke and the smell of overdone chicken.

Old man O'Brien said, "Mosquitoes as big as sparrows in Winnipeg."

When he'd turned the meat with a long fork, John brushed the pieces with his secret sauce, a secret, David thought, that should be buried for all time. John's dad, standing to one side of the barbecue like a king who has abdicated too soon, was wearing khaki shorts that revealed scraggly legs, seventy-year-old legs. Legs with a hefty mileage on them, veined and dry-skinned.

David sipped his beer. It was good beer. He didn't think his father had ever owned a pair of shorts, not since he was a boy in Belfast anyway. The only time he'd seen the old man in any sort of undress was on holiday. In the old photographs taken at Robin Hood's Bay with the Schroeders, he was wearing a full swimsuit as if, in those days, the sight of a man's naked chest might drive women to frenzy.

"David?"

"I'm fine."

"Another?"

"Not yet, thanks."

Having made his enquiry as a good host, John went back to wrapping corn cobs in foil and arguing with his father about the correct procedure for a presidential resignation.

I'll come if I have to walk there, Mum. Would he tell her he was unemployed if she called him and warmly said, Hello Love, how are things? *I'm fine, Mum. I've lost faith in the market, that's all. It's witchcraft. Trying to sell people on numbers. It might as well be pentagrams and incantations beneath the moon, 'the visiting moon.'* Four nights as Antony in the school play, for that brief while an actor, a star, had led him to mention RADA at home when he was seventeen. Dad: *A very chancy thing, acting.* Mum: *You were very good, dear, but.* Richard Higgins, his Cleopatra, sexily breathing into his ear, 'Let's do it in the Roman fashion,' always getting it wrong, and Mr. Burrill shouting 'high!' and the cast collapsing in laughter, remained the sum of his theatrical experience. Suggestive jokes about doing it in the 'high Roman fashion' pervaded that entire final year at school. It was too late now to learn how to project his voice and become a different person every evening and twice on Saturday.

He might have been a major with a swagger stick but two regimented years of folding blankets exactly so, polishing everything in sight, being shouted at by thuggish sergeants had been enough. Sandhurst had been dangled like a carrot in front of him but he'd passed up that chance for future glory. Later on, Joseph Heller and Evelyn Waugh had destroyed any military myths he might once have cherished.

"David!" This time the call came from the kitchen.

"Got anything yet?" John asked as he walked by.

"Prospects."

Mr. O'Brien patted his shoulder in a gesture of sympathy.

He went into the cool basement kitchen where the women were and was pleased that of these two, Linda was his. Diane with her kind face and plump hands was motherly, earth-motherly. She had quickly forgiven John for his 'fling' with a colleague in Guelph three years ago. Linda would never have been so forgiving, neither would she have expected easy absolution for herself. Not that she would . . . not that he would . . .

She turned now and smiled and, looking like a priestess in her long white and red robe, she held out a large wooden bowl to him. *Here is the sacrificial heart removed from the living victim with my obsidian knife.*

"Outside?" he asked.

"The picnic table, darling," she replied.

She only ever called him *darling* in company. It imprinted her brand on his forehead. He was hers. And he was glad.

Diane spoiled the moment by saying, "How's it going, Dave?"

He went outside quickly to prevent her hearing him mutter, "How do you think it's bloody going," and tripped over the step.

"Steady there," John said. "How many beers is that?"

David set the bowl down with care, not sure how he could get through the rest of the evening without biting somebody's head off. So many companionable meals they'd shared with their friends in this neat walled garden with its apple tree and the vine, planted by the previous occupants, hanging over the trellis. Nights they'd spent drinking and talking beneath the 'visiting moon' had been moments of sanctuary in their hectic lives. Here they had discussed the coming and goings of prime ministers, the war in Vietnam, books they loved. Sometimes there was a larger group, sometimes only four. Never till now had he felt out of place. He took another beer from the cooler and returned to the chaise longue: Let the others wait on him.

He went through his daily exercise, the possible interview:

Why do you want this job, Mr. Parkes? Because I need the money, you stupid bastard. How did you come to lose your last job? I told the boss to get stuffed. What kind of men do you admire? (A crafty question, that.) *When I was a kid, I read everything about Scott and Shackleton. In the war, Field-Marshal Montgomery, spitfire pilots and, secretly, Rommel, were my heroes, Mr. Interviewer. Since then, no one in particular.* The expected answer was John D. Rockefeller or Henry Ford or J. Paul Getty, any tycoon who had made a fortune through the sweat of others, or by downright theft. He realized that he was fondling a loose thread from the chair cover in the way his father used to feel a strand of wool or a piece of cloth to test for quality.

They were all asleep in Kelthorpe by now.

"Wake up, Dave," Linda was bending over him, offering him a plate with chicken and corn on it. She was beautiful, more than she knew. Her hair was loose and shiny, her eyes, even though there were lines now underneath, were bright with humour and life. He hoped she would never be a sad woman.

He took the plate and smiled. "Wasn't asleep, just calculating market odds."

John's dad said, "Eggs in one basket. Always a mistake."

John wanted to get back to the excitement in Washington. "Imagine, having to walk away like that from the most powerful job in the world, from the centre of the universe."

"He should've hired better help," Linda said.

"You get what you pay for," Diane said.

"Sometimes less."

"Where would you advertise for a professional burglar? What references would you ask for?"

"Thinking of going to burglar school, Dave?" John asked, and then bit into his corn to hide his face.

These were the moments, the *faux pas* moments, David knew he had to accept and deal with graciously in his current situation, or rather lack thereof.

31

"Might run one," he replied. And then to shift the tone of the evening, he pushed John's hobby horse in front of him, and watched him climb happily onto it. "And talking of running . . . "

Beer had given way to wine. Chicken bones and stripped corn cobs were piling up on the table.

"They have asked me, David."

"They know a good candidate when they see one. I mean how many men—or women—are there with your qualifications?"

"I wouldn't go that far. It's more a matter of being known and of what you stand for. When it comes to health and education, we have to get more value for the same money and it can be done. There are three of us round this table who know where the wastage is in the health system. And I want to make changes so that our grandchildren will be taught history, literature, art, in a way that makes sense instead of the narrow curriculum they're subjected to today. They leave school with enough reading and arithmetic to get them round a supermarket and sometimes not even that."

"Come on, John," Diane said.

"Greg reads very little," Linda said, agreeing.

"Oh yes, he's just about illiterate," David said, angry that she'd thought it necessary to throw their son to these aggravating lions.

"If I do respond to the call, Diane would have to agree. Public service is disruptive of family life. I wouldn't even be thinking about it if I didn't have an agenda and a feeling that I have something to contribute." He smiled at his wife.

"And you have a great deal to contribute," David said.

The two women got up and left the room taking piled up dirty plates with them. Old man O'Brien said, "I told him years ago to get in there, into politics. He was always a good talker. No one these days knows how to debate without calling names. We took him to Ottawa when he was twelve and went on a tour of the House."

"I'd say that I have fifteen good years ahead. Maybe more. So

I could follow through with my ideas. What we need in this province, David, is a policy that will carry us forward into the next millennium wealthy, with our infrastructure up to date and companies knowing this is a province with a long term commitment to business and all its . . . "

David kept his eyes on his friend's face but let his mind travel to England where it was now about two o'clock in the morning. What would they do tomorrow on Maggie's first day? He'd lay any money on Bolton Abbey. Or maybe they'd go to Knaresborough and stop at the well, Old Mother Shipton's petrifying spring. *Carriages without horses will go*, she'd foretold, and mentioned the ensuing accidents too. A woman way ahead of her time, she'd warned of the Armada and the Great Fire of London, and predicted submarines and telephones. He and Richard had cycled there sometimes in the holidays and touched the glove, the child's shoe, and other objects that had been made solid by the minerals in the water. How long would it take for a whole man, continuously dripped on, to be turned to stone?

" . . . real estate. If I were you, David, I'd take the Real Estate course. Inflation can't go on forever although analysts do say it could be a year or two yet. Start now and you'll catch the upturn. Take this house for instance, when we bought it the market was way down and now . . . "

The lines on John's face had developed into runnels over time as if there'd been pain in his life or the pressure of work had caused him to stay up at nights, thinking and writing by a dim light. His face was like a map. The roads all led to old age and a decline of the senses. He had a habit of tapping the table while he talked. An impatient man. A woodpecker of a man who wanted a wider audience but would for now make do with the one he had.

"What about the way people are moving out to the suburbs and beyond?"

"We have to bring them back. To make this city into a truly world-class place—a place where international conferences are held, top-level—and we need to develop the lakefront. What our grandfathers did to that lakeshore was a crime."

"Not mine," David said. He could hear the women talking in the kitchen and envied them. "Mine were minding their sheep in Yorkshire."

"Nor mine. But you know what I mean. The railway line. The highway. For Chrissake. What were they doing?"

"They were screwing up the landscape the best way they knew," David said, offering the required response.

John was in his fifties. He and Diane had been married forever. Their daughter was in medical school and their son was top of his class. Their house displayed no excess. Worn comfort was how it would be described in a magazine. Worthiness was their virtue. They were good people, an example to all, and yet they barbecued chicken to death and pudding was never a certainty. Diane might even now be arranging grapes and melon tastefully on a ceramic dish.

"But what about you, David? Here I am, going on."

"I have plans."

"To what?"

Diane came out of the house with a bowl of peaches and a platter of cookies and said, "Help yourselves."

Linda set down a pile of paper napkins and followed Diane to the bench under the trellis. The two women looked remote and dim and out of reach. *Oh, the moon shone bright on Mrs. Porter.* It irritated David that he could remember lines of poetry from school but couldn't recall enough of his physics lessons to explain to Greg the uses of a fulcrum. Perhaps in his old age the poems would surface whole again in his memory.

"You think there's a chance the Conservatives can be defeated?" he said to John, setting him off again.

"Bill Davis is riding for a fall. Thinks he can get away with anything. By the law of averages alone, there has to be a change. If Trudeau hadn't brought in the War Measures Act and frightened people off we'd have a Liberal government in this province right now. I'm betting that in two years time . . . "

By the time they got home it was five o'clock in the morning in England. His parents and his sister were in bed. Linda leaned on him as they went in the door.

"I want to be up early," she said.

"Why did we stay so late?"

"We drank too much."

There was a note from Greg on the stairs: I am home. Where are you? Don't wake me before nine.

"Your name means flower," David said as he followed his wife up the stairs.

"That doesn't mean I'm about to be plucked," his wife replied.

He lay awake for a long time and the clock by the bed moved from 12:30 to 1:00 to 2:00.

Robert sat up too quickly and felt dizzy. The phone never rang so early in the morning. Frieda in the other bed, her hearing aid on the bedside table, lay on her back snoring. He got out of bed and put his feet into his slippers. He held on to the rail going down the stairs. Held on carefully. If he fell and woke the women up, Maggie would want to know why he hadn't had a second phone put in upstairs. There was one simple reason; a lingering fear of Frieda picking up the extension and hearing a stranger's voice say, *We have your pictures, Mr. Parkes.*

He looked at the brass clock on the mantelpiece. Ten past seven. He shivered. If the phone had been ringing, it had stopped. In any case, who would call at this hour? David would be asleep. Local people were not up and about yet. The only people who rang at strange times had stopped calling him long ago and it was very unlikely that they would be getting in touch with him now. He must have been dreaming of the old days.

I served my time. I am too old for adventures, he said to himself, to 'them,' and to the birds outside the window, as he put the kettle on. He caught himself smiling as if suddenly he could pack, leave a note, *Will be gone for a time*, and set out to meet perhaps a beautiful woman, though that had never once happened—not in the way of what he did for 'them.'

It was exciting then, coming back from a journey across Europe, stopping in the London office and telling 'them' that he'd heard talk of a new ship being built in Kiel, of troop movements on the border, of men meeting in secret to oppose the Hitler regime. He was a young man living a double life in those days. And enjoying it. *Some of our contacts invent things, Mr. Parkes.* That was always said in a threatening tone as if liars were made away with, dropped to the cellar from the chair patented by Sweeney Todd. No money was offered, therefore it couldn't be taken away. It was a simple matter of patriotism. *We all want to serve our country, don't we, Mr. Parkes?* And after the inquisition, he'd make his way home carrying the secrets he never told and the suitcase that contained presents for his family and the Belgian chocolates they all loved. A bracelet or necklace for Frieda that she might wear once and never again. The cuckoo clock hadn't been well-received either but it was one of those gifts that would neither break nor wear out. It had hung in the kitchen for twenty years and would be here on this wall if it hadn't been crushed in the last move. For Maggie he had brought the music box she still cherished and for David an intricately made model car.

That last year of travel, 1939, not knowing it would be the last for six whole years, he'd been fairly sure that in a few months, the men who crossed the Channel would be carrying something very different from samples of raw wool. That was when he'd brought back the copy of *Struwwelpeter*. Happy tales for children aged three to six. Illustrated cautionary tales. The little girl who played with matches was set on fire and that taught her a lesson. Konrad stood there dripping gore after a visit from a tailor who cut off his thumbs with his shears. *'Klipp und klapp.'* Try sucking them now! What kind of a man was Dr. Heinrich Hoffman that he offered such nasty images for little kids? Of course Maggie and David couldn't understand a word of it but they soon knew when to shout *'klipp und klapp'* as he read, and kept on using the words as a kind of code long after Frieda had put the book away because the stories were written in a hostile language.

The war had kept the plummy-voiced men in London occupied in other ways. And then on an April morning when people were beginning to hope, to think of buying flags, and letting light leak out through the dark curtains, there was another call. This is the last thing we'll ask of you, the voice said, the very last thing. The last terrible thing. If there'd been no phone in the house, and not everybody had a telephone then, would he have been spared? Telegrams were too easy for prying eyes to read. Or suppose he'd been away or he'd let the phone ring, would they have gone to the next name on the list?

There could be no reason for them to approach him now. An old man of seventy-one doesn't get recalled for action. In books maybe or in pictures but certainly not in real life.

He put three mugs on the tray. Was it too early for Maggie? Did she take sugar? Did she still drink tea in the morning? Why didn't he know? He turned on the radio. A woman was talking about the best way to grow celery. "It can be difficult," she said.

"Why bother?" he responded. "It's a ratty, stringy vegetable."

He moved the dial to the other station and found soothing, meaningless music. He took the third mug off the tray and reached into the glass-fronted cabinet for one of Frieda's prized Spode cups with its saucer. Blue with a white design of flowers and pleasantly fragile, it was delicate to touch. Beside it he set the sugar bowl and milk jug. Now the glass jug was out of all proportion so he took the Spode jug from its space and poured milk into it. Spidery dust floated to the top. He tipped the milk out into the sink and washed the little jug under the hot tap and got more milk out of the fridge. Now the tray itself looked wrong. He took a cloth from the drawer, a white starched cloth, and folded it over till it was the right size. Removing everything from the tray, he patted the cloth down and replaced only the Spode. It looked nice. All that was lacking was a silver spoon. The kettle boiled. He poured water into the teapot to warm it, swirled it round, and tipped it into the sink. There were three kinds of tea in the cupboard, Earl Grey, Lapsang, and something simply called Breakfast tea. This was a special occasion; he put a spoonful of each into the pot, Parkes' special blend. He poured in the hot water and let it stand for the full three minutes.

Out in the garden, starlings were pecking at the grass and beyond the fence the cows in the field were grazing as if it was the start of another ordinary day, a day which he would spend with his daughter. Right now there was a decision to make. On the tray, there were two mugs full of tea, one with milk and sugar, one with only milk, and there was the nice arrangement of blue china. If Frieda saw the precious crockery, she might shriek out, tell him to take it downstairs at once. He could take his and Frieda's tea to their room first and then the tray to Maggie. The thing was to set the tray down in the bathroom, take off the mugs and then deliver Maggie's tea to her. *Good morning, sweetheart, it's so good to have you at home.*

He stood at the bottom of the stairs with the laden tray in his hands. It was a long time since he'd managed to walk up without holding onto the rail. A wooden Everest faced him. The carpet's sagging folds on the fifth and ninth steps were hazards like ice falls and there was no sherpa, no rope. He saw himself falling backwards and lying there covered in a mess of hot tea and broken china. *What we need, Mr. Parkes, are people who can think their way out of tight corners.*

He set the tray down.

Frieda woke up and reached for her hearing aid. She always put it in right away for fear of missing alien sounds. She liked to hear the sparrows in the garden and the sheep out there on the side of the moor. And today there was a child at home. A child who might cry out because there was no doubt that the child had come home with a load of pain. It was obvious in Maggie's face and in her silences and in her eagerness to please. For all she must have been tired out last night, she talked of trips they would take, she would hire a car, get used to driving on the left side of the road. Did they still have the picnic basket? As if she and Bob wanted to sit down on a rug in a damp field! She shivered, remembering damp summer days when her own father had crouched over a Primus stove waiting for the water to heat. It rarely boiled. And as they drank the tepid stuff, he always said, "It tastes much better when it's made alfresco."

She heard the rattle of china from downstairs. Bob had got up early and was probably making tea to impress Maggie. She went to the bathroom. It didn't do these days to linger in bed first thing when she had to pee. She arranged her hair and put on her blue housecoat and got back into bed and sat up ready to smile and say thank you although the tea would be too strong and possibly tepid just like her Dad's awful 'alfresco' brew, and he would have forgotten the biscuits. Every now and then he did some redeeming thing to remind her that she was fond of him. It was a trick he had. Just when she began to think that even though they were both over seventy and the children would be distressed and it would be a financial strain if she left him and went to live in Chichester, he saved the day by making an effort to be helpful and kind. These little endeavours of his didn't even begin to add up to the great effort she'd had to make twenty and more years ago. She would've liked to forget about all that and the letter and the tears and the excuses but some things stuck in the mind like lint on a wool cardigan and no one had invented a special brush to remove them.

It was never clear because he'd never confessed but there was no doubt that the woman in her alpine place had lured him back after the war into renewed infidelity. Those trips weren't all about selling wool, she knew that. Carrying his brown case full of tops and noils, he'd visited countries abroad that she would have loved to see but he had never once asked her to go with him. But there were the children then and it wasn't like today when parents would leave their offspring with baby-sitters they hardly knew. And Bob had returned, and had unpacked, and had sat with her talking by the fire, but there were gaps in his story. He glided over some days as if the events were unfit to be told, like the stories in those awful books he brought back from Germany written in gothic script no one could read but him.

She could hear him now, reading aloud to Maggie and David in a language they couldn't understand. They'd sit there listening intently, waiting for one intelligible word, with that kind of trust kids have, humouring him probably. Nowadays a psychologist would make a great deal out of that. She was glad when the war gave her an excuse to throw the book out. And glad when the warnings began and foreigners were advised to return home. Goodbye and good riddance, Miss Bohm. She had sighed with relief when the Swiss woman left and they had the house to themselves again. But no one in her right mind could be glad of war though it had been exciting in some ways. Bob at the ARP post once a week. All those foreign airmen in town. Serving them in the canteen and nursing and rushing home again to make quick meals out of what was left of the rations. There was a freedom because everything was excused. Almost everything. And looking back, some things had been excused that shouldn't have been. It was because there was no safety that so much was forgiven. On any night, death might come down from the sky or a jackbooted foreign army might march down the road looting and pillaging and worse. Who was supposed to stay sane and moral and ordinary with all that going on?

Bob was coming up the stairs. And then he went down.

Yes, there were the children then. He had stories to tell when he came home but they were not the story she knew was there—never the one that still remained to be told.

He was going back down the stairs. He forgot things now, they both did. Names, places, ideas. They could only look forward to a continuous gentle erasure till there was a complete blank. There he was, coming up the stairs again. It was a real worry, the fear that one day your mind would be an empty shell. He was on his way back down.

She adjusted her hearing aid. If she had forgiven those times, why did she still think about them: And was she going to accuse him on his deathbed or hers? She wished quite often these days that they hadn't stopped going to church. Once more he was coming up. She stopped herself from getting out of bed and going to the top of the stairs and shouting, *What in the name of all the saints are you doing*? She waited. He was going down again.

In the other house, in those days before the war, the telephone had been in the dining room by the window. There'd been no direct dialing then, every call had to go through the switchboard. *Could you put me through please*? And then you had to tell the number. It was that day near the end of the meal when the phone rang. They'd been having meat and potato pie for dinner, more potatoes and pastry than meat. Maggie and David wanted to know if they could have fireworks for the day peace was declared and she'd just told them it was never good to count chickens before they were hatched and David said how could you count them before they hatched and Maggie said count the eggs stupid and he'd replied that some eggs got eaten. In the middle of that argument, Bob got up from the table and picked up the receiver. He hardly spoke to whoever it was but listened and put the phone

41

down and stared at them in a kind of trance. Then he'd caught himself and smiled and said it was a wrong number. She'd never forgotten that look. A ghost might've reached down the wires and grabbed him by the throat to make him gawp like that. She'd asked him what was wrong as soon as the kids had gone off to play. "Who was that really?" Then he'd looked at her as if she was a phantom herself and answered, "It's just that I don't feel very well," and sat down to finish his meal. And then he'd said, pulling himself together, "It was Mr. Herman, I have to go to London tomorrow and then to Ireland." And the date was April 14th, 1945. Two weeks later, there was Alf Kindle at the door, hang-doggy, *something you ought to know*. She wondered still what had prompted Alf to toil up the hill on that wet day to give her the letter. There on the piece of blue paper, spelled out in flowing, foreign handwriting, was a message beginning *Mon tres cher Robert . . .*

Today they'd have fish and chips for supper and tomorrow a nice chicken roasted with all the trimmings. Maggie had always been easy to feed. She liked her food and hadn't put on a lot of weight. She was still lovely. She had his family's Irish blue eyes and near black hair. And living in that climate, more sun made her face darker. But was she happy? What stopped her and Theo, who for all his German name was nice enough, from having children? When she'd been here a few days and they went into town for coffee, she could ask in a tactful kind of way.

Bob had come back up the stairs and was now walking very slowly across the landing. She didn't want to think about the time when he'd need a wheelchair, the time not far off when they couldn't manage this house. He was in pain a lot of the time but he struggled on. A lot of their life was about pretence. She pretended not to notice when he held on to things to get around. He pretended he could do the things he'd always done while gradually, little by little, she took over the household jobs that had been his. Changing light bulbs, putting the clean curtains back on the rail, seeing to the rubbish— she got tired some days of her own ability to cope. *I am the strong one.* She did recognize a kind of pride in the feeling that she was the one who held the place together.

At times, she wished she had been made small-boned and fragile.

When he'd reassembled the blue china one piece at a time on the tray for Maggie, he went back downstairs for Frieda's mug and carried it up with care and left it on the little table outside their bedroom. He knocked on Maggie's door and went in. She was hidden by the duvet, only her hair like a dark animal showed on the pillow. He set the tray down on the table by the bed and looked at her for a moment before he crept quietly out. It was a wonder how children grew the way they did and developed lives of their own often without a decent road map. Too late he'd realized how much more he could have done in the way of direction to help her and David through life's jungle. If they had listened. If they had seen him as more than an all-the-same man.

He went into their room and there was his wife sitting up in bed, waiting.

"Tea, dear," he said.

"Where's yours?"

"I drank it downstairs."

"Well, thank you. Are you coming back to bed?"

"I—no." He would've liked to. He was tired. All those trips up and down the stairs had worn him out and his knee was crying out for rest but something had stirred in his mind. Of course *they* hadn't rung. But, truth to tell, a little of the old excitement had returned, as if he was able now to set off to whatever country *they* considered an enemy and to lurk about listening in to unsuspecting natives. Being old and arthritic was an excellent cover. Who could suspect him of anything more than a little end-of-life tourism? He might sit about in outdoor cafes, a nice old gentleman, a sympathetic listener. Of course, his usefulness would depend on the language spoken.

"It's going to be a nice day," he said. And his wife smiled at him over the rim of her mug so there was a fair chance that it would be. While he washed and shaved, he recalled the code. Respond in one hour after the first call. He'd transferred the number from diary to diary for thirty-one years and always written it backwards for security. But in all those thirty-one years, he'd only had to use it once. And that once made him regret he'd ever agreed to help 'them' in the first place. 'This is going to be unpleasant, Mr. Parkes, but you can speak the language and you've signed the agreement. We need someone right away. It's the Yanks.'

That's what they'd said then. That fateful, dreadful time. And he'd gone along because it had been easy, really, all the pre-war stuff, and he thought he could cope with something that was only 'unpleasant.' There was also his sense of pride. Men his age and older had gone over there and fought and some had died. David's friends' fathers were heroes and he was a stay-at-home, selling wool to the factories that made uniforms, a lowly warden in his spare time. No cause for family pride there except that he was not doing nothing, or worse, making money on the black market. The truth was that he answered the call out of guilt. *Herr Rosenbaum won't be working here any more.* And he could only think, then, that the man who had always treated him kindly might have been betrayed by something he, Robert Parkes, had said in that paneled room in London.

'Of course,' he'd replied and, next day, before he'd got over the feeling that at last, so late in the game, he was doing something, he was there in a place he'd been afraid even to imagine.

He looked at his own image in the mirror and beyond it he saw the drawn skin and hollow eyes of those other faces. That vision, that first look was more than an ordinary human could bear. I am not a soldier, he had shouted in his soul. I cannot stand this. But the bodies lying there had put up with more, much more and so he stood, he interpreted, he explained. A piece of his heart shrivelled in that place. And he'd allowed them to take his photograph as if he wanted a souvenir! Why didn't he just say, I'll take a skull, a foot! He shuddered. It could do that to him still.

"I thought we might go to the Black Horse," he said to Frieda when he came back from the bathroom. "We'll see when she gets up."

"Do you think she's all right?"

"Why should she be?"

"What do you mean?"

"Who is ever all right?"

"Are you all right?"

That was one question too many. Soon they'd be in the usual pit of unanswered queries. To put an end to it, he said, "She's fine. She will be fine. Leave her alone. She's come for a rest, for a bit of peace."

"Did she tell you that last night?"

He was tempted to say, Why would she? but let it alone. He glanced at his wife, her face down to the mug, sipping tea that couldn't be hot any longer. She was his life partner and the gap between their beds was no wider than one pillow but as deep as an alpine crevasse. It wasn't that they never spoke at all. They had ritual talk about the children. David's doing well. We always knew. When he won that prize at school. Lately though it had been, She keeps him there. She can't be an easy woman to live with. As long as he's happy. But that was as far as they got because neither of them believed that their son should have left his job in Leeds or emigrated or married Linda Grewson. Though for his sake, even though he was thousands of miles away and couldn't hear, they'd given up referring to her as Miss Gruesome.

They talked about the golf they watched on TV, and they made small decisions. Perhaps it was as much conversation as any long-married couple ever had.

"How's your knee?" Frieda asked.

Maggie had heard her father come into the room but stayed under the covers. She couldn't bear it that he had brought her tea in bed. A very old man, damaged by arthritis, was waiting on her! She couldn't force herself to look out and smile and tell him it was wonderful. Besides, she'd been in the middle of a new scene in which she would tell Theo that he was blind to the needs of third world countries and that the nights of sex they enjoyed, the music, the movies, their hikes in the ravines couldn't ever make up for their political differences and it was time for them to take the other route. I will be a thirty-nine-year-old woman who lives on her own and likes it, and every now and then I'll meet a pleasing man and we'll have love-you-and-leave-you sex. I'll travel to France and Germany next year. I'll be fine. What about you, Theo?

She reached for *The Accidental Man*. She'd saved it for the journey but between meals and the movie on the plane and chatting to the woman beside her, she'd read very little. The love scene in the first pages had made her smile even though she knew that a happy beginning to a Murdoch novel usually meant trouble ahead A breeze from the open window ruffled the pages and brought in different words.

"There's nowt left. You drank it last night, you greedy sod."

The 'greedy sod' didn't respond. Val next door was probably hanging out her laundry to dry in the wind that was blowing off the moors. Her sheets would be white as white and all her clothes would smell of daisies and buttercups and cowslips. Maggie regretted that none of her own linen, hers and Theo's, knew anything but the fusty inside of an electric dryer.

She looked at the tray with its white cloth and the blue cup and saucer. Her mother's precious Spode. The jug too! She couldn't recall it ever being used. It was never taken out of the cabinet except at spring-cleaning when everything had to be lifted out and washed and polished and returned for one more year. It wasn't the price of it that mattered but there was a sentimental value attached to it which her mother never quite explained. It had to do with the other man, the man who came back damaged from the first war. The man she might have been happier with.

What was her dad thinking! She laughed and looked round the room. They'd put books on the table that they thought she'd like and old copies of *The Dalesman*. There was water and a glass on a little mat, and a yellow rose in a thin vase that she hadn't noticed last night. The desk she'd had in her room in the house on Gledhill Avenue stood in the corner, and her old chair. On the desk was the china statuette of a woman dancing that she and David had bought in weekly payments for Mother's fortieth birthday. Watching her open it that morning had been a breath-holding moment and then, for a second, Mum was amazed; she couldn't believe they'd managed to achieve this purchase all on their own. And David said, to spoil the wonder of the occasion, 'We didn't steal it.' Then they all saw that there was a crack in it. They'd been had. But the saleswoman wouldn't take it back. Two kids like that. They'd likely dropped it on the way home. She had cried. David had gone silent. Mother had said she would always treasure it. Dad, without saying as much, thought they'd been extravagant.

Maggie added milk to the cold tea and drank it quickly. The china had to be washed and returned to its place before its escape was discovered. The cup slipped and some of the tea dripped onto the peach-coloured duvet cover. It was peach and lime and rose and now had a spot of beige on it. The only thing to do aside from dragging the cumbersome thing into the bathroom was to fetch some water and try to soak the stain out.

She opened the bedroom door and could hear her father talking. He was downstairs alone. There was no answering voice. She hadn't heard the phone ring. Old people did talk to themselves. Wasn't it why she'd come back, to check on their progress and report to David? She opened her door and heard one sentence spoken loudly, "How do you think I could get away?"

What on earth could he be up to? Who could have called so early in the morning? To speak in that way, it had to be someone he knew. When she was fifteen, sixteen, seventeen, she'd lived through her mother's suspicions. The war had been over a few years and Dad was going to the Continent again. He'd set off to the station without a farewell kiss from his wife. The atmosphere in the house was bleak. And her mother had turned to her and said, "Should I go see him off?" So they went together, she and her mother, and saw him hurrying towards the platform. They shouted. He turned and waved but kept moving, and they heard the great chuff of steam from the engine as he ran and hurled his bag in the door of a compartment and climbed in after it as the train moved off. He leaned out and waved to them again. "That was the train to Leeds," her mother said. And they both knew he should have been going in the other direction.

But there could be no reason for her mother's jealousy now. He had a bad knee. He was going deaf. He wasn't surely the Casanova of her mother's fancy. And yet the words she'd just heard him say had no other meaning except that someone wanted him to get away, for an hour, for a month, forever, and that he was considering it. She felt as if a foundation had been knocked from under her and she wanted to call Theo. And stopped herself. She had just instinctively thought, I have to call Theo. To tell him that her seventy-one-year-old father was having an affair?

She wished they were in bed together under this duvet which was as hot as six blankets. *My parents are about to get a divorce, Theo.* Father? Dad? Don't go. *Father, dear Father, come home to me now, the clock in the steeple strikes one.*

But maybe in this house which smelt of age, she too was getting deaf and had misheard the words. Or they referred to a meeting of the Antiquarians. How was he going to get away with his daughter there on a visit? It could be as simple as that.

"Gerron out of it." Val was still out there probably shooing a stray cat or waving off an aggressive magpie, living her morning drama while her quiet old neighbours were getting ready to begin their day.

Maggie went into the bathroom and came back with the cup full of water.

Her mother was standing in the doorway of her own room, looking at her and at the precious cup in her hand.

Greg had heard his parents come in. When they weren't back by midnight, he'd worried that they were in a car crash, his dad driving after too much wine at the O'Briens'. For a while he'd imagined what he would do, an orphan, owner of a house, a whole empty house. He could fill it with friends and die young of parties and sex and drugs. Or Maggie and Theo would take him in and be kind to him and Theo would treat him as a project, watching him, propelling him to an unwanted career all the while telling people the sad tale of his parents' death. Wearing black at the funeral, girls would see him and wish to comfort him in any way they could. And lying there, he could think of many ways.

At any rate, the relief when he heard the door open and close and then their draggy footsteps up the stairs was real. They were weird in their different ways, but Jason's parents were a good deal weirder.

He put his light on again and began to read *The Hobbit*. He hadn't liked *Lord of the Rings* much but everybody at school thought it was the greatest thing since books were invented. He preferred real stories. Truth.

In the summer, if he could earn enough money, he'd decided

to go and see his grandparents. Granddad had whispered to him
one day that he had a secret, something to tell. Perhaps he knew
where people had hidden their treasures during the war, perhaps
he knew of a place where the enemy had landed on the moors,
perhaps he knew the real identity of a German general now
calling himself Briggs and keeping a pub in the village like that
TV programme set in South America . . . down in the cellar was
a spider, flat and brown, shaped like a pancake, the size of a saucer
. . . and a girl with spangles in her hair was stroking it . . .
Argentina . . . where they danced and were naked in the sun.

"Up in the attic, there was a spinning wheel."

"Bungalows don't have attics, Mum."

"This one did."

Maggie had heard the story often and wasn't sure why she'd
chosen this moment to argue about the layout of a holiday home
she'd never seen. There was something like a wall between her
and her mother at the moment. She knew it was the strength of
the tie between them that stopped feelings from becoming words.
It was like a light that was too bright to bear or a look that was
too intense to face. And she wanted nothing more on this first
day than to return the way she'd come, to back away as if from
the dread presence of royalty. She looked at the door, the window,
the chimney. Her heart felt like a heavy and treacherous animal.

And then her mother said, "I made gooseberry pie for later.
You always liked that."

Was that it? The fact that her mother remembered what kind
of food she liked? At any rate she was brought back into orbit by
memories of succulent fruit cooked between two layers of pastry.

"I suppose it was one of those bungalows with one upper
room," she conceded.

"I was afraid of the spinning wheel."

"Did anyone use it?"

"I was quite sure that at night a witch came and spun something horrid, so one night I went up there."

Her father was putting his hand in his breast pocket every few minutes as if he'd forgotten something or was making some kind of sign or had a pain in his chest. Perhaps he kept the secret pictures there. Images from his single days? A photograph of himself from the one time he'd been to Norway, with his arm round the woman who wanted him to get away?

"It was dark. And when I got to the top of the steps . . . it was more of a ladder . . . I could hear the wheel spinning."

Sitting here innocently with his wife and daughter, was her dad dying to go and meet whoever he'd been talking to, she assumed, on the phone? She didn't like to consider the other possibility—that he'd been talking to himself. She hadn't expected to be holding either of them back from their lives. Foolishly, she'd imagined her parents sitting around waiting for her or David to call. Planning for them to come, sighing with loneliness.

"I ran out of the house and down the street. I must have been about seven."

And now that she was here, she had a sense that she was in the way. This will go on and I'll get stuffed with their memories, their lives before I had life. As if everything her parents had done and known was piled on a plate and she had to eat every scrap. Think about orphans, she said to herself. Consider people like Theo with no memory before their own time. So listen! Don't leave anything on this plate. Take it all into yourself. It's rare nourishment of another kind.

"In the middle of the night. In a strange town. Only it wasn't the middle of the night really."

Maggie shrank from her mother's loving look. It was hard to bear. It took her over, possessed her, wanting more than she could possibly give.

"I got muesli. I know you like it."

"Thanks, Mum."

The room sparkled. The windows shone, inside and out. The pink and yellow curtains had been washed for her visit. The silver frames round the family pictures gleamed. The cloth on the table was starched and so white it was nearly blue. Her dad was wearing a dark blue suit as if he was going to a meeting at the town hall. He sipped his tea without paying attention. He'd broken his toast into little pieces and forgotten to eat them.

Then her mother said, "We had such good times in Scarborough," and he perked up.

The milk Maggie poured onto the cereal was as thick as cream. And the coffee had grounds floating on top.

"When you used to go with the Schroeders?" Maggie asked.

"Well that was before . . . " her dad said.

"That day Hannah started running up and down the beach pouring water on strangers. She'd gone out of her mind, poor thing. They said he was unkind to her."

"We laughed at first."

Before they could start on another series of memories, Maggie took over the agenda. "What shall we do today?"

"Whatever you like, love."

"I was thinking we might go to the Abbey."

"It's all tourists now."

"Then we'll be tourists. I talked to Ron last night about a car."

"Jim Hobson's boy. He runs a whole hire service."

"He's done very well for himself," her father said, remembering now their driver from last night. "His father was a crook."

Frieda burst into tears.

"Mum? What is it?"

Her mother got up and walked to the kitchen in a dignified, don't-follow-me way.

"Dad?"

"Leave her be. She's pleased you're here, that's all."

"Are you sure?"

"It's a build-up of excitement. Waiting and waiting. She's been looking forward to it, getting ready. Now you're here."

They ate in silence for a few moments.

"You've got the garden looking nice."

"Not me. We pay a lad a pound or two. He comes on Saturdays when it suits him."

He became silent again. Maggie picked up the morning paper and read, Nixon's advisors refuse to answer questions. North Vietnam silent on number of *POWs*.

Her father said, "War is a terrible thing."

The phrase was like an echo in a cave. She'd heard him say that in different ways and in that tone all through her last years at home. As if even after the war was over, the blood and the deaths and screams and sorrow continued to shower down on their lives, on everyone's life. She looked at her father's pale lined face and wished for a time machine so that she could roll history backwards and find her father a gentler era to inhabit.

"When was there a peaceful time?" she asked.

"There's always been a war going on somewhere," he replied.

And she remembered that her father came from a riven nation.

Frieda dried her eyes on a tissue and took a deep breath. Maggie had come but would leave, and David might never come to see them again. His wife kept him in Canada against his will. There was no way he could prefer a country like that to the place where he'd gone to school and joined Scouts and gone to university and done well. But that was silly thinking. Of course he wanted to be with his wife and there were chances over there that might not have come to him here. As long as he was happy—if he was. They'd only started to call Linda 'Gruesome' after that weekend in the cottage by the lake in Ontario. The smell of pine trees, even of pine-scented floor polish, could bring the memory back. They'd seen what they'd seen and then wished they hadn't. Next thing they knew, Linda had foisted Theo onto Maggie. She had given him Maggie's address when he came over to Leeds and now there they were, both of her children, mismatched and living far away.

She watched the cows in the field amble down the slope towards the fence. Sometimes she thought they played a game to see which one got to the fence first without increasing speed. She jerked her mind back to the here and now and told herself not to be an old idiot. There'd be time enough for senility later. Her only daughter was sitting there at the breakfast table, yet she had begun to cry for no other reason than that she wished David was sitting there too, and she felt guilty and ungrateful for even thinking it. A host of thoughts flitted round in her head like bees. Children come and go. It was to be expected. Leonard had taken off in a flimsy plane and not returned. Time passed. The cow with most black on it had got to the fence first and now put her head over it and was looking straight at Frieda as if to say, They took my child and ate it so what have you got to cry about? Has anybody slaughtered one of yours lately? The cow could only have in its big fat head images of other cows and juicy blades of grass, but her own head contained a huge album of pictures: Scenes and faces and places going back, if not the whole seventy years, then sixty-six. First old Mr. Bowers handing her a birthday gift over the low wall that separated his house from theirs. A wooden jigsaw puzzle, handmade. *For you, little Frieda.* In the next clear picture, a policeman was bringing her home after she'd wandered off and got lost. From then on the memories piled up, over-laying each other, getting dimmer the closer they came to the present. Alf Kindle on the step holding out the letter with his 'I thought you ought to know.' Bob's denials seemed sincere at the time but behind them she'd sensed something darker, as if the matter were of little account.

All of the stand-out memories were framed in the heightened

colours and sounds of war. Like the fighting on the Bayeux tapestry, both wars were by now still, silent battles fought across a woven landscape. Dear Leonard was one of the knights wearing embroidered silver armour and a flying helmet. A stain stitched in darkest red ran over his breastplate onto the field. The Swiss woman was there in colour, indelible but not, alas, lying on the ground with a spear through her heart.

My name is Gerda. We'll call you Miss Bohm. There are the children to think of. It wouldn't do for them to call you by your Christian name. Take her things up to her room, Bob. I hope you'll be comfortable. Thus she'd welcomed the snake into her own house. She'd even told Maggie and David to respect the snake and not to go into her lair without being invited. The back bedroom is hers, a foreign country now. Keep out.

In the time of peace: A small hotel, a double bed, Constable's "Hay Wain" on the wall. She and Bob running on a beach together hand-in-hand. Bob was wearing an old-fashioned bathing suit and she had on the silk beach pyjamas she'd kept for years, more for the memory than that she might wear them again. The smell of the sea, the seagulls squawking, the slippery pebbles under her feet. Bob reciting at the top of his voice, 'I must go down to the sea again.' The Schroeders had gone off to get dry and order tea. She and Bob found a deserted rocky inlet, a cave with a carpet of damp soft sand. Perhaps after all, they should have christened David "Alexander" so that they could call him Sandy for short.

She put two more slices of bread in the toaster, reminded herself that she was the one who held this little world together, and returned to the others, smiling.

"Sometimes you remember things," she said.

"I'm going. Going now," Greg said.

"Close the door on your way out, gently."

"Me and Jase might go to the new Bond movie this afternoon."

"Not the same without Sean Connery."

"It's *Live or Let Die*."

"Don't be late."

The door was closed with ironic care. Linda gave David her but-we-are-happy-here-aren't-we smile. He'd never yet been able to respond to that smile with a loud and definite NO, though now and then something in him wanted to. Desperately. She looked at him across the table. He looked down at the day's news which was yesterday's news served up in simple, slanted bites.

"He's a good boy," she said.

The good boy had just gone out wearing a pair of black jeans that showed the top of the crack in his ass. David sighed. In his twelve years here, the fine word arse had become corrupted into a word that signified an animal, a silly person, as well as a backside. The good boy was also wearing a shirt that said to the world, *I may be stupid but I can lift heavy things*. He was probably going to his friend's basement to make excruciating sounds on his electronic keyboard until the neighbours complained, and then he and his friend would remove themselves to the street to wander and talk and look for trouble in the shape of girls.

I've become an old man, a man who doesn't understand the young. I'm an old man who pretends the danger on the streets is sex because I don't want to contemplate drugs and violence.

Linda, on the other hand, like the other women roundabout, stayed young, in touch. Perhaps every single one of them had a lover. Linda? He looked at her and smiled back. Did she and her friends snort lines of white powder to enable them to hit harder and leap higher and win? No! Health was their goal, not just for themselves but for everyone within range. Her skin was smooth and soft. She added colour but didn't need it. Only the lines under her green eyes were a clue to her age.

Once a week or so, he had a fantasy of going off to live on his own in an apartment. That apartment was equipped with a sound system that would flood the place with the pure sounds of Bach, Bon Jovi, Eric Clapton. He would recite *Hiawatha* in the bathroom at the top of his voice. And in the wall-to-wall fridge, there would be a selection of ales and Guinness and a medley of rich cheeses. The drawer in the bedside table would be full of pictures of women bound and unbound. The dream stopped there and moved into nightmare. On a local tennis court lay a toy boy with thick blonde hair beaten not quite to death with his own tennis racquet. *I'm not a violent man, Judge,* the killer said. In France it would be called a crime of passion and thousands would take to the streets holding placards which read, 'Free David Parkes.' *Bollocks*, replied the judge. *Twenty years without parole.*

"Trudeau says Senator Martin will be given a very senior job shortly."

"That's nice."

"It means putting him out to pasture."

He put the paper down and looked at his wife. Her hair was hanging over the script she was reading. A poet might have said her hair was like a raven's wing, hiding half her face. Whatever she washed it with, it shone and he liked it. Liked her. He wished he could help with the show and would be called on later to perform the simpler tasks of taking tickets and counting money, but for now there was nothing he could do. His previous efforts at editing had left too many long pauses and his ideas for moving actors around a stage apparently lacked subtlety.

"What are you going to do today, love?" he asked.

"I'm playing tennis this morning."

"We could go to the flea market to look for props."

"I can't give up the court."

"I might come and watch."

"Why don't you cut the grass?"

Because I cut it last week. Because I don't want to. It's a make-work project, an alternative to welfare. I am a flightless bird at the moment. But I am not going to sink into ennui. I will not succumb to adust. Blight will not enter and rot my soul. The bastards who have rendered me unemployed will not make me unemployable. They don't know my plans and if I had any I wouldn't reveal them. I will appear to be sitting around happily in this bright land waiting for something to turn up.

He saw patience set into her face when she said, "It has to be done sometime. And I thought it might be good for you to have some exercise."

So he'd become an expensive pet which needed walking to keep it sleek and in condition. He compensated for his mean thought by passing her the main section of the paper before he'd finished reading it.

He stared hard at the help wanted ads as if, just by looking, a hand would reach out and drag him into a new office, a new situation no longer vacant. *This is our new financial manager, janitor, short-order cook. Let's all give three cheers for Dave.*

"Theo called while you were in the shower," Linda said.

"What did he want?"

"Maggie's gone to England."

"We know that."

"He's afraid."

"We'd've heard if the plane had crashed."

"He's afraid she won't come back."

"Or afraid she will?"

"Don't be an idiot."

Idiot, idle, infest, infidel, infidelity, inextricable. The air was filled with significant words beginning with i. His wife stepped out of the back door. She didn't kiss him or say when she'd be back. Her back was implacable.

Linda stepped out of the door lightly because she was afraid of shouting at him to get off his ass and do something. She couldn't wait to get to the court and smash balls into the netting at the far end. With each ball she would mentally scream out one of what she had identified as her five main problems: Lack of sex. The new personnel director. Greg's lack of interest in his future. Her forehand. David out of work.

You must not, friends, magazine wise women and TV personalities advised, let him see that you are frustrated. Not even when he's sitting about speaking in oblique phrases? Staring into the air with a blissful look on his face although he is now contributing nothing to the household expenses? She feared he had moved into a Buddhist phase and had decided that striving for money and saving for retirement was unimportant. When they'd met, that was their shared philosophy: The world was a materialistic hell which could only be saved by self-sacrifice and love. Well, they had changed and come to understand that the universe needed their efforts if it was to go round in a decent and orderly way. Love had seemed to become less important than the struggle to move the country along. His job was to keep the ship of finance on an even keel while she helped a large hospital to run like a well-oiled machine. Her spare time occupation was no less worthwhile in that it offered entertainment to many, and to a few a chance to hone their thespian talents. Who was she kidding! She directed plays because she liked doing it and because she loved actors and their chameleon ways. She laughed to herself at her own efforts at self-deception: Linda the noble martyr. She parked her car and locked it.

She wished she hadn't invited Theo to dinner. A quarrel would erupt before she brought the dessert out of the fridge but a quarrel might be an improvement over the quiet accepting look on David's face as he made remarks about the colour of broccoli or the advantage of carrots. As for Theo himself, she could only put down their brief affair to the fact that she was young, and the later moment of damp lust all those years ago to the fact that she was drunk.

Walking through the little clubhouse, she said hello to the few already there but didn't stop because she saw two women she'd had to reject for the role of Shedra. Each of them was still waiting for her to see the light and change her mind or better yet, for *A Perfect World* to fall flat on its face. She went onto the court and began to smash balls into the net.

She saw Gerry watching her. In an exaggerated pantomime of fear he dodged past her to the other end of the court.

"It's too hot for this," she said. She'd put on a white shirt and slacks and wished she'd worn shorts. The sun was beating down through a steamy haze.

"It's Toronto," he answered.

"Let's move to Vancouver."

"Is that a serious offer?"

"My turn to serve first."

"Hey! I'm not your enemy, Linda."

"I'll be gentle," she said to him.

"Theo, come in. Dinner won't be ready for several hours. About eight in fact."

"I just thought I'd drop these off."

David tried to love Theo like a brother but Theo wasn't the kind of brother he'd ever wanted. His imaginary brother was like Maggie but with more muscle. His brother would drink beer and like hockey and football and own a boat on the lake. Theo had brown facial hair that made him into a type. He looked like a save-the-worlder who thought that only shaving the skin round his mouth below his cheekbones helped the environment and made him look sincere. He was also deprived in the height department and always seemed to be looking up. He handed David two bottles of wine in a bag marked 'bottles.'

"One of each. I didn't think to ask what we'd be having."

"I bought steaks yesterday."

"Great. Where's Linda?"

"Playing tennis."

"Ah."

"Coffee?"

"No thanks. She's directing a brand new musical, Maggie said."

"Premier performance. I tried to talk her out of it. The composer calls every other day to say the libretto is garbage and the writer complains that his words are being drowned out by the music."

"I don't know how she makes the time."

"Well that's it. She makes time." *She crochets minutes and hours together into one bright pattern of office and exercise and drama.* He could see the warp and weft of the cloth that Linda wove out of her days. Her work ethic was hard, imprinted on her by her background, a long trail of antecedents going back to the eighteenth century. Pioneers with drive and foresight, they sowed their crops and harvested wealth and position.

His own forbears, far back in time, had probably been hairy fellows who died young in tribal warfare before the Viking invasion. He liked to think of them as short, dark Brigantes, members of a tribe driven to live in the harsher northern climate by the Romans, fighting a rearguard action all the way; not shepherds but soldiers. Mixed then with Norse blood, many of their descendents were tall and fair-haired like him.

"It was sudden, Maggie's decision to go," Theo said.

"Had you had a disagreement?"

"Only the usual. Has she called you?"

"No—but then why would she? Why don't you call her?"

Theo made a couple of turns round the kitchen and then said, "I hope the wine's okay."

"Would you like a glass now?"

"It's a little early for me."

David poured a glass of wine for his guest and got a beer out

of the fridge for himself. Linda had no doubt invited Theo in the
first place because he was on his own, but also as a companion
for him so that she could leave the two of them after dinner and
go back to the play. But she surely hadn't asked him to come for
the whole damn day.

Theo was turning over the pages of the newspaper, snorting
every now and then at displeasing items.

"Look at this," he said, pointing to pictures of glossy and richly
dressed couples at a charity benefit. "Why don't they just send
their clothes?"

"They wear them more than once and then they give them to
the poor."

Linda had come from that world. A world where people still
now and then dressed formally in the evening, where dinner
was a ritual, a place and time for candles and conversation, and
a stand-up cocktail hour before. This evening, she would run
downstairs dusty, wearing jeans and an old shirt, and forget
about candles and eat quickly not saying much. He had
brought her to this, a downhill move. *Life is for ascending, not
descending:* A saying of his dad's. It was a depressing idea. It
isn't possible to go upstairs all the time. He tried to remember
the name of the poet who'd said it. A long French name. His
dad had often mentioned the guy. Not quite French, more
Dutch-sounding.

"I picked this wine because it's Californian and I think they're
producing some really good stuff these days," Theo said.

"Verhaeren!" David shouted.

"Californian?"

"Belgian I think. Yes. Belgian."

"Do the Belgians make wine?"

"My dad used to go to Verviers when he was selling wool and
he met a relative of Verhaeren's and every time he went there
the family invited him to dinner and they used to talk about their
cousin the poet."

"Ver—who?"

"Sorry. It's funny how things just come into your head sometimes. I suppose Verhaeren would have said they come to your mind because they're necessary. He believed that people could live together in harmony and that the world would go on getting better."

"They should and it would."

"Then the war came and he saw what men were capable of."

"Awful to have your faith shattered like that."

"Doesn't it happen all the time, Theo?"

"What made you think of that just now?"

"I sometimes wonder whether you weren't meant to be a psychiatrist instead of a journalist."

"Curiosity is necessary to both."

"To tell you the truth, I was thinking about Linda and that she made a downward move when she married me. Her parents used to dress for dinner. They always had silver candlesticks on the table and lots of starched white linen. Her mother sipped sherry."

"If I were a psychiatrist, I'd say you were depressed."

Theo smiled at him and looked boyish and clever and David wanted to say that he was as happy as could be but the words came out differently.

"I wish I'd had a job like my dad's."

Theo said, "Why don't you go to this town in Belgium? Check out the places he went. You can travel a damn sight quicker now than your father did."

"Then it wouldn't be the same."

"You could find slow trains."

"Or a bicycle, or a barge! My dad wanted me to have a better job than his but I don't honestly think he believed there was one."

"It sounds to me, David, as if you have unresolved issues here. Perhaps you're beginning to feel trapped. You see, with a job like mine, I can come and go and work my own hours."

"All my hours are mine at the moment."

"That can be another kind of trap. Caged in by the expectations of others. Seriously, you don't have to go back to Bay Street."

"It's what I know. It's all I know."

"It's the easy option. Look. I don't really want this now." Theo set his glass on the counter. "I'll be back around six. David, this time out might be a gift for you. Use it. If you're afraid of flying, go by boat. But go."

David heard him close the door and thought about Europe. In Verviers they made the chocolates, *langues de chat*, that Dad always brought home from abroad. He could taste that refined smooth sweetness now. The oval tongues were the perfect shape to slide between your lips and hold in your mouth as they melted. He added Theo's wine to the marinade and poured it over the raw steaks and reckoned it was two weeks since he and Linda had made love on the green silk sheets.

They were at Bolton Abbey and he was walking in an alpine meadow with Gerda. There was a carpet of edelweiss. A bed of soft grass. A bed in the back room when Frieda and the children had gone away for two days to visit her mother. Mountain streams tumbled over rocks, murmuring. And the ghost of the Shepherd Lord was always present in this place.

"We're going to walk through the woods a little way," Maggie said.

"Be careful."

"We're not going far."

The River Wharfe was wide and slow here, slurping unhurried over the stepping stones and he liked to think of the monks lifting their robes, tip-toeing from rock to rock to keep their sandals dry. Monks lifting their heavy brown woolen robes, woven from the wool of their own sheep, washed most likely in this very water. The holy men knew a thing or two long before the wool trade moved North. The soft water that gave children rickets pampered the fleece and made the fibers easy to spin and weave.

How many of those cloistered men had tried to jump over the Strid where the river narrows and deepens. It had tempted many a victim. Only last week a man on his honeymoon showing off to his beloved and shouting, "Watch me, I can do this," had been drawn down into the swirling gyre.

"I'll be fine here," he said.

It was a good place to see ghosts, this, to consider the shepherds who'd driven their flocks all the way from Somerset, Cornwall, Devon, and stopped to wash their fleeces in the river. When they saw how the wool lathered up in a white foam, they lathered themselves with excitement. They hadn't known about the limestone but had stopped by chance in the place of the 'broad ford.' And there they settled, having no idea that one day cities humming with trade would grow up nearby, or that an ordinary man would be asked to do a bit of spying along with the commerce. Every age thinks it knows a thing or two but very little is made clear.

He watched them walk away from him. Maggie who'd grown to be five foot six after all the misery when she was twelve and thought she was set to be a dwarf. Frieda was still an upright five ten or so and not all that overweight. Tweed skirt, tweed jacket, jumper. How much of that outfit was man-made? Hardly anything was pure wool any more. Synthetics washed better and didn't crease. Scientists kept trying to reproduce the fine feel of real wool with chemistry and machines but nothing came close. He hoped it never would.

A family walking towards the river turned to stare at him and he realized he'd spoken his thoughts aloud again. It was becoming a habit. He sat down on a wooden bench and looked around. Close by here, the Shepherd Lord himself had lain on his back looking up at the stars. There were a lot of moments in history which he would have preferred to witness rather than the ones that were forced on him because he was alive in the twentieth century. In 1215, he could have stood behind King John at Runnymede and watched him sign the Magna Carta. In the seventeenth century, wearing a wig and dressed in silk, he might have welcomed Charles the Second when he returned to the throne. But most of all, he would have liked to see Lord Clifford striding into the House of Lords after the Wars of the Roses to claim his inheritance. Was he barefoot? Was he still wearing a shepherd's coarse garments when he walked up the aisle of that aristocratic place? Or had his mother bought him a rich robe to wear? After all those years of living in a cottage hidden among simple folk, he likely spoke their dialect. *Ah've coom to claim what's mine bi right.*

It was a comfort to know that long before the old Priory was destroyed, a truly good man lived here; a man whose fortunes, like so many since, were changed for worse and better by the vagaries of war.

The women were already strolling back towards him, not giving him enough time to finish his thoughts and to put gracious words into Lord Clifford's mouth when he confronted those who had brought his family down. At the end of that imagined speech, he always said, at least in Bob's version, *And ah s'll continue to tend t'flock.*

Maggie was holding a fistful of bluebells though he was sure there was a sign somewhere that told people to leave the wild flowers alone. But she lived by her own rules, did Maggie. He felt a bit sorry for Theo. He'd come over with her twice and seemed nice enough but edgy and took up a good deal of space as if he'd been brought up in a mansion. It was a good thing she'd come without him this time. He had things to tell that he didn't want shared with an outsider.

"Dad," she waved the bluebells at him. He went towards them and not seeing a large leaf nearby, bent down to wet his hanky in the shallow water of the river as he would have done all those years ago, to wrap round the stems and keep the flowers fresh till they made it home.

"You'll fall," Frieda shouted.

When they got closer, he saw that Maggie wasn't holding flowers at all but had been waving a blue scarf at him. He didn't tell them that his left foot was wet. They hadn't noticed him slip as he held out a hand to Frieda when she stepped off the last stone to dry land. When they got to the car park, he insisted on sitting in the back saying he wanted to stretch out his leg, as if there was room to stretch anything out in this box on wheels. He tried to reach down and dry his shoe with his sleeve.

"What are you doing, Dad?"

"I dropped something on the floor."

It was three o'clock when they got home. Maggie worried that her parents were wearing themselves out for her. Her dad had taken his left shoe off and was limping worse than ever. They'd had lunch in a little café with hard chairs and he seemed to be shuffling all the time. Now her mother had gone next door to return a plate to Val and might be gone for a while. Her dad was in his chair, his hand inside his jacket as if he had indigestion.

"Are you all right, Dad?"

"Being old is no joke," he replied.

She didn't have an answer. Three clichés sprang into her mind but she held them in. It's better than being dead wasn't a good response.

He went on. "But it's important to know that you did something a bit worthwhile. Even if it's just having loved someone. Being old doesn't matter so much then. We all have to die sometime. We're the only animals who know we'll die. Dogs, cats, hyenas, go through life thinking they're immortal. And especially rats."

She laughed.

"I want you to know Maggie that I'm very proud of you—and David. When I was in the trade, none of us ever thought of synthetic material. They're the thing now. Pure wool, real linen . . . "

He tailed off and she could see he was back in the warehouse at Kleemans or in Budapest showing his wool samples to a buyer and hoping to make a sale.

"A lot of people can't afford wool, Dad. Synthetics give people a chance to buy clothes that are smart and cheap."

"I know, love. I know. You're doing a good thing. But it was a bit of a shock at the time. We should have seen it coming. Haldane and Huxley and others had given us enough warning. Huxley was a clever writer till he went to America. Never wrote anything good after that. But he and the others, they foretold a lot of things. I'm afraid it's all going to come true. Designed children. Automatic people. Machines for doing everything except wipe your arse and I expect somebody out there's inventing a machine to do that. 'I grieved to think how brief the dream of human intellect had been.' I've never forgotten that—H. G. Wells, *The Time Machine*. It's as if you can see things declining. People are beginning to let machines think for them. We all watch the telly and let it put ideas into our heads. It stops us from talking. In a way, I'm glad to be on the way out. But . . . "

Something had come into his mind that brought a light to his eyes.

"Dad?"

He leaned forward and said, "There's one thing I'd like to do before I go. The Concorde. I think they're letting people go on trial rides."

"For a price."

"'If there were dreams to sell, What would you buy?'"

"'But there were dreams to sell . . . '"

"I'd like to do that, Maggie, go up in that. Can you imagine the sensation of it, flying through air at that speed? 'Just like the man on the flying trapeze.' What do we need our bit of money for? You and David won't want it."

"Dad! You and Mum could live for another twenty years!"

"Aye. Well, she could. But still. Think of it. It's sleek and smooth, like a greyhound. A really fantastic machine. Wells and Verne knew something like this would come. It'll go faster than my words are coming to your ear. I'd love to hear it break the sound barrier. Mach Two they call it. The first time I flew was in a twin-engined prop plane and it took three hours to get to . . . to get to . . . and we were . . . when we got there, well. It wasn't exactly . . . "

"It was a jet, Dad. When you flew to Canada. And it took seven hours—more going in that direction."

"That's right. Yes. No, Maggie." He stopped and she waited. "Remember Marley's ghost. All those chains. It's almost as if I won't be released until I've told someone."

"Released?"

"From here. Allowed to shuffle off this mortal coil."

"That's not going to be for years."

"Remember how I used to do the Rheingold?"

She laughed again but without pleasure. The memory of his imitation of the whole opera was a party piece that brought the house down and embarrassed her and David as they grew older. He used to take the head off the mop and wear it as a wig and prance from side to side playing different roles. Why was he thinking of it now? Was he about to give her a list of his infidelities or the whereabouts of the other family she'd imagined living in Switzerland?

"Herr Rosenbaum gave me those tickets to Bayreuth. They'd been given to him. He couldn't go, he said. I remember his voice when he said that. And I went with his secretary. It was the year you were born. It was grand—grand opera. I'd never seen anything like it in a theatre. It wasn't exactly my cup of tea. You need to be brought up to that kind of thing and we weren't opera lovers."

She bowed her head. Here it came. His guilt. His old-fashioned guilt at spending the night with somebody's secretary, a German woman with a charming accent and thick blond hair worn in a plait that reached her bum. In another man she wouldn't have minded but this was her own father. Did he have to be held to different standards? The answer, however often she asked that question, was yes.

"But why couldn't he go, Maggie?"

She knew but shook her head.

"That's the whole thing. And when I used to clown around with the Rheingold, it was a kind of revenge. I see that now. Because I couldn't bear it. And not all that long after, the war came. We knew it was coming, could see it a mile off. All except Chamberlain. He'll go down as a villain in history. It could have been ended much sooner if we'd been ready. He was as thick as two short planks that man. Of course even though we saw, we hoped. We kept hoping. Just like I hoped Rosenbaum would be back in his office the next time I went there."

He was astride his hobby horse and on his face was the look of sad frustration that she'd seen so many times.

"You can't forget. And I don't know if I should or if it would be better. But when . . . when I went to Ireland. That's what I said I was doing. Going to see your aunts over there. Your mother thought . . . and I did wonder at the beginning whether we should have sent you two to America . . . for safety, but what would we . . . it would have been another . . . could we have saved . . . "

His mind was wandering. His eyes still seemed focussed. She touched his hand. It was warm and not trembling. He drew it away and reached into his inside jacket pocket and said, "While there's just the two of us."

For a moment he looked at her as if he wasn't quite sure whether even now she was old enough to share his secret. She held her breath, afraid of whatever package or note or picture from his past he might bring forth.

"Maggie . . . " he whispered.

"I'm back," her mother shouted from the door.

Linda looked at the maquette and wished the actors were small enough to fit into it. People two inches high could be directed to move here and there easily, and if the writer became troublesome she could put him into the tiny trunk and push him offstage. She set the minute table down on the left and put the fragment of wood that stood for the knife on the chair. Tomorrow, in the church hall, she had to be ready for the actors' queries, the writer's inadequate responses; his weary look of well I wrote it, now be grateful and act it. She wanted to be well prepared before Gilles arrived on Wednesday with the music. When she had so eagerly agreed to direct the show, she hadn't realized that having two components more than doubled the problems. Which took precedence, the music or the words? The words or the music?

From below she could hear the rumbling voices of David and Theodore and hoped they hadn't already begun to argue.

In the night, she had thought of backing out of the project, saying she needed to be at home. But it would have been a weaselly move. Dottie had been rehearsing the songs for a month. Harold in his best moments could keep a scene going on his own. Three of the tunes were hummable. It would work. It truly would. The applause on opening night would be deafening; standing ovation. Bouquets. *Author! Composer! Director! Thank you everyone.*

My job, Linda said to herself, lying on the floor and looking into the maquette like Alice peering into the rabbit's house, is to motivate the actors. Motivate them and move them. In turn they would move an audience and make an amateur production into one of those rare electric nights in the theatre when everything came right. If only it could be as easy as that at the hospital, *go there, do this*, the place would run a damn sight better. Director was her title there too but direction at St. Anthony's was by committee and consensus, slow and not always right.

The phone rang and she wasn't prepared to answer it but it was time anyway to join the men downstairs and assemble the salad. By the time David called out, "It's Louise," she was in the kitchen. She picked up the receiver and said, "Hi!"

To Lighting Louise nothing was more important to the production than her chiaroscuro effects.

"Linda, I have this new idea of making it totally dark when she goes offstage."

"Harold won't like that. He might fall."

"Fluorescent strips."

"We'll discuss it tomorrow."

"You don't like it?"

Steak was already sputtering under the grill. Theo was pouring small amounts of wine into three glasses.

"I'd like to look at it. I really have to see it, Louise. Tomorrow."

She hung up and smiled at the men. She was in this scene now and might as well play it for what it was worth. She took the bottle from Theo and added wine to her glass till it reached the top and then she got the greens out of the fridge. Light and dark green lettuce was a poor excuse for a salad. She wished David had bought radishes, radicchio, mushrooms. She wiped a garlic clove round the wooden bowl and added oil and vinegar and mustard and black pepper and salt and beat them together before she tossed the lettuce into the mix.

"How are the steaks, love?" she said.

"Yours is ready." He held up her rare steak on his fork.

"It looks perfect," she said.

"Why aren't you a vegetarian?" David asked Theo.

"It doesn't necessarily follow," Theo said.

"What are you working on now, Theo?" Linda asked.

"I could say, my soul, my spirit. My life."

The steak dropped from the fork onto the floor.

72

"Sorry, sweetie."

"Isn't that what all of us should be doing?" Theo asked.

Linda speared the steak with her own fork and took it to the counter. She scraped the underside of it and set it down on her plate.

"It'll be fine. In what sense, Theo? Those are huge thoughts."

"We go on day to day, looking at the little questions and never, never getting to the big ones till we're terminally ill and haven't the energy to deal with them."

"And then death is a merciful release," David said. "Here's yours, Theo. Medium well."

"Thanks. No one cooks a steak like you, Dave. But you see what I mean?"

"It comes down to fear," David said. "Salad?"

He knew what Theo was talking about but wasn't about to say so. Last Wednesday, spooning the froth off a cappuccino at the Can o' Beans, he had begun to realize what was missing from his life besides a job. His sense of entitlement had gone, fled, and left him wondering how it was that he could sit there enjoying a cup of coffee that cost three dollars and fifty cents when he was a non-earner and people all over the world were starving. By Thursday he'd moved on to demand what was expected of him. His life, unemployed and comfortable, was at odds with the universe. In another age he would have set out to fight dragons or, at a later time, gone off to be slaughtered for a noble cause. There in the coffee shop, he only knew that he wanted to be tested. He wanted a Lenten period in which to deny himself comfort. Consider what had happened in Washington. A man who had risen to the very top, had fallen, had been brought down by over-reaching. It was a lesson in making right decisions.

"And I'm also working on three articles, a series about the polluting factors of dyes in the polyurethane business."

David tuned in again and heard Theo's words as a dig at

Maggie's work. "Is your steak ok, Theo?" he asked, wanting to snatch it from him and throw it on the floor and walk on it.

"Fine," Theo answered. "But what I was saying is that the world can't go on like this. We're ruining it. Starving half the world's population. Destroying air and water. Letting whole countries sink into a state that's six degrees below Third World."

"If," David said, arguing against his own feelings, "we shared one of these steaks between the three of us, if I'd only bought one, where would the other two go? Would they end up on the plates of the poor?"

"You're being frivolous."

"I'm not. I truly want to know."

"It's the old consumer argument."

"You're saying you don't know."

"I'm saying it's a ridiculous question. You know very well that if people like us stop spending our money, the butcher, the baker and the candlestick maker lay off their employees and the economy goes to hell."

"But this goes against all the stuff you write, Theo."

"It does not!"

Linda said, "Have you heard from Maggie?"

Both men turned to her and answered, "No."

"I made lemon pie for dessert," she said, and their faces softened a little. There would be a sweet truce for the moment.

"But," Theo said, "it's all very well for you to keep quiet, Linda, but you must have some thoughts about this."

"I think you're both wrong and both right. When you've got it sorted out, let me know. It's time for the news. Do you want your pie in the other room?"

"Great response from the oracle," David said.

Linda lifted the pie out of the fridge and held it for a moment as if she might push it into her husband's face. Instead she cut it into four, leaving the largest slice for Greg.

*

"Why are you standing there like cheese at fourpence?" Val's voice broke into the Sunday morning quiet. The door to her house was open and the 'cheese' was perched on the front step, half in and half out. Maggie hurried on down the hill to the newsagents to avoid being caught up in a family argument. She stood for a moment inside the shop and looked at the jars of sweets, the chocolate, the magazines, postcards and papers. She was inhaling the scents of her childhood, recalling the pleasure of buying a comic and a bag of licorice allsorts and hurrying home on a dull afternoon to enjoy them. Tears came to her eyes for no reason at all.

"You want summat, love, or have you come in to browse?"

"Mr. Parkes' *Times*, please. And *The Independent*."

"How is 'e? I've not seen 'im lately."

"Fine," she said and paid for the papers quickly before she was tempted to spend pounds on Pontefract cakes, pear drops, dolly mixtures and copies of *Beano* and *Film Fun*.

She walked back to the house the long way round past sloping terraces of what once were workmen's cottages. The slated roofs all cunningly fitted together, adapted to the steepness of the hill. She walked along the High Street and looked in windows, the chemist's, the baker's with doily-covered plates in the window, empty till tomorrow. And the wool shop, last remnant of the industry that had once driven this town to prosperity. She crossed the bridge and stared for a moment at the old church and the moors rising behind it. She'd left this ancient landscape for the new, for love, for opportunity. Could she see herself in one of the old cottages, fixing it up, re-attaching herself to her roots? After her trip to Europe, she could consider it.

When she got back to the house, her mother had made coffee and for a time there was silence. Frieda took the sports section of the *Independent*. Her father had all *The Times*. He complained that the crossword was a muddle these days and some of the writing was rubbish but he sat back to read it with a little smile of contentment. And Maggie felt the comfort of being at home on this day, wanting nothing better than to spend a few hours reading with her parents close by. She knew well enough that by Thursday she would find the close atmosphere in the small room, her mother's insistence on second helpings of food, *you always liked this*, and her father's pain, too much to bear.

He looked up and said, "This fellow Nixon. They get carried away with their own power. After a time, they forget that other people matter."

Her mother said, "We'd better get there by twelve. It's crowded on Sundays."

Maggie came to with a start. She'd fallen into a sleepy state thinking of Theo still in bed. Today he would call. And she would say to him, I've decided to travel, Theo. Keep the duplex. I'll come back to wind down my project at work and then I'm off to Europe and might never return.

Her mother went upstairs and her father leaned across to her and said, "This government's going to ruin the country. They want to nationalize everything that's left. I'm all for taxing the rich but it's what they'll do with the money."

"It says here widows will be better off under Healey's plan."

"That's going to be a worry to a lot of old men. In Wales, the druids had to hold their ceremony inside. The grass was wet. You wouldn't think that mattered to druids."

"Perhaps they were barefoot."

"Two Scots—ten years for storing gelignite for the IRA. I'd lock them up for life."

She went to get ready, leaving her father to his magpie-like gatherings.

Robert managed to clamber out of the car and follow the women to the pub. These were the women of his life now and he was an old man who did as he was told. Around him were the faces and voices of the place, the atmosphere in which he spent his days, all collected in two small rooms. A couple of men he knew from the Historical Society waved to him. Women who used to be young smiled his way. Women who used to be straight and slim were bent forward over their food.

"I thought you'd like to have lunch here."

The pub had been brought up to a high standard of nineteenth-century quaint. The 'wooden' beams were worm-free plastic and the 'brass' ornaments would never need to be polished. Tankards hung in a neat row over the bar. One wall was covered with pictures of the town from the 1700s on. The centrepiece was a copy of a much earlier document, a testament from the local people to their 'much-loved Lord of the North,' the Duke of Gloucester, soon to be Richard the Third. Beside the dartboard, the cricket schedule showed all the games between local teams for the next two weeks. He found a table squeezed up against the stone fireplace.

"They've ruined this place with their modernizing," he said. "Now when I used to come here on my way to Todmorden . . . "

"I'll get the drinks," Frieda broke in. She got up and moved to the bar.

Her father leaned forward and whispered to Maggie, "Remind me to show you those pictures when we get home. Don't mention it to your mother. It's something I've been wanting to do for a time but you'll have to keep it to yourself."

He turned to respond to someone at the next table while Maggie cast her mind down a list of possible events which had to be kept from her mother. Home for a couple of days, and being with your parents was always 'home' no matter how long ago you'd left and or what kind of house they'd moved into. But this time there was a subfusc strangeness. Her father had an unusual kind of energy as if he was about to take off somewhere. And what kind of pictures? What secret had he wanted to tell her yesterday? Was there some other family—a woman in Brighton, two other children just as much loved? Children who had . . . but she dismissed the thought. He couldn't have had time.

Or did he want to tell her about the Swiss woman, the misunderstood stranger, who had changed the atmosphere in the house forever? She wanted to tap her father on the shoulder and say, *It was a summer Saturday. I was walking round the house in my velvet party cloak, blue with imitation ermine on the collar, pretending to royal birth.* Dad and the Swiss woman had come in late from the office, and the words came out of mother's mouth, a kind of howl, *I know where you've been.* In that instant, the princess had become an orphan child, bereft of adult harmony.

It was the year Dad kept on muttering about the shame of England.

A week or so later, she'd been overheard by her mother telling David that Miss Bohm was a witch and was made to say she was sorry. On another Saturday after lunch—offices were open on Saturday mornings then—Miss Bohm beckoned her into her lair. My name is Gerda. I am tall and slim and proficient and I wear hats because smart women wear chapeaux. I am proficient in three languages. She who can translate holds the key to power. That was a hindsight impression. What the Swiss woman actually said was 'I'm not a witch, little one, but I can enchant. Say after me, *Je suis enchantée de faire votre connaissance.* Hold out your hand. There is no chocolate as good as Swiss chocolate.' Her room was indeed a foreign place. She had brought her own lacy pillows to put on top of the ones that were there although a great fuss had been made about her mother buying new ones. There were several books on the little mantel over the fireplace, and a dish on the dressing table containing fruit. A picture of a red chalet on a green alp spattered with white flowers hung where the gypsy dancer had hung for as long as Maggie could remember. "This room was mine till you came," she'd said, knowing very well that it was rude.

In another memory, a still picture, they were gathered on the steps, the stone steps that led to the front door of the other house. The tulips were out. The sun was shining. Kathleen, who came twice a week to clean, had scrubbed the steps as usual and whitened the edges. There must have been traffic, it was a busy road, but Maggie had no recollection of any sound at all. In her head it was a silent movie. A taxi drove up. Dad helped carry the cases that contained the small lacy pillow and the books and the picture of the Alps and probably chocolate. Miss Bohm climbed into it. And then the silence was punctured by Dad's voice, hollow, a seagull's cry, "Aren't any of you going to say you're sorry she's going?"

Her father turned back to her, smiling.

"You were talking about pictures, Dad."

"Was I? Yes. When we get home. Not here."

"I'd better give Mum a hand."

"She does very well, doesn't she? Hardly any arthritis. I bet she could still play hockey."

Maggie smiled and touched his shoulder and then followed her mother to the bar.

There was no denying *them*. They'd always made that very clear. When they called, you had to respond. "We'll let you know the time and place." They'd always spoken as if they were legion but he only ever met with a single man at a time. The first one in the thirties had said, Just call me Mr. Smith. He was a natty fellow with a superior accent and the look of a pawnbroker's son. He wasn't sure now why he'd thought that except that Smith's clothes and attitude seemed to be secondhand and more like a disguise than his own choice. The last one, Michael, who'd met him in Leeds and driven him out to Yeadon in 1945, had been a serious older chap with a Scottish accent who must by now be a hundred, or dead. But to begin with there was the man who called himself Roper who'd overheard him speaking German to a tourist in a pub near Kings Cross. That small innocent and helpful act, answering the woman's question, 'Wo bitte ist die St. Paul's Kirche?' had started him on a track to the worst sights he had seen in his life. They'd summoned him then as if he was a genie in a bottle. Just like that.

They weren't about to call on him now and hand him a ticket to Vietnam to observe the aftermath. That was not our fight. It had to do with fear and aggression and greed. You can't expect me to make that long flight with my bad knee and I can't speak any variant of Asian tongue. He smiled to himself at the idea of being, at the end of his life, an ancient, creeping spy. Besides, all he knew of the East he'd learnt from Somerset Maugham and it mainly had to do with planters and their unfaithful wives. Not very useful. But he could hear that refined voice now, For your country, Mr. Parkes? 'They' were welcome to what was left of him. This night your soul shall be required of you. Morbid thought. The women were taking their time with the beer.

Frieda, at seventy-three, walked like a soldier, a heavy soldier but straight, and no crumbling joints let her down. She'd been an athletic kind of girl, a girl who could run up and down a hockey field like a gazelle. Right wing. Speed and aggression were what she'd contributed to the West Riding Young Ladies Hockey Team. Her hair still had some brown in it. And her face, well it was the face of an old intelligent woman, the peaceful face of a person who didn't hear very well and who'd come to realize that not everything was worth hearing. Their daughter was not the lovely girl who'd gone off to Germany and returned sad. Sadly, she had gone off to Leeds every day to university, then moved to Manchester and become happy again. Then moved to Canada to live with a journalist. And that was all right. But she was lacking something. It didn't take a genius to understand that whether it was children of her own, or real love, or excitement, there was a gap in her life.

They were carrying three glasses of beer and set one down in front of him. Now this was very nice, sitting here with these two. The pain in his knee had eased up and he felt pleasantly in tune with everything and it was on the tip of his tongue to say, *I imagined that the men from London called me again yesterday morning,* and then spill out all the rest of the tale in one long stream of incredible words. But he sipped his beer and kept quiet.

Frieda was watching him. He'd become shifty and kept looking from side to side now and then as if there could be someone after him. Minds went like this. Paranoia set in with age. She saw it happen at Safe Haven. The change in some of those men and women from one Monday to the next was astonishing. One week they'd be as pleased as punch when she and Mary came in and then the next week a man who'd been polite and a bit cheeky would accuse her of stealing his shoes. She'd seen it too in the hospital during the war. Some of those old people thought the enemy was behind every corner or under their beds at night. They weren't helped by all the slogans. *Careless talk costs lives. Be like Dad, keep Mum.* He'd kept her and she'd kept him and there it was. He looked as though, with all kinds of shadows flitting across his face, he was telling himself a story with different voices in his head batting words to and fro. She had always, well maybe not always, but for a long time, known there was something in his past that preyed on him. Once or twice she'd tried to get him to speak of it but she had never found the right question. And perhaps that had been deliberate on her part. She truly did not want to hear about a woman in his life who was more attractive, more sympathetic, had nicer hair. Even the thought of that brought out a touch of resentment. If the secret he was holding so close was something else, something of which he was afraid to speak, she wanted to hear it. She could keep her counsel as well as anyone. She could bear a burden. In the difficult years of the war and now in these years of old age, she had to be strong. There was no other way. She catered and she coped. It was only on some days she wished that her mother had taught her how to crumple and weep and ask for help.

"I think I'd like a bit of a rest this afternoon," she said. Maggie looked grateful. About this time, jet-lag hit them when they'd crossed the Atlantic like that. And Bob would gladly fall asleep in his chair.

The waitress set down three ploughman's lunches on the table and Maggie looked at the pickled onions on her plate and got up quickly and went off towards the loo.

"When they were little, David told her they were eyes," Frieda said. "Boiled eyes."

Robert removed them from his daughter's plate and pushed them under a lettuce leaf on his own. Suddenly they looked like boiled eyes to him too.

In the church hall, with its pictures of saints, its ghosts and props from other productions stacked against the wall, Linda faced her cast. It was the exciting first day. The day when everything was possible. Linda inhaled the smell of oranges, dust, old socks. The actors round the table were looking at her as they would look at her for the next four and a half weeks, waiting for words of praise and encouragement. They were her family now and she would love and coax them for this short time; they would be a team.

Dottie was still able to spring about the stage with energy and would be off book in a week. Make-up would subtract ten years from her age. Harold Wilbur always took till opening to learn his lines and would play the husband, Bart, in the way he played all his roles, as a Noel Coward afternoon man. Linda hoped she'd be able to rein him in. And then there was Jenna, small-part Jenna

Boreski, who could do wonders with brief appearances and had a sweet voice. At the end of the table sat reliable Jeffrey Black, the only one who'd acted professionally for any length of time. A good-looking man for his age, known for his portrayals of smooth villainy.

Glenda Jones from X-Ray had volunteered to be stage manager and would bring more enthusiasm than efficiency to her role.

"Time to begin," she said.

Linda began.

"I'm very happy to see you all here. This is an exciting new production. We are the first people ever to work on this musical. You've listened to the music and read the words. Because our rehearsal times have to be fitted in between working hours, it will mean that you have to practice the songs at home. This musical is not Carousel, not Oklahoma, and it's not Brecht either. It's a play about reconciling ourselves to the fact that the world we live in is an unsettling place, good and evil cohabit, and we have to manage as best we can. The title isn't altogether ironic. I think as we go along we'll all find things in it that we can relate to. We won't get into singing till Wednesday. Today we'll do a quick read through and then we'll talk. You've met our writer." She nodded to Boris Shaw who was sitting on a stool a few feet away from the table with his script on his knees.

"I'd like it if we just went round the table and said who we are and what we've done lately," Harold said.

Linda didn't want to let him take over but it was part of the ritual and she'd forgotten it.

"More fun to do it after the reading. And then Boris will answer questions."

There were nods and murmurs of agreement.

Boris said, "I'd just like to say that when I was in Paris five years ago I went to two play rehearsals and it was the custom for the author to read through the whole play himself, in one case, herself, on the first day, so that the actors could get a sense of the writer's intentions."

"They do things differently in France," Linda replied.

The music began: strident, attention-getting chords led into a lyrical tune.

"'I knew you'd come,'" Dottie said, beginning the scene in which she had to make clear that although she had clairvoyant powers, she was keeping it secret.

The four actors read on, mangling lines, destroying meaning, but occasionally giving a hint of life. When they came to the end of the first act, Shaw said, "It's not often that my own words move me but I have to tell you guys . . . " He dabbed at his eyes and Jenna took hold of his hand to comfort him.

Linda knew from experience that after today he would have very few kind words to say, especially when she told him that he had overwritten the second act and that the words didn't fit with the music.

David was at the door when she got home. All she wanted to do was close out the voices of the day and have a drink and watch something idiotic on TV. But David, pregnant with news, took her briefcase from her and led her into the living room.

"Maggie called," he said. "It's Dad."

"Oh, David." She hugged him.

"Not that. She thinks he's having an affair."

"Come on!"

"I know, but love is mysterious."

"He's over seventy. He has a bad knee. What's brought this on?"

"Something she overheard. And then when they went to the pub, he nipped out and said he wouldn't be long. He came back half an hour later looking pale and never explained."

"It's an old man's problem. They try to pee and they can't and it takes an age. He needs to see the doctor, that's all."

"She heard him say to someone, 'How do you expect me to get away?'"

"She's got jet lag and her ears aren't right yet."

"I can't stand you being so practical. How can you direct plays if you can't make leaps? Where's your imagination?"

"That's a little part of my life. Weekdays I work in a place where being practical is a matter of life and death."

She was getting into dangerous territory.

As though reading her mind, he said, "I've got three interviews next week."

"That's great, love. Where? D'you need the car?"

"Close together. Around King and Bay. I'll take the subway."

"Tell me about them."

"After. When I come back."

"Good luck, darling."

"I'll wear my lucky tie."

She sat down beside him on the couch and held his hand.

"Is Maggie upset?"

"Mystified. And I guess, yes. I mean kids get upset when their parents split up. It's traumatic."

"You aren't kids. And I really don't think your father's about to run off with the barmaid from the Drum and Monkey."

"Give me another hug anyway."

"Nice." The ironic boy opened the door and passed by, brushing David's shoulders as he did so. "Flakes, Dad."

"Hi, Greg!"

"Got homework for tomorrow," their son replied as he went towards the kitchen and the fridge.

A romantic moment ruined. The ruination had begun when the boy was in the cradle—his cradle or rather large wooden crib. The elf looking over the rail as David took Linda in his arms. *He's awake. He's always bloody awake. He's a daytime sleeper. He'll have to get a job as a night watchman when he grows up.* So their lovemaking had become surreptitious and quiet. And now they usually waited until he was out of the house before they had sex.

Linda looked at her husband. 'Husband' was a word she had loved and it still sounded foreign as if it didn't belong to the English language. Her husband's face had taken on a mellow look. He appeared to be enjoying his life of leisure while she, coping with several things at once, knew that lines were deepening under her eyes and a thousand more hairs turned grey by the day. Soon he would be on the prowl for someone younger and she would be the older nagging woman left weeping in a small apartment and Greg would never visit. His children would grow up without knowing their grandmother and she would die alone surrounded by cats.

"What's wrong, love?" David asked.

"Nothing," she said and patted his hand. "What's for dinner?"

Maggie knew it wasn't reasonable to expect her parents to give up their regular lives just because she was there but she had to stifle a nasty little jab of resentment when her mother said, "It's my night at the Home. It's only a couple of hours. Why don't you come? Some of them remember you. Seeing a new face makes a nice change for them."

It would have been a good chance for her to stay in with her father but he seemed to be willing them both to go out as if for some purpose of his own he wanted the house to himself. To speak to the person who wanted him to get away? To decide which of his mysterious pictures were suitable for her to see? She sighed and followed her mother out to the car.

The Home smelled of age. There was a sickly sweet scent of whatever had been used to mask the complex odour of sadness, of decrepit bodies, of long nights, of fear and pain. There were twenty or so old women sitting randomly about the room, and a few old men. Three people were in wheelchairs. One, almost a skeleton, sat bowed and dim as if he'd already gone and was waiting only to be removed. The management had made some effort to brighten the room, though Maggie thought the travel posters on the walls added a touch of cruelty to the pink and yellow wallpaper. There were books on a shelf in the corner and a pile of games and all she wanted to do was to turn and run. To scream and get away. This is the future. This is how it all ends. It's what we come to. Theooooooooo!

Her mother took her arm and led her towards the cluster of armchairs in the corner. "This is my daughter, Margaret."

Time-ravaged faces turned to her with pleasure as if she had indeed brought some sunshine with her when all she truly had to offer was a newer face, a younger face and a promise that there was life out there still. But their thoughts came at her like poisoned darts: *We were like you once, not so very long ago. Even yesterday we too walked in a sprightly way and had good eyesight. You might as well book a space here. It won't be long.*

"You could turn the pages," her mother said as she sat down at the piano as if Maggie were eleven or twelve and had to be useful.

One of the women pulled at her sleeve and told her to sit.

"I can't talk up to where you are. You're so tall."

Maggie sat beside her and smiled.

"It's just this," the old woman said. "I can't say it to your mother. But tell your father—he is still alive, is he? I suppose so or she would have said. We would have known. We always look at the deaths. A few of us in here knew your dad very well. That was in our younger days. Hard to believe now. But it comes to this. It always comes to this in the end."

"What would you like me to tell him?"

"Sssh. She's starting. She's very kind. She does it for us but some of us'd rather be playing cards. Don't tell her that."

Maggie took her stand by the piano and looked out at the history in the room; the accumulation of years, the lives lived, the excitement, the sex, the good times, the tragedies. It was all there. But it was over. All the work and good deeds and bad deeds, the passions and jealousies and lies and adventures. This was the Limbo they'd talked about in Religious Studies. These people were here to be assessed.

Her mother played the first bars of 'Some of my favourite things,' and a few voices piped up. From the back a bass voice, not old, not straining thickened vocal chords, repeated the words an octave lower than the rest. Maggie looked up. Ron Hobson was standing by the door.

"Page please, Maggie," her mother said.

Her mother's hair was growing thin on top. She was upset by the sight of her mother's skull and wished she could cover it with a hat, a wig, a shawl, anything. She turned the page too soon. Her mother segued into older tunes that had been fresh when these people were fresh. 'When I grow too old to dream.' 'Little old lady passing by.' Not much 'lavender and lace' here. The men and women made a patchwork of dark blue, assorted tweeds, flowered prints, home-knitted shawls. There was a glittering of rings and necklaces, brooches and badges of service. Many of these old folk had served their country in large or local ways.

The voices grew tired. Her mother picked up speed. She'd left 'Land of Hope and Glory' to the end and that roused the ones who could be stirred. Reedy voices grew momentarily strong and the faces shone and Maggie had tears in her eyes and forgot to turn the page so they went back to the beginning and started again. At the end, there was applause. Her mother bowed and began to play a little background music.

Ron came up to Maggie and said, "You haven't changed much."

"I was here two years ago."

"I don't think I was looking then. You were talking to my mother."

"She wanted to tell me something."

"Pay no attention. They all feel they have to tell their secrets before they go. Or else they want to let you know they were important. You can't blame them, can you. It's like people writing their names on bridges and rocks: *I was here*. And here comes the tea. Watch them rush for the chocolate biscuits. Even the lame ones. You could get knocked down."

A young woman wearing a pink overall wheeled a trolley to the front of the room. There was a slow uprising of ancient men and women, a retarded eagerness, a slow rush towards the tea urn, a gentle grabbing of biscuits.

Maggie tried to get away from Ron to return to his mother but he had hold of her arm.

"You have a fine voice," she said to him.

"It goes with my work. I'm an auctioneer in my spare time. Livestock."

Maggie smelt cows, she smelt sheep, she saw curving dry stone walls and heather and lone houses standing on bleak hilltops. She drew away from him and took a cup of the strong tea and went to sit beside the old woman again.

"You wanted me to take a message to my father?"

"I remember you when you were right little. Your dad used to bring you to my house and you played in the garden while him and me had a chat." She laughed. "He was a fine, fine man. I wish he'd pop in here sometimes to say hello. You say to him, when there's just you and him, when your mum's out of the way, say Joanie Hobson wants to see him again. He'll understand."

But will I? Will I ever understand?

Her mother was handing out tea to the ones who found it hard to move, going round the room with the plate of biscuits. There was a look on her face of pleasant intimacy as if she knew all of these people and loved them.

"We were air-raid wardens together, me and your dad. I were a carder at Clements for thirty years," Joanie Hobson went on. "We worked hard in the day and what went on in that air raid post of a night was all the fun we had. Well, we played dominoes. Then we'd go out on the streets. Anybody we didn't like we'd find some chink in their blackout and wait till last thing to knock on their door and tell them to fix it. We had such times. And then we'd be at work next morning, tired out like. I used to wonder why they didn't give us extra rations."

On the way home, her mother said, "There's Grassington. I've always liked it there. And Linton. And perhaps if you don't mind the drive, your father likes that café at Malham."

Maggie wasn't sure her mother really wanted to go on all these trips, or whether they were planned for her enjoyment. Either way, she wasn't going to get into a morass of cross talk that began, If that's what you'd really like. That would end in each of them trying to imagine what the other wanted and they'd get nowhere. It was easier to follow Frieda's lead, pretend it was exactly what she would most enjoy, pray for rain, and hope that on at least one day, she could go shopping in Leeds on her own. She didn't mention Ron's offer to drive her to the fair in Dent next weekend. She didn't mention either that she knew very well what he wanted and that she'd said yes.

In bed, propped up on fat pillows, she read more of *The Accidental Man*. She closed the book on Matthew saying, '. . . there are movements of the spirit which break down resentment, which let love and pity in . . . ' because the thought was too hard to get hold of in her tired state. She would consider it tomorrow.

David hadn't enough breath left to shout *Eureka* but it was definitely a Eureka moment. He'd had to run along Dundas to catch the streetcar and the feeling of his feet on the sidewalk, *klipp, klapp, klipp und klapp*, at once gave him the answer to his problem. The office door had closed on him but on the other side of that door was the whole wide world. *I will run home to Mother. The Atlantic will be a problem but problems are there to be solved. Tomorrow, I will buy the perfect shoe. Today, the planning of distances.* Maps would be required to find the names of cities and towns on the route and to find out how many miles he needed to run each day, not to the end of the world, only as far as Kelthorpe, Yorkshire, England. It would be a hobby, a healthful hobby, and while he was running, he could figure out what to do with the rest of his life.

For an outlay of a few hundred dollars, at least to begin with, he could own the city and way beyond. Klipp and klapp! He and Maggie had used those words to refer to their parents in a kind of secret code when they were kids. Ma was Klipp because she wore those slides to keep her hair in place. He couldn't remember why they'd called Dad Klapp, probably by default and a few years before they knew what it signified.

"Are you all right?" the woman on the inside seat asked. He had apparently been jogging his feet to the rhythm of his thoughts and possibly, although he wasn't aware of it, muttering aloud.

"Sorry," he replied and kept still. He glanced at her, she was about forty and was wearing a nice scarf tucked into the top of her jacket and clutching a briefcase to her chest. In profile she was attractive but profiles could be deceiving. The two halves of a face weren't always co-operative.

"My life is small," he said.

She moved away.

His life was small, encompassed by these streets, the walls of his house, his child, his wife. And those were not bad things. Long ago, in his second year at university, or maybe the third, he had come to understand that he would not be prime minister or a chosen confidant of princes, or a great artist and it had been a great relief. So he had built his life on figures, on pounds and dollars, pennies and cents and made a decent home for his family. Years ago, on one of his history essays, Mr. Glyn-Jones had written, 'You are too easy with yourself, Parkes.' And maybe old G-J had been right.

He leaned across and said to the woman, "Perhaps you've never had an epiphanic moment."

A giant of a man standing by the door said, "Is he bothering you, lady?"

David pulled the wire for the next stop and went to the door quickly before she had time to reply. He only wanted to tell her, anybody, that he had found an occupation. While he was running, oxygen would flow to his brain and give him an idea of what to do with the remaining decades of his life. 'But go,' Theo had said. *Just go.* He would go, not away, not to abandon his loved ones, but simply to move his life, his efforts into a new and demanding sphere.

The new office supply store was really a warehouse with rows and rows of shelves stocked floor to ceiling. He wandered up and down admiring the latest in electric typewriters, paper for every kind of function, pens and pencils, envelopes and wrappers. All of it made him feel like a tiny figure in a forest of usefulness. He was a bewildered pygmy with no purpose; a life-waster. And then he saw the stacks of Bristol board in various colours. He touched the purple and the green and finally chose white.

"Shall I roll it for you, sir?" the fellow at the counter asked.

"No thanks."

"What's it for, Dad?"

David looked up and saw his son. " Is this where you work?"

"I told you last week."

"Sorry. I hadn't realized it was this store. Isn't it a school day?"

"Teachers' conference."

"Right." He looked at Greg with pride. His son was a wage earner. A step above night watchman. There was hope for the lad.

"That's a dollar fifteen. So what's it for?"

"Do all your customers have to account for their purchases?"

"We're the chain that cares."

"You'll be home for dinner?"

"Late."

*

When he got to the house, David took the pristine white sheet into the basement, to the corner cordoned off by two bookshelves and a filing cabinet which served as his office. He found three thumbtacks in the dish shaped like a hippo that Maggie had given him long ago and tacked the board to the paneling over the desk. With a red felt pen he drew a rectangle in the top left hand corner topped by two sloping lines. He added a door and from the door drew two short lines; the beginning of the road to Elsewhere.

By the time Linda got back from the office, he'd chopped up a red onion and an avocado and arranged the chunks in concentric circles on lettuce. The dressing would go on later. He set the large saucepan beside the sink to be filled with hot water which he would later boil for the fettuccine. The can of clams was ready and the garlic. The bread was sliced and covered. He had a few moments now to greet the worker.

"Did you have a good day, dear?"

"All right. You?"

"Yes." He replied with an enthusiasm that made her look at him but he wasn't about to explain. This wasn't the moment. He poured two glasses of wine and doused the dancing imp inside him that wanted to shout his plan to the world.

"I'll just have a wash," Linda said.

"Sit."

She sat and took the wine from him and gulped till the glass was half empty.

"It was an awful day," she said, and tears began to trickle down her cheeks.

Now the fire in his breast except for one tiny spark was almost extinguished. What was he thinking, letting his wife work so hard while he was contemplating an activity that could in many ways be regarded as self-indulgent? Or was it heroic?

He lingered on 'heroic' and said, "Tell me about it."

93

"I've been working on that plan for a month. And now that bitch from the States who's only been in our office since May is taking it over."

"How can she?"

"The draft dodger."

"Oh him."

"He has a degree in hospital administration and another in ergonomics. He fled his country to avoid going into the army. And they come here to live in comfort. There's a whole lot of them, a damn invasion of cowards and castoffs."

They'd had this argument before but he had to say, couldn't resist saying again, "If we were Americans and Greg had been old enough?"

"Those are two big ifs."

"But what if and if?" he asked, knowing she wouldn't answer. And knowing too that she would have hidden her son in a closet, paid for him to live in Canada, Peru, anywhere, rather than have him sent to be killed in a useless war.

"So what happened?"

"Jurgen let him take the files and the papers and I'm supposed to assist him. And you know why, don't you?"

David knew why she thought it was and he didn't want to get into that morass. He could see that it was important for his sanity and for the well-being of the household that he hold onto his idea and that tomorrow he buy some first-class running shoes. He went to the kitchen and came back with the bottle, and some crackers and a wedge of cheese on a plate, prepared to listen and advise.

Linda had slipped off her shoes and put her feet up on the couch. She'd moved the phone to the little coffee table and was telling the story of her awful day to Gerry. She smiled at David and held out her glass for a refill. He sat near her for a few minutes making the kind of faces that he hoped conveyed that she should get off the damn phone and talk to him instead.

"It's discrimination, Ger. How long is it going to take? It's one step forward and three steps back."

David went down into the basement and added an inch onto the path on the board. He sat and contemplated the fine white space that was to be his world. It was an arctic emptiness for which early explorers would have given all their gold, and did often give their lives. *I am setting off into the unknown.* Names like Igloolik and Invialuk also began with 'i' but sounded a lot more friendly than 'infidelity.'

Obsolete. Obsolescence. Out of work. Last day at the office? Had his habit of alliteration been the final straw? We suggest, Les Baker had said, as if there were ten people in the room instead of only the two of them, that you take time out. He had gone on to 'suggest' that with the problems in the market at the moment, David might be glad to look elsewhere. *Of course we'll always be glad to have you back should conditions improve.* By which he meant, should *you* improve, Parkes, and stop freaking the clients out by staring at them as if they have two heads, and trapping them into silly word games. Just because one stock beginning with 'p' is skyrocketing, it doesn't mean you tell our clients to invest in pork bellies, plastics and perfume. He left no space for David to tell him it was a joke and that he had only mentioned the idea to one client he knew very well and that, in fact, it had paid off. At least in the case of stocks beginning with 'g.'

Stomping footsteps overhead signified that the son and heir had returned to the family seat so he went back upstairs to heat the water. The kid had his head in the fridge.

"Tell me about your day," David said.

"Oh Dad!" the lovely boy replied and clattered off up the stairs.

"It'll be ready in fifteen minutes," he called to Greg and to his wife.

'No answer came the stern reply,' a favourite saying of his dad's.

*

Linda heard the call from the kitchen but couldn't face the underdone pasta and clam sauce that was his specialty. She wanted seared halibut with mushrooms and baby spinach and a starched tablecloth and a waiter to put a napkin over her knees and say, will there be anything else, madam? Failing that she wanted her kitchen back. Guilt, fear of being thought redundant in every part of his life, had led David to assume the role of cook. It was too early to lay down rules, but soon . . . soon she would open up to him the wider world of real housework, cleaning shelves and the slats of the blinds and the stove. Meanwhile, there was only one thing to do; she went into the kitchen and hugged him and told him he was wonderful.

Next day at Walk in Comfort, David picked out a pair of shoes that were white and navy. He turned them over to check out the price.

"Can I help you, sir?" the salesman asked.

"I could buy a pair of hand-made leather shoes for this."

"Could you, sir?" the man replied. "Why don't we try them on."

David wished he hadn't spoken because last month he would have paid up without a word. A new reality had set in. Money was not growing on trees, or growing out of his daily labour either. Headhunters weren't beating a path to his door. *Services no longer required* was written on his forehead for all to see.

The salesman eased his feet out of their stern leather shells and encased them in pillows of man-made comfort. David stomped around and looked at his feet in the mirror. In these shoes he could walk to the edge of the world with ease. He wiggled his toes and hopped from one foot to the other. His feet expanded, flattened out like happy fish.

"I'll take them," he said. "Don't wrap them, I'll wear them."

"I have to take the tags off," the salesman said as if he suspected that David would run out into the street without paying, now that he had winged heels. This too was something he had to get used to. He was out and about in the city wearing casual clothes at a time when a man his age should be boxed in, on a perch, at the office, the store, the plant. He handed over his credit card as if it had a million dollar limit. A few moments later he glided out onto the street, Hermes, Mercury, Roger somebody the four-minute-mile man.

As he moved, his worries slid away. After all, there was money in the bank. They had a decent portfolio. Linda had a good salary. He would sit down with her this very evening and draw up a balance sheet. By shopping on a Thursday, buying the special bargains, they could save ten bucks a week on groceries alone. And with careful investing they might even be better off than before. He would use all his expertise to increase their holdings. And he would be free to run. The shoes were magic. He lifted up his arms to let the air flow down his body. He didn't care if people stared. He was a free man. Free to consider what he wanted to do with the rest of his life: actor, soldier, lawyer, teacher, long-distance lover.

It came into Robert's dreams often, and into his waking moments too, that memory of himself, woozy and tired from the short flight and the long car journey, standing in a forest of tall men in uniforms. The lieutenant with his twangy accent wasn't pleased to see the limeys. "This is Mr. Parkes," Michael said.

With military precision, the American moved forward and said, "This is not going to be a picnic, gentlemen. Follow me, please," paying no attention to the woman in the group.

He couldn't remember now what the path was like or how long it had taken to walk from the makeshift office through grey drizzling rain to the caged-in ground. He'd asked where they were but had only been told 'in the mountains.' At first he'd looked up at the sky because he was afraid to look down.

Yards away, was the great gaping hole of the tunnel, a tunnel with no light at the end of it. Darker and darker, like the minotaur's maw, it swallowed people as if they were pieces of cheese, strawberries, sweets. He couldn't stop staring at it because he knew now where it led. On the way from the aerodrome, Michael had said, "The Yanks want as many witnesses as possible because it's unbelievable. They want it seen."

Why then had he been told to keep it secret? He knew why. It was because he mustn't reveal what he'd been doing in his travels in those pre-war years. And one revelation would lead to another and another. There was movement not far off. Wheels. A trolley. And shouts of "*Herein. Hier ist es.*"

The smell was the vilest stench he'd ever known. It made him want to lose the power of smell forever as if these odours would rule his life and no scent in the world would ever wipe them from his memory. And then he did look down and what he saw made him almost willing to give up his sight too. He wanted to lose all his senses at once and become an insensate being, an Aldous Huxley robot.

They had been men and women, once were people. So small, the bodies might have been a pygmy race. And then he saw that some of them were children, and that none of them were alive. And one of them could well be Heinrich Rosenbaum, another, his wife.

"Are you all right, sir?"

"Why isn't . . . " he began to ask.

"They're beginning to move them now."

"Who did this? Why have you brought me here?"

"It was important that this be seen by civilian observers."

Why me? That question must have been asked in this place a hundred times a day. It was as if some punishing force was pushing his face down and saying, 'Look, stare, take all this in. You aren't free from blame.' There'd been hints out of Germany from time to time, and from Poland, but no one had ever described anything on this scale. He wanted to weep but the men around him were all in uniform, even Michael, who had always been in civvies when he sat behind the desk in that London office. This was the first time they'd met since the Spring of 1939, after his last commercial journey abroad. He was horribly aware of his own appearance, navy blue suit with grey pinstripes, shirt and starched collar, discreet tie, a white hankie sticking out of his top pocket, his trilby hat; the uniform of a Yorkshire wool merchant. Michael had lent him a leather flying jacket for the journey but it covered nothing. He removed his hat for a moment in a late and totally useless gesture of respect.

Ancient cries came into his mind. He wanted to shout out, Who has done this to thee? It wasn't a matter for tears. It was beyond the horror of battlefields. The Baptist God of his parents, of his brother, had turned a blind eye to this. He followed the group, walking as if they were tourists in a gallery. The soldier led them back to the shed and someone handed him a cup of tea with far too much sugar in it. All he wanted to do was smell bluebells and sit on grass, to be at home with the children in a time that was innocent.

"We'll be getting back then," Michael said. He saluted the American officer, and the American privates saluted him.

They got into a car and were driven along a winding mountainous road past a checkpoint, the way they had come. The woman MP who had come with them and disappeared while they were walking round that fearful place was sitting beside him choking into her handkerchief. She was probably vomiting but he felt paralyzed and couldn't help. Possibly he would never move again. Even when she lay back gasping, pale against the black leather of the seat, he couldn't reach out to her. Only when she went strangely silent did he tap Michael on the shoulder and suggest that they stop the car. The car behind them halted too. There was a conference between Michael and two soldiers. He was asked to get into the other car and did as he was told, an obedient zombie.

He read the woman's obituary in the paper the following week: A heart attack suffered at her home in Kent. She was spared from carrying the memory, the picture of those bodies, in her head through life. Like those young soldiers, half his age, he had to go on. He had to go back home, carrying a secret bigger than himself, stunned in all his imaginings. From then on it was pretence. As if it were a miser's treasure, he had to hide that horror and would take it eventually to the grave with him. And all those years at work and at home, he dragged the story with him like Marley's chain, and the refrain in his head ran, *If they knew, if they knew, if they only knew.*

He was startled into the present when Maggie said, "The photographs you were going to show me?"

"Maybe tomorrow, Maggie. Not now," he said as if she'd asked him to take her to the park to play bowls and was too tired. "Later."

Her father closed his eyes and sat back. Whether it was to sleep or to close out the world, she didn't know. She wanted to shout at him, Who were you talking to on the phone! Are you going to run away? Leave? Desert the family? What's the matter with you?

Theo would call tonight and perhaps suggest coming over. *I can't do without you, my life here is empty, my love.* If he didn't call, she certainly wasn't going to call him. She was here in this little town among people who spoke her language, surrounded by the beautiful country of her childhood excursions. The woods and moorland, the sheep and fells, gentle rivers, a compact landscape. Here was history and silence, love and calories. And a large, bluff Yorkshireman had offered to drive her deep into the Dales.

Her mother brought in a tray with a teapot and cups on it, and a plate laden with scones cut in half and buttered. She seemed to sense something of her daughter's thoughts because, as she poured out the tea, she said, "It doesn't always do to be obstinate, Maggie. I remember when you were little, you'd never give way. You'd stick to your guns no matter what. A little thing you were, standing outside that sweet shop."

Despite her inclination to scream at hearing this story for the fiftieth time, she smiled and let her mother go on.

"And the man came out to coax you inside but you just stamped your foot and said no, no no. I had to apologize. And you didn't get your toffees that day."

There was a tap at the back door and it was opened and her mother murmured, "For goodness sake. She always knows."

"Hello, Frieda. I'm not stopping. I've just come to have a look at your Maggie. It's been a long time."

Maggie went into the kitchen to get a fourth cup. When she returned she saw that it was unnecessary. Her father had de-materialized. At any rate he was no longer in his chair and Val had settled down on it and moved into her own life, an ongoing tragedy which she was willing to tell and re-tell as often as there were ears willing to listen.

"So he said, I'll be home Wednesday. And I said you'll find t' locks changed. And 'appen I'll have another man in here. You just watch out. And he said, I'll throw 'im down t'steps. You and whose army, I said. And he said, it's football, lass. We're playing away. I know what you're playing, I told him."

Maggie hadn't conceived of changed locks. Would Theo, could he be so hostile to her and her work that he would shut her out and put all her clothes and books and discs out on the sidewalk? Why was the thought of loss so disturbing when she'd decided anyway to leave him and to travel?

Her mother was saying, "Now Val, it's the boys all together. They drink and shout and act like idiots. Then they come back."

Can this marriage be saved? Should this marriage be saved? Maggie set herself up as counselor to the anguished. When did you last have sex? Did your father desert your home in his old age? What have you to complain about?

"I'm at the end of my patience," Val said. "And he will be sorry."

She was a large woman. All the features in her round face were a few millimetres larger than the standard. Her hair was a natural rich brown colour, thick and drawn back with two large butterfly clips. She leaned towards the older woman and murmured a few words as if she thought Maggie was too young to hear what she was saying. Then she turned her attention to the larger world. "I told him it was a crime not to vote even if he does vote different to me. If I'd been one of them suffragettes, I'd've chained myself to the railings. Women put up with too much for too bloody long. Is it better over there, Maggie?" she asked but didn't wait for an answer. "We're still the ones left at home doing the work while they bugger off enjoying theirselves and then come home telling bare-arsed lies and expect their dinner on the table."

Sipping her tea, Maggie wondered where her father had gone. To get upstairs he would have had to pass the kitchen door and she would have seen him. There was something so fragile about him now that there might be a real possibility of him disappearing into thin air. Then she saw his pale face look in the window and away again. He was in the garden, probably pulling up weeds that had dared to pop up between the flagstones since her arrival.

"And so he comes back about eleven and . . . ."

"Will you be wanting anything from Asda? Maggie's rented a car and she'll fetch it for you."

"That's nice of you, Frieda. But he went and got what we needed in the van. If I think of anything."

Maggie admired her mother's way of breaking the stream of words long enough to set Val on another track.

"So tell me what it's like living over there, Maggie? And do you see a lot of your David?"

Her mother got up quickly nudging the tray so that two of the scones dropped onto the floor.

"I'll put some hot water in the pot."

"No more for me," Val said. "I'll be off in a minute."

"The climate's a bit extreme," Maggie said.

"You get a lot of sun."

"It's bright. Yes."

"I couldn't do with too much of that, me. I need shade. Clouds. Too much light bothers me with my skin. In summer, the doctor give me these pills to make me less sensitive."

And they work, Maggie thought. Perhaps we all need some.

"I'll be off then. It's been nice to have a chat."

She walked out of the front door and called back. "You'll come and have tea with us before you go."

The little clock on the mantelpiece told her that it wasn't quite lunchtime in Toronto. The hearing was in three weeks time. There was still some research to be done, preparation so that when the environmentalists asked about the chemicals released into the water, Brian would have the answers ready. He was the spokesman, assured, smart, chosen for his look of innocence. Maggie dialed the office number. Like a rope attaching her to the ground, it made her feel safe. The phone at the other end rang and rang and then Gina answered. The others were all in a meeting.

"I just wanted to know that it was all going on."

"It is, Maggie."

"Fine," she said, as efficiently as she could. "I'll call in a couple of days."

It had to be jet lag, that feeling of being cut off from all that made up her 'life.' She cried out, startled. There was a face at the back window. It was only her father looking in again. He must have dodged down the side of the house when he saw Val leaving.

There was something furtive about him today. And was there a reason why she couldn't ask him who he'd been talking to on the phone on Saturday morning? Why not simply say to him, Who were you talking to so early? Or if he wasn't talking to someone, what was she to think? Or do?

She went out through the kitchen. Her mother was standing with one hand on the sink, staring at the cows.

In the garden, her father was tying bacon rinds onto the bird-feeder.

"The tits like it," he said.

Frieda could see Bob out there; as usual he'd run away. He'd never seen the necessity for neighbours. He couldn't stand Val and her stories. He had no sympathy for that kind of complaint. Or what he saw as complaint. If asked, he would have said that she should think about the true tragedies of the world. That in her comfortable house with more than enough to eat, as you could see by looking at her, she should try to think outward. But what if she did do that, if they all did that, could any of them do anything to help the world? No more than those large animals in the field.

There were days when she wanted to go to some country where the population suffered from disease or starvation and to work with them while she still had strength, but she knew well enough that no agency would accept a woman of her age without qualifications. On other days, most days, she wanted to get out from under the dark shadow that hung around Bob. She wanted a last chance. Unrolling the past through her mind, she knew very well how much of her life had been a matter of waiting upon others, waiting for their decisions, adapting to their plans and days. She didn't regret it, most of it, but now she wanted to get up one morning and say, *I'm going away*. She often thought of Chichester but it wasn't far enough. There was one place in the world she had always wanted to see, and that was the Tyrolean Alps, the Austrian Tyrol. Mountains and a gentle kind of forest and waterfalls. She had enough money in her secret savings account to pay for it. Enough to get her where she wanted. Not as far as Australia or Japan but at least across the Channel and well into Europe. And there she would stay . . . 'with the birds and the bees?' The kids had loved that rhyme. 'Until they could learn to say please?' Until David came back to her? Until Maggie was happy and had a husband with a name that wasn't foreign?

She might have said once or twice to Bob, I'd like to go to the places you've seen but he never answered or maybe he had made soft promises that meant nothing. Their holidays these last years had been little trips to Scarborough, to Ireland, to familiar places where he stood on cliff tops or on the seashore saying, What could be grander than this? Other than their trip to Canada, they'd done nothing adventurous. Now, as if there was a calendar on the wall marking the years, she saw how little time there was left. A short time ago she'd been Maggie's age. Now she was an old woman whose body was falling little by little into disrepair.

She checked off the hours in a day she spent waiting. Looking up from her book and thinking it was still an hour till she could put the kettle on, still half an hour to dinner time, to bedtime. When she'd cleaned all that might be cleaned and the meal was prepared, there were gaps. Just now, with Maggie in the house, those spaces were happily filled, in contrast to the time before Saturday and the time two weeks from now when the slow cycle would begin again. Except that she had decided to make her move as soon as Maggie had gone.

The family might all be startled. They might feel let down. But she had a right to do what she wanted. She stood up straighter and tidied up the dishes and put the milk bottle out. She looked up at the darkening sky. It covered a wide, wonderful world and she wanted to be out there where there were different trees and other languages and people who would make her welcome.

*

David felt entitled to one last cappuccino. He'd run a mile in his new shoes and every time his cushioned soles hit the paving stones, he envisioned himself slim and healthy and needing no other purpose in life than this. The financial world was rolling along without him. Others were writing reports on the stability or otherwise of companies and organizations, examining charts, and keeping an eye on market fluctuations. Money was being made and lost without his help. He dodged past a large man who was standing in the doorway, and jogged up to the counter.

The man followed him and said, "First off, you need a pedometer."

"A cappuccino, please."

"Make that two, " the man said.

"Hey."

"I'll pay for my own."

The stranger's voice was deep and harsh as if he'd spent years smoking outdoors in inclement climates. He brought his coffee to the same table and snatched back the packet of sugar that David was about to tip into the mug.

"Boomer's my name. Coach. Coached Olympic runners before they got to be Olympic material. I could tell you some names. I do it freelance now. Men like yourself, you start running after forty with no style, no method, you end up with wrecked knees, bum ankles. Problems the rest of your life. We start with a plan. A daily regime. In three weeks you can run five miles without losing a breath."

"I'm running for distance, that's all."

"You get home today, your calves'll be as stiff as boards. Did you stretch before you set out? Were you planning to stretch when you get home?"

David looked at the overweight man opposite piling sugar into his own coffee and felt that he lacked as a mentor.

"No," he said.

Boomer's face was ruddy, matching his outdoor voice, his eyes were blue and sharp. He was wearing a tracksuit with the words 'I am an Olympian' printed on the pocket. Miniscule letters underneath spelled 'eater.'

"Won't charge the first two days. After that it's ten bucks an hour."

David moved to the next table.

"Then you need some real shoes. Work with me and I'll have you ready for Boston by Spring."

"I just bought these shoes. I don't want to run in a marathon."

"You all say that at the start. But after a couple of weeks with me, you'll wonder how you got on without me."

"I'll manage," David replied.

Boomer wiped the froth off his face and smiled. It was a warm, encouraging smile. It was the smile of a man who wouldn't be deterred. "See you here tomorrow. Ten sharp."

"Leave me alone," David said. His moment spoilt, he left the café, walked slowly till he was round the corner, and then ran the rest of the way home. Why was there always some expert waiting to tell you that what you were doing was wrong?

The wicket had changed in England's favour after the storm. The spin bowlers' dream.

Pakistan had come back, hitting hard. *What about a trip to Lord's tomorrow, ladies?* But Maggie had never liked cricket. David enjoyed it but couldn't catch a ball to save his life. The only real sportsman in the family was Frieda and she wasn't one for a day out watching others play.

She'd gone to bed, their child, looking pale and tired. He felt pale and tired himself. He'd walked a fair bit more than usual. His knee was telling him that. He picked up the book Maggie'd brought him and looked at pictures of great steam engines. Those were good days. Trains that had a rhythm to their wheels and went chuff, chuff and left a trail of smoke. Today's diesel monsters were fast but had no magic. If 'they' asked him to meet them again he would only go if they offered to pick him up in the Concorde. He laughed at the thought of that great silver machine landing in the market place.

Frieda looked up from the mystery she was reading. He nodded. She turned on the telly. No need for speech there. They were getting to be like two monks in a silent order, the men who'd once walked in the woods at Bolton Abbey or the two in the picture over the fireplace. Where had that painting come from? Why did they keep it there? The announcer's face appeared on the little screen through dissolving lines and his voice broke the silence. "In Washington today, President Ford . . . " *In Ford today George Washington said, I never tell a lie.*

Frieda paid attention to the men and women who spoke from the box. She listened to strangers, not to him. And he had things to say, important, interesting stories to tell to the woman sitting there in the other straight-backed chair. They'd been together a long time now. He'd lost count. The woman was his wife. That was clear. There were ideas to talk about, a world to speak of. He tried to lean forward to tap her on the knee but felt dizzy. And what would she answer, the woman, his wife, if he said to her, Did you know, did you know that Huxley, in his *Brave New World,* foresaw much of what's happening now? And what about Darwin? Evolution changed what humans had believed for nearly two thousand years, and that's only the western people. Other groups had entirely different ways of seeing how the world began. Some believed it all started on the back of a turtle. He wanted to tell her his ideas about art and about the paintings he'd seen in the galleries in Budapest and Vienna and the music he'd heard and how little he understood and how much more he wanted to understand. He knew too much and too little both at once. All this and more he wanted to say. He wanted responses from her but he had no idea really of the stuff that was in her mind. He didn't know what filled her head and what she considered when she was baking, dusting, making beds, doing all those things that left room for thought. Did she recite Tennyson to herself or recall days at school when she'd run up the field dribbling the ball with her stick and dodging past the opposition? Did she think of her brief attempt to get onto the city council? Her only vote-for-me moment? And what did she wish for? He feared to ask that question aloud because the answer might be freedom, freedom from him. Had she ever, he wondered, wished him dead? If there were dreams to sell, what would *she* buy?

In the classroom in Belfast. *Mr. Parkes! Are you awake at the back? What would you buy? Please condescend to join the rest of us and tell us your dream.*

Television was a great gap-filler. Evenings were taken care of and during the golf season, parts of the day too. There was no need, even if he could have thought of a way to begin, to say, What do you think of the Conservatives' foreign policy? The men and women in the box had all the answers. Arguments in this house were rare. They exchanged a few facts every day. The Carters are moving. It's going to rain. Milk's gone up again. But they never sat and talked for an hour about anything interesting or got so deep into a subject that one of them eventually looked at the clock and said, My goodness it's long past bedtime.

Alte Liebe rostet nicht. Had Rosenbaum talked to him of love? Or was it Gerda under a rosebush. And was it true that old love rusts not?

When he got back from the continent, he could have said, I went to the Volksoper in Vienna, they were playing Strauss, and led into a discussion of the end of the Austro-Hungarian empire. Instead, he'd played with the children, distributed his gifts, taken her to bed and made love and said, I missed you. They had made love. Satisfying, pleasing love. But that part of life had rusted, seized up, become a useless bit of machinery.

The secrets he had to keep put a gag in his mouth that blocked the words that could have flowed over there to the quiet woman. If he mentioned Budapest could he stop himself from talking about his meeting with the man in the café whose name he never knew? And later, after that April journey in '45, every mention of death, every reference to life, to the war itself, could have led him to blurt out, 'If you only knew what I've seen.'

If he'd ever told her, she would be burdened with a secret she didn't deserve. Besides, if those words ever came to the surface, he would cry for the whole damn human race and might never be able to stop.

"Look at that!" Frieda said.

He looked at the screen and saw coffins being unloaded from a large plane somewhere in the United States. Soldiers were standing to attention; a guard of honour for the flag-covered coffins that were taken one by one and placed into a hearse. Weeping relatives were watching, and perhaps considering that their loved ones had died far away in a cause they couldn't understand and in a war that had been over for a whole year.

"They just found their remains," Frieda said.

Robert was bewildered and afraid. He thought about the cemeteries in France and Belgium. In those two wars, they would have needed another army, a permanent welcoming guard if all those bodies had been returned to their various homes. Factories going night and day to manufacture Union Jacks and coffins, an ongoing fleet of little boats toing and froing across the Channel with a morbid cargo. An office full of people occupied with notifying the relatives: Be at Dover on such and such a morning and if the tide's right, your dear one will be returned to you. Imagine having to check which bodies belonged to which family. The amount of paperwork alone would keep hundreds busy. And what about those people who had no cars, no way of carrying the corpse home. He saw them waiting at bus stops with their unwieldy burdens, walking along narrow streets carrying bodies of sons and lovers. He was responsible for all this and he had no idea how to set about the huge task. A thousand angry men and women were screaming at him, what have you done to my boy, my husband, my daughter?

"When I was in Belgium," he began. But Frieda gestured towards the television set to silence him as if she had heard everything interesting he might ever have to say.

When I was in Belgium and I went for the last time to Verviers to see my good friends the Van den Kerkes, that was in 1952, they thanked me for what I'd done. They knew, you see, because Jens, the son, was in it too. Mine was a small part but they treated me as if I was the entire Army of Liberation. Verviers is an ancient town. I'd like to have shown it to you. It's on the river Vestre and in those days . . . Anna Van den Kerke was beautiful. A generous woman. There was wool there. And chocolate. She always called me Bobby and kissed me and said, "I've made your favourite cake." We spoke French together and she read her grandfather's poetry to me. One afternoon in a place not far from Frankfurt . . . One evening lying on a grassy slope behind a chalet, Gerda said, Stay with me . . . All kinds of memories had twisted themselves together like the strands of a rope that he was making a great effort to unravel. Field Marshal Montgomery marshalled his thoughts and marched them to the top of the hill . . .

"I want to tell you," he said.

There was a great shushing sound in the room, so loud that it filled the world. *Do you remember when I came back from Germany in 1935, you were pregnant.* His heart was pounding. *When I stopped in London on the way.* She would kneel down and say, 'My hero,' and shower him with questions. At first she might be incredulous. But he had evidence. *When the warehouse burned down.* We will talk to each other. His thoughts were so loud that she must surely hear them but she sat stone-faced watching another face on the little screen. No he said, no, to the images that piled into his mind. Stay back! Begin at the beginning. One at a time, please. *And when I came back in '45 and you thought I'd been to Ireland. I'm going to tell you what I saw. Why should you sit there in that comfortable way and drink tea the way you like it and not know?* He waited a moment and the room was flooded with colour. He, Robert F. Parkes, was going to be recognized finally for what he truly was. He pulled on the new garments bought by his mother for this important occasion and leaned forward to speak.

"I've something to tell you. Dora . . . ," he said.

PART 2

The Legacy

"Are you sure, Mum?"

"Go, lass, go," Frieda said. "I'll be all right. It's a grand drive." She managed not to say *enjoy yourself*; it was hardly appropriate.

She watched Maggie, smart in grey slacks and navy jacket, walk down the path and climb into the black car beside Ron Hobson. She waved to the back of the car as it moved slowly down the hill and turned at the bottom towards the road, towards Dentdale. Her daughter's face had been sad and pale but by the time they got to Skipton, as like as not, young Hobson would have made her smile.

Bob's hat and coat and stick were gone from the hall stand as if he had just set out for a walk into town and would be back soon. She took the vase of sickly-smelling lilies and put them beside the back door. She was able now to entertain the thought that 'Dora' was some long ago one-time woman, forgotten till that last moment. In any case, he'd hardly been in any shape to go chasing after this one and that in the past few years. One part of her mind allowed for a measure of forgiveness. She recognized that he was a man who had perhaps never felt quite safe, quite secure.

She'd looked through his drawers and his father's old writing desk where he stored the bills and household documents and found nothing to incriminate him, no love letters or photographs signed to, 'my darling Bob.' The undertaker's man had brought her the stuff out of her husband's jacket pockets. She'd cried over the keys and the wallet, and given Maggie the envelope with her name on it. The parcel addressed to David had been in his shirt drawer and was now in Maggie's suitcase, to be delivered. She hadn't bothered to look inside it. Bob would never have sent evidence of his illicit love life to his children. Love life! Just when she thought she was feeling all right, the rage would come back as if it was simmering under the surface all the time like a hot spring, and she wasn't ready to let go of it just yet. There were reproaches that had to be stated even if they were unheard. *I was here looking after the children while you picked up your cases and travelled abroad being Mr. Businessman, Mr. Important.* He's happiest when he's packing for a trip, her mother had said once, as if she needed to be told that. Her list of unspoken regrets began with, I too could have had a career or a lover. I could have stayed on working in the newspaper office, moved up, become a journalist, traveled on my own. After the kids were gone, I might have taken up archeology or mountain-climbing. Coaching young hockey players was a pastime, not a life. She wanted to tell all this to Maggie but Maggie was on her way to the Fair.

Once the busyness of the funeral had died down, the relatives and friends gone, Maggie had been preoccupied. Her kindness had seemed almost mechanical as she made tea, encouraged her mother to eat, asked if she'd slept. Of course she was sad that her dad had died. She had loved him. Frieda was glad she'd never done what some mothers did and run her husband down to the children. They'd had a stable home, she'd seen to that. She had provided a decent place for the four of them and then for just two. But what was the value of it now there was only one?

My husband was a travelling man. Those journeys had meant so much to him. When he came home, he was often silent for a time. And sometimes there was a look on his face as though he'd been into a world he had no power to describe. Somewhere neither she nor anyone else could follow. Those were the times she imagined him on a February evening in a chilly hotel room a long way from home, disappointed about a sale, missing his family, looking for company.

My husband was a thinking man. She had tried to understand when he talked about Huxley's ideas but to her they were so impractical, so far from the real world, that she soon turned back to her own kind of book: *Tess of the D'Urbervilles, Notre Dame, Emma,* and, in these later years, the library's stock of thrillers. For years she'd been meaning to read *Bleak House* but the title put her off.

"So she's gone?"

Val walked in carrying a small sponge cake on a plate. The cake was filled with jam and fresh cream and sprinkled with icing sugar. She'd sliced it into six and was obviously expecting to be invited to have a cup of tea.

"I've got so much food in the house," Frieda said. "I think you'd better take that home. But it's very kind of you." She vowed to keep the door locked from now on.

"Your Maggie'll be hungry when she gets back tomorrow."

"They'll eat on the way."

" 'appen they will."

Frieda waited. Her neighbour was pregnant with words. She anticipated the flow and was ready with her defenses.

"Now Frieda, you're being brave. You've carried on like a right trouper these few days. But next week, Maggie's going back to Canada and you'll be on your own. Jim and me are worried you'll sink into depression. You'll give up eating. I mean even Jim, who as you know isn't one for feelings, was disgusted that your Bob's last word was another woman's name. It makes you wonder what kind of man he really was. I've heard tell of a woman who helps people through times like this. You've got grief on top of grief like. Death and unfaithfulness all in one."

"I just need time to think things through."

"I knew you'd say that. You think you want to be independent but you'll sit here by yourself, crying and wishing he could come back to life so you could tell him what a pig he was. And that's not good. I've talked this over with Jim and he's agreed that I should come and spend evenings with you. You'll come to our house for your tea and then we'll come in here and watch telly or play cards, whatever you want."

"No!" Frieda said and hoped she hadn't shouted.

"It's what Maggie would want. It's what your David would want."

"I won't be alone," Frieda replied. "It's very good of you and Jim but I'm expecting David." It was an impromptu lie but when had she not been expecting David?

"When he's gone then."

"When he's gone."

Frieda felt blessed relief. That burden lifted for the time, she offered Val a cup of tea and brought plates and forks so they could both eat a piece of cake even though it was only eleven in the morning. The cake was soft and the cream melted into the raspberry jam and every bite was a treat. They each had a second piece and a third and in no time the plate was empty and they looked at one another and laughed.

"You've got cream on your nose."

"We've eaten a whole cake," Frieda said.

"I do know some things about mourning," Val replied.

Frieda hugged her good neighbour and saw her out. There'd be no need to make lunch now. She was full of sweet buttery stuff, slightly sick but more cheerful. She took the tray into the kitchen and looked through the window. The cows were still there but Bob, Robert F. Parkes, was gone, disappeared, extinguished.

What had she really known of him? The young fellow introduced to her at Hannah Smithers' Christmas party? Hannah who was to be Mrs. Schroeder that spring said, Come and meet this fascinating Irishman. And there he was, standing by the mantelpiece, one hand in his pocket, slim, black hair, deep blue eyes, an exotic creature in that landscape of fair-haired girls and heavyset young men. He told her he'd come to work for Kleemans for the summer and as he talked, she was charmed by his accent but not particularly by him. He's nothing to write home about, she told Hannah later.

But he began to come and watch the Saturday hockey games and cheer for her team. It wasn't long, it seemed, before they were making love on the floor of that sandy cave and she was wearing a quickly bought dress and standing beside him at the altar.

Tears came to her eyes because there had been so much love then, love that stayed between them while he went on his journeys and came back and read to the kids and went to bed with her and made plans for their holidays. When did it happen, when did they begin to step back from one another? There was one answer, and that was Mademoiselle Bohm. Did he call her 'Dora' in his passionate moments? But there must have been others, other hazards, other women.

What had held them together for the past thirty years? Why didn't he walk out? Why didn't she? Perhaps that was the 'mystery' of love; all those days and years when they kept on, simply kept on living in the same house, sleeping in the same room, eating at the same table, saying the same things to each other. Had they settled for neutrality, for peaceful co-existence?

All that talk about life and its being a one-time thing had never meant much to her after Leonard. Leonard was a boy when he disappeared, chewed up in the greedy jaws of that unreasonable war after which there was to be no other. 1917, they were both children. She'd remained alive to read *Idylls of the King* without him, keeping on with life in the way they'd been told to do, not expecting another boyfriend ever because so many young men were dead. And then Hannah Schroeder nee Smithers said, 'Come to my party,' and she'd gone because the war had been over for three years then and it was all right to dance.

"I always tried to keep the house neat and make good meals without too much fat and sugar in them," she said aloud as if she had to impress Bob with her virtues now. "I spent my life . . . " the word 'spent' hit her like an arrow. She caught sight of his photograph and the books he'd treasured, the few he kept on the table beside his chair. She pulled the picture frame apart and took out his image and ripped it into tiny little bits. Grabbing *The Time Machine*, she shredded page after page, ripping the paper and shouting, "I am tired of my virtues! You lived off my good behaviour! If I'd known . . ."

But she had known. Deep down she had known. She felt suddenly tired. She fetched her shopping bag and took out the travel book she'd picked up at Bradley's while Maggie was in Boots yesterday. She brushed the flakes of paper aside and turned Bob's chair to the window and sat down as if she were squelching him flat. Turning the pages, she found Austria. Her tears dripped onto the picture, making a lake.

In the three days she'd been back from England, Maggie had only called once. She'd been abrupt on the phone and there was something in her tone that made David reluctant to call her. She must be jet-lagged, sleeping at odd times. But he was eager to talk to her. He wanted to know about the funeral and how his mother was and whether his dad had left him some kind of a last message. At the same time he dreaded an avalanche of justifiable reproach.

While he waited for the phone to ring, he tried to think about running. He could easily cover the distance from Toronto to Iqaluit by next Easter, five miles a days for two hundred days, and still afford to take a few days off. In winter he planned to run round the track at the Y. As well, he could add on time in his daily life. Was it cheating to wear the pedometer all the time? Round the house? Running errands? At the supermarket? It would be interesting to know how far a shopper walked picking up items from produce to meat to the dairy section to snacks. He clipped the little device round his ankle and went upstairs to clean the top of the stove.

From Iqaluit to Manchester was about two thousand more miles. Add on the sixty or so to Kelthorpe. Four hundred days, give or take a few. *I'm on my way, Mother.* He lifted the burners up and then put them back. Music was required for a chore like this. John Coltrane. 'Trane,' the sax magician. It wasn't the kind of sound his father knew but he might have grown to like it over time. *I want you to listen to this, Dad.* He put the cassette in the player and turned the volume up. A slow, dreamy melancholy filled the room. 'The very thought of you,' and he was dancing with Penny Anderson at the Harmony ballroom the year before he met Linda. Penny, his ideal girl, had drifted away in someone else's arms out of his life, out of the country. He lifted up the burner trays and put them in the sink. The spilled and burnt-on tomato sauce from last week's spaghetti had formed a shape like Australia. He scrubbed at the edges with wire wool till it was more like Wales.

In late summer, the year the war was over, Dad had taken them to Wales for a holiday. They'd stayed in a cottage on a cliff top and it had rained a lot. The rain and endless card games were all he could remember—besides his Dad looking for a telephone booth in the middle of nowhere when they were out for a walk one dry afternoon. He had to call the office, he said, as if he'd just bought a load of wool from the backs of the sheep in the nearby fields and must let Kleemans know right away.

The wire wool wore the stain down to a series of spots.

There was a strange drumming sound behind the lyric. He went to the player to change the cassette and saw a face trying to peer in through the stained glass design in the hall window. He opened the door carefully. Who knew what kind of maniacs preyed on women at home alone in the daytime? But it was only

Theo, grinning; his eyes were shining, his hair was hanging over his forehead, and his shirt buttons were undone.

"Have you won the Irish Sweepstake?" David asked.

Theo said, "Better than that. You must come round now and tell her it's wonderful. She's upset. She can't stop crying." Tears began to run down his cheeks.

"Our father has died," David replied, ashamed that his own eyes were dry.

"We're going to have a baby," Theo shouted loudly enough for the whole street to hear.

David embraced him. A couple passing by glanced at them and made a thumbs up sign, and the man shouted, "Way to go, guys!"

"This is wonderful," David said although he wasn't sure that *wonderful* was the right word.

"Where's Linda?"

"At work."

"Come on. We'll call her from my place."

David locked the door and followed Theo out to his car, swept along in the wake of the other man's delirium. He was still wearing his shorts and T-shirt but it was the day when fall had suddenly descended on the city and he was cold. Labour Day had just gone and the leaves were turning but the dahlias and chrysanthemums were still blazing away. He breathed in the misty air and thought that Maggie's news was a good thing. She could hibernate and give birth next spring. Lambs. Calves. Tadpoles. Renewal of life.

"So she got pregnant in Yorkshire?"

Theo drew his arm back as if he was going to smack him on the jaw. "Two and a half months," he said. "Ten weeks to be exact."

"I meant she found out over there," David said. "It's just that I never thought you would."

"You think I'm impotent!"

"No, Theo. But her age. You've been together ten years."

"Ah. Well, Dave, I'm not religious as you know but I've found myself praying lately. If that's what wanting something with all your might is. Yes, praying. And here we are, expecting. It's a miracle. It's all happened at a difficult time with your Dad dying and I don't know what to say to her. It's as if there can't be a good thing without a bad thing to balance it. As if joy can't be unconfined. I've given some thought to this and I think I'll write a piece about it. You could look at it the other way too, that in despair there is some joy but that's not always the case."

So I'll be an uncle, David thought as he followed the babbling Theo and climbed into the passenger seat of the Chev. He relished the idea of going to toy stores again. Those Christmases they'd spent in England after Greg was born, he'd gone to Hamley's and spent hours among train sets, remote control cars and sailboats, Lego castles. But Theo and Maggie were on the doorstep of middle age. What would they make of long nights, a shaken schedule, the randomness of life from henceforth?

"There'll be unexpected things," he said as Theo continued to drive down the middle of the road far too fast. "Slow down, Theo, please."

"She should be listening to Mozart and walking in gardens, and going to art galleries and staring at the Impressionists. I've tried to take the photos from her but she just keeps looking at them. I liked your father. He seemed like a harmless, gentle kind of guy. All the same, I can't help wondering if this isn't some kind of posthumous nastiness along with what he said to your mother at the end. She seems to be taking it oddly well, by the way. We don't always know what our parents are really like, do we? I mean, I never knew mine at all so I've no idea. It's just what I've observed. I'm only glad Maggie waited till she got back here to look at them. She'd tucked the envelope in her bag without looking at it. There was a funeral to arrange and your mom to look after, papers to sort out. Then yesterday and the day before she was too jet-lagged to care about unpacking. She still has morning sickness but it's not too bad. And I take her lime juice and crackers to bed before she gets up. She doesn't like it much but I think it helps. I tried the bottled stuff but now I buy limes and squeeze them. Some are a lot juicier than others. I suppose it depends on where they're grown. And some have much thicker rinds. It seems a shame to throw all that nice green peel away. Does Linda know how to make marmalade?"

"What photos? I'll run from here if you let me out," David said.

"So this morning, she was clearing out her travel bag and she found the envelope. David, I want you to reassure her about this and get the damn pictures away from her. He should have given them to you."

Maggie was sitting on the sofa hunched over in a way that was surely bad for the child. Her hair looked unwashed and she appeared to be twenty pounds heavier than when she'd set off to England nearly four weeks ago. She was wearing a loose, dark blue tracksuit which signified that she wasn't going anywhere or making happy plans. She looked like an untidy piece of furniture in this well-appointed room and she was staring down at four photographs that were spread out on the shiny coffee table.

"There you are," she said.

"Congratulations, love," David said.

"How can I? Into a world like this? We are not human. We have not progressed. Look!"

The pictures were about three by four, black and white, and at first it was difficult to make out the shapes. He looked from one to another seeking definition. His new glasses were in his jacket pocket at home. Slowly, as if they were emerging from a mist, the figures appeared. Clearly there was an American soldier. David knew he was an American because of the shape of his helmet. The soldier appeared to be twice as big as the civilian beside him. Both men were looking at the ground. Not far from their feet, lying about in crazy bony angular shapes, were dozens of corpses. He thought at first it was a battlefield, the aftermath of a bloody fight, and then he realized that these figures had not been fighting men. Some were probably women though it was hard to tell. They were all nearly naked. Their mouths were gaping as if they'd given out one final unheard scream. They had been human. They were the wrack of human beings who'd been starved and worn down to nothing in misery, deprived of love and beauty and music and even of language itself. It wasn't distant history, some ancient slaughter among savages; the civilian was wearing modern clothes and the uniform of the GI was Second World War issue. Theo was right, Maggie shouldn't be looking at pictures like this.

"Mother put these in your bag?"

"They were in a sealed envelope. She didn't know."

"She must have known." He tried to envisage his mother going upstairs to Maggie's room and placing this awful package in her bag, like a drug dealer foisting a pound of heroin on an unsuspecting traveler.

What Theo had been saying in the car on the way over began to make sense. Maggie always responded to things with her whole imagination. She'd be seeing the 'before' images of these men and women in their daily lives, once laughing, dancing, talking, part of a neighbourhood, shopkeepers, teachers, students, owners of cats and dogs. Two of the pictures showed no live figures, only the terrible hellish charnel house enclosed in a mesh fence as though any of these people had the strength to climb and run. He put his head down. He sighed. He could only think that inside Maggie was an embryo who should not be taking this knowledge in through Maggie's skin and brain.

"Look," she said to him but for the moment he had looked enough. "I always knew he'd seen terrible things. When I was ten, I knew he'd seen terrible things."

She had to mean the photographs. Their father had been given them and had carried them in his wallet and stared at them from time to time to remind himself of the evil that men do to men. In the war, Dad's uniform had been the navy blue serge outfit of the ARP. He'd killed no one, no friends had died beside him of bullet wounds. The three bombs dropped randomly on Kelthorpe had caused nothing more than a fire in Greens department store and one casualty—an over eager warden had tripped over a sand bucket and broken his leg. Their father was a bystander, a man whose only medal was one of tens of thousands given to those who'd served at home. But he'd kept these pictures.

There was a sound from the kitchen of metal dropped onto the floor. David started.

"Jesus Christ!" he said.

Maggie said, "Look!" again, and put her finger on the edge of the fourth picture.

David peered at it and saw what she was seeing. It couldn't be right. He looked away for a moment but when he looked back, the photograph was exactly the same. There was no mistaking the identity of the civilian in the picture—a man with a slightly lopsided stance, wearing a leather jacket that couldn't have been his own, his trousers tucked into rubber boots, a trilby hat on his head, small beside the soldier.

"Bloody hell," he said.

"Yes," Maggie said. "That's our father standing there."

David leaned back. He felt weak. The solid image of his father, the man present always in his mind, dissolved into wavy lines. "Did he say anything?"

"No. He kept wanting to but Mum was always nearby. On that last afternoon, he seemed too tired. He'd told me a few times that he had some pictures to show me. The envelope was in his pocket with my name on it. All the time, I was thinking it had to do with another family that he kept in Switzerland or somewhere."

"Has Mum seen them?"

"I don't know. He seemed to be keeping them from her."

"But obviously he wanted us to see them."

"He was more than we knew. His life was larger. That's what he wanted us to know, David. He did do something in the war besides sit in the Air Raid Post at nights playing dominoes and flirting with an old woman called Joanie Hobson."

David couldn't shift his mind from the scene before them to the cozy schoolroom where the wardens, playing games for pennies, waited all night for the sirens to howl. He could only see his father standing there amid this human wreckage. He looked at the skulls and bones inside sagging skin and considered that perhaps even the day before the pictures were taken, these shapes had been breathing, thinking, sentient beings. There was an awful cruel geometry in the way they were lying. And this had happened in his lifetime! Why hadn't all the decent adults he knew prevented it? He kept on staring at the fourth photograph. Yes, Robert F. Parkes could speak German but so could many Englishmen. He had traveled in Europe but he was only one of hundreds of salesmen who spent weeks abroad every year peddling their wares. So why him? What hand had dipped down into the grab bag of English life and plucked him out to view this horror of all horrors? The people who ruled over these things, the bureaucrats who ran the lives of spies and subversives, must have known him. That silly song came unwanted into his head, *Lloyd George knew my father, Father knew Lloyd George.* Someone in a London office had known his father and his father had known that someone.

"Were there any strangers at the funeral?"

"What do you mean? Of course there were. People I didn't know like the men from the Historical Society. They were old and kind and said they'd miss him. The cousins came from Sheffield, and Kathleen's daughter, Martha. She cried more than anyone. It was a sunny day. The minister said that bit from John Donne about no man being an island. Why am I bothering to tell you all this? If you'd come you would've known. I had to explain to the relatives why you weren't there. I told them you were sick."

"I was detained." He didn't tell her about driving to the airport or about the ticket he'd bought or the way he'd tried to move his steps towards the departure lounge and heard his name called three times. *Final call. Air Canada 361 to Heathrow. Mr. David Parkes.*

"Try telling Mum that."

They were both quiet as if the corpses laid out on the table were in the room with them. It was a full minute before Maggie spoke again.

"It has to have something to do with his travels all those years ago," she said.

David wanted only to go away and take in this new idea of his father alone. Three weeks ago, he'd begun to mourn the father he'd always known. Now he had to consider him as an entirely different person. Who was the man who had helped him with his French homework, tried to teach him to play cricket, looked for him when he ran to hide? He needed information. He needed truth. And he wanted to search for it on his own. To put his sister off the track he said, "Look. It was long ago now. I mean thirty years. Leave it alone. Forget it."

"Forget! He saved these all this time as if he was saying, Don't you ever forget this. As if they were his last words. I always knew he'd seen awful things. He came back from—oh David! He said he'd been to Ireland that spring the war ended but it was this. This is where he'd been. And he came into the house looking pale and afraid. I know I was only a kid but I remember that look. It frightened me. I thought he was desperately ill or knew something that was going to ruin our lives. I never felt safe after that."

"You were only nine and you had an imagination like a box of monkeys."

"I was ten and that doesn't make sense." But she couldn't help smiling for a second.

"Listen, Maggs, you're pregnant. You're going to have a child. That's what you have to think about."

"Awful things aren't going to stop happening in the world just because I'm pregnant."

"But you don't want to dwell on them."

"I can think my father was a hero."

"And a philanderer apparently."

"What does that matter when you see something like this?"

She was forgiving the lesser sin and acknowledging that there was license in times of desperation—license to be licentious when death was all around. He turned that thought over in his mind, smiling to himself at the image of his father as a dashing James Bond killing and fucking his way round Europe, a sample of wool in one hand and a machine gun in the other. He heard his sister say again, "He was a hero."

"Yes," David said. And he couldn't help feeling a touch of schoolboy's pride. See! So there! All those years at the Grammar School, while the other boys boasted of fathers who were pilots and submariners and gunners, his dad was a lowly air raid warden. But had he truly in fact been some kind of cloak and dagger guy? Maybe he *had* been involved in the struggle.

Who really were the buyers he mentioned when he came back from his journeys abroad, those men who were kind and often invited him to their homes—in Berlin and Vienna and Budapest? Once a Herr Goschen had come to the house on Gledhill Avenue and spent an hour in the front room with Dad talking the language of *Struwwelpeter*. There was a whole spidery network of sticky threads around their collective past now. Nothing was what it had seemed to be. Their father had been living a double or triple existence while the rest of them went about their simple days: School, homework, football, evenings spent listening to the wireless, playing cards. What had Dad been thinking when he read those incomprehensible and cruel stories to his children? *'Klipp und klapp. Klapp und klipp.' This is how I speak to my customers over there*. Was he offering them a code to his secret existence?

Come and find us, Dad! Hiding under the massive archways of the old aqueduct had been fun mixed with fear. Water dripped from the stones overhead. Strange sounds echoed from wall to wall. And sometimes when the search had taken too long, there was a moment of chilling dread, of being abandoned like Hansel and Gretel with no breadcrumbs to mark the path home.

He held his sister's hand and they stared at the photograph together. She'd carried back from England not ashes but a mystery and this was their father's legacy. *Come and find me, children.*

As the elder brother, he'd seen it as his duty to enlighten his sister about Santa Claus and the tooth fairy. When they were in their teens, he'd given her some hints about the danger of getting too close to certain boys. She'd laughed at him then. Now, he feared he was seeing a darker meaning to this part of their father's life—if there could be anything darker than what was before their eyes—and this time he would say nothing.

"Maggie," he said. "I want to explain why I didn't go to the funeral."

"You don't have to explain to me," she snapped. "Explain to Mother." When she was angry, her Yorkshire accent became stronger. "You always left me to do the heavy lifting."

"That is not true and you know it," he replied, wanting to pinch her arm till she cried out.

"Who was there when they had to move?"

"That's years ago. If you're going to dig up old stuff."

"Couldn't leave work, you said. As if my career was of no account. And now look at you."

"Tea." Theo came in with a tray. He set it down between them on top of the pictures.

Maggie moved the tray aside and picked up the photos. She

put them into a yellow envelope and tucked that into her purse. "Sorry," she said softly to her brother.

There was a teapot on the tray and three mugs, plates, sugar, milk and a large chocolate cake hacked into rough chunks.

"You're eating for two now, " Theo said to Maggie and put a slab of cake onto a plate for her.

David figured Theo had bought the cake on his way to their house and that by the time the baby was due, its parents would be as big as elephants. And perhaps Maggie would give birth to an elephant. He imagined it cute, with a little trunk, huge ears and notional tusks, letting that image drive out the pictures for a moment.

Maggie was beginning to cry.

"You'll have a lovely baby," David said. "You can call him Theodore or her, Theodora."

The phone rang. Theo rushed out to answer it.

"I don't want it," Maggie said.

"The baby?"

"Cake."

He took the slice from her and ate as much as he could quickly, crumbling the rest, and handed the plate back.

"Or the baby."

"You'll change your mind," he said. "You must change your mind. For its sake, Maggs. It's there now. It exists. You must think of him."

He knew it wasn't the right thing to say but he knew that it was true, a real imperative. He went on, "Mother must be pleased."

"I haven't told her yet."

"It would help her get through this time."

"You don't understand. I tried to tell you on the phone when I called you the day after the funeral but she kept coming through the room carrying piles of his clothes. She was too angry to think about anything except getting all his stuff out of the house. If I hadn't stopped her she would have thrown it all onto the street."

"All you said was that he'd mentioned this other woman, Dora."

"His last word to her, David!"

"It might have meant something else. It could have been the beginning of a longer word."

"Grow up for Chrissake! When he called her 'Dora' that night, Mum shouted at him. She said all the stuff she'd thought all those years. Terrible things. About other women and how he'd never taken her to Austria. Just yelled. I ran downstairs. He was crouched over and I thought it was because he was upset. Val heard the row and came round and she touched him and said he was gone. And suddenly Mum was like a collapsed balloon. She sank down onto the floor."

That was the scene, the awful scene that would replay in Maggie's mind forever. Their quiet, loving father, small in old age, had left behind a huge shadow. David waited for his sister to break into hysterical sobs.

But she said, "And she gave me all those postcards from his journeys. The ones he kept in the shoebox. They're from all over Europe."

"Send the cards back to her, Maggie. People rush to give stuff away when their loved ones die and then they regret it afterwards."

"And the photographs too, I suppose! That's just like you. Get rid of anything you don't want to know about. You have not been listening. She's looking back on him with hatred. She doesn't want anything of his."

Theo rushed in. He seemed to be living at twice his normal speed. "Linda's on her way," he said and then looked at Maggie's plate and patted her on the head. "Good girl."

He didn't notice the crumbs rolling down David's shirt onto the rug. Then Maggie began to laugh in a mad way and Theo tried to embrace her but she was resisting him with her full strength. David got up to leave. Linda would come soon and mop up the tears and the crumbs. It was a woman's job. He kissed Maggie on the cheek and said, "I'll take you for walks. I'll be a good uncle."

Maggie groped into her bag and pulled out a lumpy packet wrapped in shiny brown paper and said, "Mother told me to give you this."

David's impulse was to go at once to the kitchen and drop the thing into a sink full of water. He tried to bend it so that it would fit in the pocket of his shorts but it wouldn't give. He waved to Maggie and Theo from the doorway. They were side by side on the sofa and took no notice as he left.

Theo said, " If your Dad had known you were pregnant, Maggie."

"Then what?"

He poured tea into a mug for her and added milk.

"I don't take milk," she said.

"You do now. He wouldn't have given you those photographs. Let's put them away and look at them later. A few years down the road. Our son should have a cheerful start in life."

Maggie sucked in air. All the people lying in those camps had possibly had a cheerful start in life and where had it got them? Their mothers had sung lullabies to them, their fathers had played trains with them. Their teachers had praised them for getting good marks, or they'd been carefree truants who laughed their school days away. And they had ended up in the direst of places, dying a slow and hopeless death. Her father staring down at those corpses in bitter sorrow was maybe all the funeral service they had. In her heart and her belly, she knew that Theo was right and tomorrow or the next day, she must brighten up. Lighten up. But her father had died without telling her the secret of his life. Her brother appeared to be living on another planet and now her sister-in-law would come through the door like a whirlwind and tell them what kind of crib to buy and what colour to paint the spare room. She couldn't think of anything to do but sip the awful milky tea, wishing it was coffee, and pat Theo's hand.

Theo said, in his careful way, "We don't want to ignore evil, Maggie, but we have to believe in good. We have to know that it triumphs. It does win."

"It's often too late," she said. "And I'm not sure I do believe in it right now."

My father was a good man. That had been a given all her life. Now she felt betrayed as if he'd been unfaithful to her too. Who was Dora? Had the affair gone on all through their lives? She felt a sadness that reached to the bottom of her heart and the deepest recesses of her mind. In the days after the funeral, she'd watched her mother take over the finances, clean out her father's dresser with a single-minded kind of vengeance. 'I'm not angry,' she'd kept saying as she threw socks into a plastic bag. 'I just wish I'd known. I could have made up my mind how to act.'

But she hadn't said what her actions might have been.

David sat down on the wall that enclosed Theo and Maggie's front yard. It came to him like a brick hitting him on the head that his father had died, that he had behaved badly towards his mother and that he was the worst of sons. The pictures, the baby, the godforsakenness of some lives, overcame him. There was an infinite amount of life and history and humanity that he didn't know. I'm a stupid ignorant bastard, he said to himself, and useless besides. And my dad is dead and he never taught me how to fly a kite. He began to cry and found that he couldn't stop. Linda came and sat beside him and offered him a Kleenex.

"Thank you," he sniffed.

She kissed him on the head and said, "Come on, let's go inside."

"I don't know who my father was," he replied. "You go and talk to Maggie. I have things to think about."

Linda took hold of his hand and tried to pull him towards her but he didn't move so she went inside the house herself. Theo offered her tea and chocolate cake and left her with Maggie who was obviously and reasonably worried about being pregnant for the first time so late in life. Theo had only said on the phone that she needed calming down. Panic was natural in the first days, she'd told him. It was due to fear of not being able to cope. She sat beside her sister-in-law and smiled at her.

"This is wonderful news. A baby!" There was no response. "You're in good shape. And thirty-nine is nothing nowadays. You'll find a good ob/gyn and do your exercises. It's going to be great. You can decide whether you want to keep on working after or stay home for a year or two. Theo earns enough surely so you don't need to worry. I see these older mothers around and they look so calm, you know. They don't worry as much. You've had a difficult time and then the flight. You need a rest. If there's anything I can do."

"Tell Theo he mustn't fatten me up like a prize cow."

They both laughed and Linda saw Theo peep round the door and smile. What a simple idiot he was! Then she said, "Let's go look at the spare room. And next week if you like we'll do a little shopping."

She seemed to be having the required effect. The smile had very quickly gone from Maggie's face and she was sitting still, tugging at the edge of the top of her awful outfit as if she was already too large for it but she no longer appeared to be about to cry or scream.

Linda let the quiet settle in the room for a moment. She looked at the large picture of the sea opposite. She'd never liked it. It wasn't a peaceful scene. Menacing shadows suggested monsters beneath the waves and the occasional dark red patch looked like the blood of a shark's victim. Beside her, Maggie was beginning to shuffle and sigh. It was time for the gift. She brought the lion out of her briefcase, a soft spineless lion with a benign look on his furry face. It was still brand new and had been in her office drawer since the last Christmas party. A telling gift from the staff. She handed it to Maggie.

Maggie drew back and yelled, "You think a few stuffed animals will fix everything! A nice teddy bear! You are so stupid. You are all stupid."

She reached into a flight bag that was beside her on the couch and drew out an old envelope. "Look at these pictures, Linda," she said.

David knew it was time to open the package that Maggie had brought from home. He'd talked to his mother that morning but hadn't asked about the contents. Since the name Dora had been spoken aloud by the man she now referred to as 'your father,' she had become more talkative.

"I know now why you stayed away," she'd said to him. "You knew, didn't you, David. And you couldn't bear to tell me. I wish you had, that's all, but I can see it's something a son couldn't say to his mother."

He accepted the false excuse and tried to give her advice about her finances and told her that from his savings he could send her money if she needed it. He invited her to come and stay with them for as long as she wanted. It was an offer that had to be made. Linda would complain for a day and then conscientiously work to make her mother-in-law feel welcome. He would try not to feel oppressed by the weight of his mother's love and distress. He imagined looking at her over the top of the newspaper at breakfast, trying to find the right words to make her smile.

"I won't be late," Linda said. "No rehearsal tonight."

She blew him a kiss and went out. He walked to the window and watched her hurry down the drive; a smart dark-haired woman in a green suit moving into her busy day. He was surprised that she'd shown so little interest in the photographs. After work yesterday, she'd blocked moves for the actors, listened to the music from the show and had a long phone conversation with the writer. At dinner, she'd talked about the baby and said that Maggie would need their support: Older women tended to lose confidence when they became pregnant.

David poured himself a cup of coffee, carried it to the living room and sat down in front of his mother's gift. He'd taken the thing out to the garbage can twice and brought it back. He wasn't sure he was ready to know what was inside it but then he might never be ready. The package was tied with string and measured, he reckoned, ten inches by fourteen. It felt soft on top and hard underneath and it was uneven as though it contained odd-sized objects. The knot in the string had been tied many years ago and had tightened over time. The string was yellowish like the paper. He pulled at the knot and it separated easily. There was no hiding from the contents of the parcel now.

The edges of the paper crumbled as he pulled them apart to reveal a folded piece of paper, a notebook, and a woman's handkerchief. He wanted to tie the parcel up again at once and address it to his son, 'to be opened ten years after my death.' The coward's way? The sensible way? He took up the hanky first and unfolded it. Its lace edging was coming away from the material. He knew that it was, had been, an expensive thing. He rubbed the cotton or linen through his fingers and it seemed to give off a fine scent. *A woman drops it as his father is walking by. His father bends down to retrieve it and, still kneeling, looks up into the dark eyes of a Serbian countess and . . .* There was a brownish stain in one corner of the hanky. He set it down and picked up the folded paper.

"Oh God," he said aloud. "This is Treasure Island!" But he knew very well that the map wouldn't lead to any brass-bound chest full of gold and rubies. It was no pirate's sketch. The outline showed part of Germany. Dresden and Frankfurt were marked, and the boundary with Belgium. The rest was white space except for a few scattered swastikas. In handwriting along the edge, someone had written, 'swastikas indicate camps.'

He went to Greg's room to find the atlas and sat on the bed as he turned the pages. Deutschland was huge compared to tiny Luxembourg or The Netherlands. The white area where the swastikas were should be a region of mountains and valleys where young people were supposed to tramp along grassy paths singing of birds and flowers. He looked round his son's room as if it might offer clues. The posters on the walls were mostly of baseball players. Munch's "Scream" hung beside The Rolling Stones—there was a weird symmetry in those five open mouths. On the bedside table, on top of a copy of *Zen and the Art of Motorcycle Maintenance*, was a card that read, *Teenage Pregnancy. For help call*—Christ!

There was a sound downstairs. He ran down to the living room and wrapped the three things in the paper and pushed the whole lot behind a cushion. When Greg entered from the kitchen, David was sitting upright and breathing like an old man.

"I thought you'd gone to school."

"I'm on my way to the library. Research."

"You've come a long way round."

"Dad?" The ironic boy sounded un-ironic for once.

"Yes, son?"

"Don't call me that."

"You are my son."

"I'm serious."

"Sorry."

"I came back to ask you something. It's about Jase. He's got his girlfriend pregnant."

Oh no, David thought. This is one of those friend-as-decoy conversations. For help, call? This can't be happening. This is Ossa on Pelion.

"How did you . . . I mean he?"

"It's not the how, Dad. We all know how. It's what's he supposed to do? That's what I'm asking."

We all know how! He knew how? He and his friends were kids but they knew how! Did they practice what they knew? How often? With whom? And now the local kids thought of him as the unemployed man who ran through the streets at odd hours and was sure to know the address of a back street abortionist. He wanted to lie down and listen to a harp concerto. He pulled himself together and took a deep breath.

"What does the girl want to do?"

"Marry him."

David couldn't stop himself letting out a wail of despair. "You're too young. I mean you're all too young."

"She's twenty-three. He's seventeen."

Oh yes. That would be it. She tells him she works in the bar while attending law school. He lies about his age and drinks so much beer he can't think straight. *Your place or mine, Honey?*

"Is he sure it was him?"

"Yes!"

David wanted to hug the boy who was looking at him with certainty as if there could be no doubt whatever.

"Well I don't think it's up to you or me to have any opinions about this, Greg. It's between the two of them and their parents. Or his mom and dad anyway since he's a minor. What do you—Jason feel about it?"

"He's in a kind of mad state. Doesn't know what to do. He thought she was—you know—using something."

"Nothing is safe," David said. "Nothing is completely safe."

"Nothing?" his son echoed. "Thanks Dad!"

"Has he told his parents?"

There was some hesitation. Was this the moment? He waited for his son to speak.

"He's going to."

"Greg. If anything like this . . . if you . . . not that you would. But . . . "

"Sure, Dad."

"I mean it's a huge responsibility."

"Jase would like not to have it but she says her biological clock is ticking."

"She's only twenty-three for Chrissake. That is unless . . . " He saw a thirty-five-year-old woman taking advantage of a schoolboy, groping him, murmuring soft words, lying through her aging yellow teeth. He opened his mouth to protest.

"Got to go. I'll be late. See you tonight."

No words came and the boy loped out of the room leaving a load of worry behind him. *My grandfather smoked cigars.*

"Is Dad all right?"

"His father's just died."

"I know, Mom, but he's acting strange."

"How do you mean?" She tipped the last of the bran flakes into a bowl and poured milk onto them.

"Just now I told him I wanted to go with Jason to the Stones concert in Buffalo and he gave me a hundred dollars and said, Have a good time."

"Did he?" She was disturbed. Teaching Greg the value of money and keeping him out of dangerous situations had been part of the web of safety David had tried to weave around their son. Now he had apparently given up on warnings and injunctions and told the boy to go and enjoy himself come what may.

"We have to be kind to him," she said.

"I was," Greg replied. "I took the money. It was what he wanted."

Linda looked at her son standing there in the doorway, tall, handsome, eager. She wanted to hold him there and keep him forever young, energetic, full of ideas, open to the future. She wanted to ward off the stones and arrows that life would hurl at him as he grew older.

"Stay," she said.

"I'll be late for practice."

"I only meant . . . "

But the door closed. He was gone.

David set aside the books he'd picked up at the library, three he'd promised for years that he would read when he had time: Churchill's *The Gathering Storm*, *The Trojan Wars* by Erica Persson and Homer's *Iliad*. The other two, *My Life at Camp* by Saul Derwitz and *The Truce* by Primo Levi, were part of his new research. He put them on the table and regarded them, and then turned to the accounts.

He made out cheques for the phone bill and the hydro and wrote the figures into the debit column. The balance told him that however many company doors closed on him, he should keep knocking till one of them opened. And when that door did open, it was his duty to go inside and surrender himself. Plans for a new career, for an entirely different profession, for saving the world, had to be put on hold. He looked at the letter from J. Bruce Hanford of Hanford and Associates asking him to call to set up an interview. He switched his mind to market fluctuations and picked up the phone and managed not to say, *So soon,* when he was asked to be there next morning at ten.

The prospect of having to look after a baby while the child's parents went back to school made getting a job, any job, imperative. He hadn't mentioned his conversation with Greg to Linda. Linda was likely to go round to the girl's house and demand a meeting and there would be no end to the complications. Greg wasn't a liar and if he said the problem was Jason's, then it was. Probably.

Now, while it was quiet in the house, he was going to look inside the notebook that Maggie had carried back from England. First he measured the path to elsewhere on the Bristol board. It hadn't lengthened on its own overnight. He set out the pens and markers on his desk in a neat row. Lying before him was an old-fashioned schoolbook with hard blue covers and red binding on the spine. He touched it and then smelt his fingers. Musty paper, old age, dried sweat. A ghostly little draft blew through the open window. An early fall breeze that would bring down the first loose leaves. It was a warm current of air like the one in the *Inferno* which punished sensual people by wafting them to and fro for all eternity. He'd never liked that image—lustful men and women drifting past each other reaching out but unable to touch. He always pictured them mute and naked.

By evening, it would rain.

Was there enough stew left for the three of them for dinner? How many housewives, not necessarily the impoverished, were thinking to themselves at this moment, If I eat only a little, there'll be plenty for them and I won't need to cook? Throw some grated cheese on the salad to add more protein. And there is always bread. In fact, given Greg's appetite, there wasn't always bread. He went upstairs and got a chicken out of the freezer and unwrapped the frozen carcass hoping it would thaw in time.

When he went back to his office, the notebook was still there. He touched it again and this time lifted the cover. The pages fell to one side no longer attached to the red binding. A few cotton threads were all that held it together. In what tone of voice had his mother said, Your father wanted David to have this? Was it a rejecting tone? A tone of love? Did she wonder why? Had she read it? Loose pieces of paper drifted to the floor. He picked them up and read the first one fearfully as if he were opening the door to a forbidden room.

My attempt at translating the poems of Emile Verhaeren, by Gerda Bohm, and underneath, a date: May 19th 1938. A few lines in French followed. Gerda hadn't bothered to translate the title. *Les ailes rouges de la guerre.*

There were also three newspaper clippings. One was an item about the Concorde. In spite of protests, the Americans had placed a 24 million pound order. Why, the opponents said, spend all this money on such a risky project when air traffic is declining? June 6th 1963. The next was a picture of a woman in a flowing nightgown holding a candle. It was an advertisement for the new wonder material, Terylene. *It will not crease or stretch and does not need ironing.* No sheep had been sheared to make it. It was one of the synthetics that had conspired to put his father out of work.

The last yellowing bit of newsprint was a copy of a cartoon: The squat family enjoying a hot summer day by the water. Mum and Dad in deckchairs, Dad's fishing line dangling in the river, the kids at play. Grandma in her winter hat and coat was reading aloud from a newspaper, "The U.S. has a nuclear punch of at least a hundred million Hiroshimas. This could wipe out, or 'overkill' as the Americans call it, Russia and China 100 times." Giles's Grandma always knew how to ruin a day.

David fingered these scraps, pieces of the world that his father had kept. The cartoon was an awful reminder; something that must have made the old man wonder if all the previous wars, his own work, all his life, had been for nothing.

The last fragment, a lined page torn out of another notebook, was covered with the name Robert F. Parkes written over and over in beautiful copperplate handwriting as if a forger were practicing to sign the old man's name to cheques, to documents. He admired the loops and the sway of the *r* and the *b*, the *f* and the *s*. Like the lace on the handkerchief, such writing was another skill lost to time. David spread the loose papers on the desk. Later he would try to make sense of them.

He put his wooden frog on top of the book and closed the window. He wasn't ready to find the way into his father's secret life. Spy, hero, serial adulterer? Did he, satyr-like, pursue a whole flock of women whose names ended in *a*? Barbara, Ada, Almeida, Amelia, Linda, Dora?

It was time to run.

Dorothy was still playing Shedra as tragedy queen. Linda had called an extra mid-week rehearsal after work to straighten out a few kinks. Opening Night was only six days away and there were still cards and gifts to buy for the cast and crew, all of equal value and appearance. How easy it would be if it were just the performance, if she didn't have to think about ticket sales, or the opening night party, or the critics. *For a local, amateur production, this is a pleasant evening out. The cast and director have tried to do their best with a musical that should perhaps have been left in the desk drawer.*

She drank her coffee quickly. It was bitter and tepid. She wished that Maggie hadn't shown her the photographs. She'd known of course about those camps, about the atrocities of WWII. Everyone had. But the aftermath of the war had permeated all of her childhood and she wanted to be free of it now. Her father had returned from Europe in 1944 wounded and remote. He was never the same, her mother said. And said it frequently, as if the man who had set off to fight in the ship out of Halifax that fall had been a perfect, loving, charming man who would return and be successful and unscarred. As it was, she and her mother had conspired to build a wall against his melancholy. Her post-war childhood was one of forced smiles and upbeat remarks and stifled feelings of rage and helplessness. But in thirty years, there had rightly been a forgetting. She turned her mind to the tripping music of the first act, and to reminding Dottie that she must turn on the last beat of her song and speak to Harry.

The actors were closing in round her. She looked at their faces and was reminded of a game they'd played at university: If you had to be an animal, which animal would you choose to be? She was surrounded by an amiable bovine, a snooty giraffe, a beaver and a fox. It was the fox who spoke first.

"We've been thinking," Jenna said.

Linda braced herself. They were going to quit en masse, demand equal billing, a share of the ticket receipts, bigger parts. She waited.

Harry braced himself against the doorjamb, took a deep breath, a dramatic pause, and then he said, "It's about the coffee. We all, every one of us, not Jenna because she doesn't drink it, put our fifty cents in the tin. Every time we have coffee, we put fifty cents in. Dorothy brings milk and sometimes cookies. But they," he indicated the stage manager and Louise who were adjusting the furniture on the set, "drink at least three cups every rehearsal and never put one single dime in. I know because I've watched them."

Why weren't you going over your lines, she wanted to shout at them all, *thinking about who you are in the play, getting into character?*

"They put in a lump sum at the beginning," she said, improvising. "I'll ask them how much and make sure that it covers the whole time."

"Three times six times three times two," Dorothy said, "is a hundred and eight."

"Times fifty or divide by two," Harry said.

"Places everyone," Glenda shouted. "We've only got two hours. Last scene. And then we'll do the curtain call."

"If there is one," came from the writer in the stalls.

"Standing ove," Dorothy said. "I can see it, hear it." She clapped her hands loudly but no one joined in.

"Try for that moment of surprise, Dottie," Linda said.

The music began and Dottie sang, almost inaudibly, "'Must I live in a cave and die there alone?'"

Linda gestured for her to raise her voice.

"I'm saving it," the heroine replied.

David could hear Linda shouting. He wasn't listening to the words just the tone of her voice as it rose and fell. He'd never liked opera or musicals, men and women screeching or singing things to each other that would have been better said softly and preferably offstage. He liked the quiet contemplation of chamber music and wanted to say to her, *piano, piano*.

"David!" she yelled in a voice that made him tune in. "Couldn't you have remembered this one thing? You're home all day and—oh God!"

He ran up the stairs into the kitchen and saw what she was looking at. The innocent chicken which should have been in the oven an hour ago was sitting there raw and unstuffed.

"I'm getting answers," he said.

She lowered her voice nearly to a whisper, "We can't go on with this."

"You've got first night nerves," he said.

"It's not till Tuesday."

"How's it going?"

"I'm not going to be put off. We're going to talk about this now. About you and Maggie and the whole thing."

"There is no whole thing, love. Maggie and Theo are going to manage.

"I'm talking about the photographs. It's nearly thirty years since the war ended. Your father should have thrown the pictures away."

"He wanted us to know who he was."

"Well now you know. They sent observers to those places because they wanted civilian confirmation. That's all. You and Maggie both have other things to think about. I know it's been a shock on top of your dad dying, David, but you really have to put it in perspective and not go making up some fantastic spy story around him."

"I'll have a job by Thanksgiving."

"That's a holiday," she said, smiling a very little.

"A perfect day to start."

"I don't want you to feel pressured. The right one might take a while to find, I know that."

He feared this new understanding tone. Like his mother, she was about to shoulder the weight of the family and render him insignificant.

"I'll put the oven on," he said.

"If you put the chicken in now, it won't be ready till ten o'clock."

"I'm sorry, honey. Look, if I don't have a new job earning twice the salary I had at Bakers by next week, you can turn me into the street and throw my clothes out after me and empty the bank account."

"David! You have got something. Tell me."

"Not till I'm absolutely sure."

He persuaded her to sit down with him and talk to him about the rehearsal, the writer, the choreographer and the difficulties of using taped music, while he stroked her hair and told her she was amazing. After a little while, she let him lead her upstairs and to bed for the first time in weeks. Was it sex as a reward for finding a job? No, it was sex because she was hungry for it. Her clothes were off and she'd closed the drapes before he had time to think. And afterwards when the phone rang, she didn't leap off the bed to answer it but lay there peacefully with his arm round her and said they'd order Chinese. The chicken could wait till tomorrow.

"Maggie was right. I'm pretty sure my dad had affairs," he said.

"That doesn't give you permission," she said and rolled over onto him.

"I kind of knew about the Swiss woman but—love."

His training had made him stronger and he knew that in a

little while he'd be able to make love to her again. He wondered if the pedometer could measure the rhythm of these amatory press-ups and whether it would count towards his journey and whether she would mind if he wore it in bed. He stroked her neck and told her it was lovely. He kissed her right ear and told her it was his favourite. She was purring and caressing his chest with her breasts.

"Ooooh," he murmured and heard an echo. An echo!

"Ooooh Christ!" the echo said and the bedroom door closed. They both sat up.

"I didn't hear him come in."

"How long was he there?"

"He's seventeen."

"We're his parents."

"Oh God, I was having such a great time."

"Me too, love."

"What'll we do?"

"He knows the facts of life."

"Kids believe in virgin birth. Moms and dads are supposed to be celibate."

"And there's Oedipus."

"Screw Oedipus."

"I'd rather screw you."

"What do you think he's doing now?"

They washed and dressed not looking at each other like teenagers discovered on the living room couch by their parents. Would their son run into the street to tell all the passers-by that his mom and dad were 'doing it'? Or perhaps he was calling all his friends to inform them of the gross event. The staircase seemed long. When they reached the kitchen, Greg was putting knives and forks on the kitchen table. The chicken was nowhere to be seen.

"I ordered Chinese," he said. "I thought you might be hungry."

*

Theo wanted to be joyful. When he closed the front door and walked down the street to the subway, he hummed to himself. His song of triumph, the song that came to him in the best moments of his life was always, 'Take a sad song.' There were high notes in it that he tried to reach in a whisper. It never worked but nonetheless he was singing. There was the baby coming. A child. And when that little creature lay there in her arms or in his, Maggie would smile and be loving and all would be right in the world. The doctor said that her depression wouldn't affect the child but that it would be better if she could be cheerful. Theo was glad that advice was on the health service and that he hadn't paid some huge private fee for it.

He walked by the elevator and trotted up three flights of stairs. He smiled at the reporters tapping away at their typewriters and wished the ones he knew a good day.

What the editor wanted that couldn't have been said over the phone was a pleasing puzzle. Congratulations? A request for a week-by-week series on the state of Maggie at twice his usual fee? He strode into the office and sat down across from the editor and smiled. The editor smiled back. Griffiths was a large man with jowls and a crooked nose and uneven teeth. He knew he looked like a retired prize fighter and used his appearance to alarm and command. Theo wondered whether, by contrast, his children were beautiful.

"Theo," he said. "You know we like your work."

"Thank you," Theo said, still smiling but smiling less.

"How many years is it now?"

"Man and boy, fourteen."

"Right. Very good. I have to say, though, that in these last two pieces, you seem to have lost your aggressive touch. People expect more from you. We usually get at least thirty letters in response to one of your columns. A lot of angry ones, which we like. Now it's as if you're writing for *Women's Weekly*. You're going to get requests for advice! You're turning into Ann Landers for Chrissake. That one about new life is nicely written but nice isn't what we pay you for."

"I'm expecting," Theo said.

"I know. We're all happy for you. I'm knitting booties. But."

"I'm thinking about the environment."

"We've done that. We've polluted the atmosphere ourselves with articles about it. We've used enough paper to rebuild half a forest. We need to go after two things, consumerism and big corporations. Perhaps some international stuff. This thing about Nixon is going to go on for a time. Trudeau is always good for a few lines. And like I said, North American consumerism."

"That means waste and the environment."

"Big business and over-consumption."

Theo stopped the Beatles record going round in his head and said, "Those two are part of the same thing. They're on the same side."

"Whose side are you on, Theo?"

Theo pictured the child growing rapidly to manhood and now standing behind him and wanted to say, *His*. Instead he said, getting up slowly as if he was thinking deeply, "I'll give you an outline tomorrow."

"And make sure it's got teeth," the editor said.

Teeth! Babies were not born with teeth unless they were very late. The first teeth began to come in at six months. He walked over to the Biggest Bookstore and went straight to the shelf with the child-rearing books. He found one entitled, *The First Year For New Parents*. He hadn't bought a book in three days and none of the others was first-year specific. As he walked down Yonge Street, he passed three homeless men sitting a few yards apart, begging, and gave the middle one a dollar bill. The last one, youngish, dark-haired, clean, held out smooth hands towards the passers-by. Three lines were written on a board in front of him:

Poor Work Habits. Failed to Attract Rich Woman. Hungry for Love. Theo walked on a little way then stopped and got out his notebook to write the words down. He felt a tap on his shoulder.

It was the mendicant. "Copyright," he said.

Theo gave him five dollars and the man went back to sit by his sign.

The subway train pursued its mole-like way under the city and Theo imagined an alert baby admiring the scenery as he made his way through the birth canal, seeing beauty in what to others would be a grotesque and awful dark place. But then the light at last, the world opening to him, a shriek of joy. Daddy!

"My wife is pregnant," he told the man next to him. "We'd given up trying. I mean she's not my wife in the legal sense but we are deeply committed. She's nearly forty but nowadays that's nothing. Mothers are getting older all the time. The thing is, she's had something of a shock. I think she's starting to get over it . . . "

The man said, "The resilience of the human spirit is a remarkable thing."

Theo noticed that his companion was a clergyman and continued his line of thought in silence. It was seven days since Maggie had returned with her great news and only a month ago, when she left for England; he'd been afraid she would never come back to him, had been afraid to call in case she refused to speak to him. When she had called with that sad voice, he'd shouted, No! before she'd had a chance to say, Hello, Theo. When she'd told him that her dad had died, he'd felt guilty relief and offered to go over. But she'd answered in a strange way that there was no need, her mother was fine. They were both fine. And she had come back to him carrying their child. Thank you, thank you, he said, looking up and speaking softly to a deity of unknown origin.

He got off the train at Eglinton and walked the rest of the way home. He went inside and called out, "Maggie." There was no answer. Perhaps David had taken her for a walk. He hoped they'd stopped somewhere for an ice cream. Calcium was important. He went to his study and looked at the range of books on childbirth and baby care, motherhood, fatherhood, saving for your child's education, surviving the empty nest. Not a single one told him what he really wanted to know, the day-to-day marshalling of thought and effort to make the best of the time before the baby was born. These few, countable days. He estimated there to be two hundred and thirty one left. And if he wasn't careful, he would have spent so much time in anticipation that when the boy arrived, they'd be living on the street and there'd be no money for milk or diapers or juice.

Julie next door turned on her stereo blastingly loud. Till now there'd been no need to complain. He could douse the sound with his own music or use his walkman. But when there was a baby who needed to sleep in the daytime, Julie's parents would have to be told. When Maggie felt better he might suggest that they look for a detached house, preferably one that stood alone a good distance from others. But she would have to go back to work and bring in her salary.

He glanced through the new book and saw that it was as useless as all the others. It offered a simpering kind of advice that he could have got from any magazine. Your baby needs a harmonious home. The right clothes to wear. Eating for a healthy child. It was all selling, selling, selling. Rampant consumerism again. As soon as he was born, the boy would be faced with ads for diapers, baby food, toys, furniture, running shoes, vitamins. From birth to the eventual coffin or urn, aggressive salespeople would be pushing their wares into his face. He would learn to crawl and then to walk through a billboard forest of faces and bodies, watches and shoes, underwear and cigarettes, booze and breakfast cereal. On TV, glossy men and women would lean out of the box to persuade him to buy *their* toy, *their* ice cream. How could he protect his son, everybody's sons—and daughters—from this horrible battery of voices and images?

He sat down at his desk, turned on his new electric typewriter and began to write.

Day One. The day you know for certain that you are to become parents of a mystery. An unknown person is about to enter your home and everything you do and think and feel will have an effect on him or, in some cases, her. About to enter your *home.* The word 'home' was hugely significant. Homer, home run, home-style, homely. Home! He hefted the dictionary down from the shelf and put it on the desk. *Home.* Old English: *Ham.* There was a long column of examples. He liked best, 'A place where you are free from attack.' Home free. Home base. And then he remembered Robert Frost: 'Home is a place where, when you go there, They have to take you in . . . I should have called it, Something you somehow don't have to deserve.'

Those lines, since he'd first read them years ago, had never left his memory. Sometimes he wished they would. He was going to make sure that his child would never have to 'deserve' a home as he'd had to do. Never have to look up to adult faces staring down. *Aren't you a fortunate boy*, their awful mouths had growled or sweetly said, as they patted his head with their large ugly hands. Briefly there had been an undeserved home, with his toys scattered about and a garden with a tree and two people who doted on him. He always pictured them standing under that tree, beckoning to him. Well aware of their importance to him, his parents, so he'd been told later, never flew together. Just that one fatal time they had taken off side by side in their little plane. The reason for that decision was buried with them.

He resolved from now on to cross roads at the light, drive with extreme care, exercise, give up eating fatty foods and watch over Maggie's health too. The cake had been a celebration cake. No more sugar except the natural kind in fruit.

After an hour he'd written ten pages. He didn't care whether

Griffiths liked it or not. He was experiencing one of those rare moments of visceral agitation that meant he was on a track to something good. If Griffiths turned it down, this piece would find a home of its own. He looked over the pages and recognized a beginning, a germ, an embryo. By hand he scrawled out a tentative letter to a publisher, and then a proposal for a whole book. In half an hour he had outlined ten chapters, each with its own heading and synopsis. He couldn't believe his own temerity. A book! He went to look for Maggie to share his excitement. He'd heard her come in half an hour ago. She wasn't in the bedroom or the living room. The shabby old postcards were spread out on the dining room table but her chair was empty. He found her in the basement. She was sitting in front of the washing machine, her eyes fixed on the dial.

"What are we having for dinner?" he asked.

She turned to him and said, "Those people had nothing."

"Maggie," he said. "Do you think that now you're going to be a mother, we should call you Margaret?"

"Maggie is carrying the sorrows of the world," Linda said. "Try to persuade her to go back to work."

"She's not ready."

"If she doesn't snap out of it, the child will be born depressed."

"I don't think she knows how to 'snap out of it.'"

"But David, she has to consider what she's doing. If she's going to go on like this, she'd be better off having an abortion."

"For God's sake don't let Theo hear you say that."

He patted yesterday's chicken, thawed now, and put it into the oven.

Linda said, "I'll do the veggies."

"I was going to do rice. Why don't you put your feet up? You need to rest."

"What I need," she began and then stopped.

He knew exactly what she'd been going to say. She'd stopped because an argument would have begun and she didn't want to go on with it. He wished he could reel back time to yesterday when for a brief hour all had been harmony and delight.

"The interview went well this morning," he lied. "I'll hear in a few days."

"Sorry sweetie, I should have asked. That's wonderful. When the show's opened, I'll be a better person. I'll go change and then you can tell me all about it." She kissed him on the cheek and went upstairs.

Kissed him on the cheek! What kind of a message was that? He feared that it read, *Our child has seen us making love therefore we have to become celibate until he has not only left home but has left the province, the country and gone far enough away that we know he won't come barging in any time he likes.* Unwillingly, he turned his mind back to the interview.

He had turned up at the offices of Hanford and Clark, Brokers to the Nation, that morning. At the reception desk, a smiling woman had said the dreaded words, Mr. Hanford is expecting you. The top three floors of 750 Oak Street were theirs and she sent him to the summit. Wearing the uniform, a suit and shirt and tie, hard shoes, he felt oddly hampered. Another helpful woman pointed to a door at the far end of the corridor. He walked past familiar-looking boxes containing men and women talking rapidly on phones, or staring at columns of figures, making little sounds and writing on paper. None of them turned as he walked by. Dismay swamped his mind but he made himself move on.

In the office of J. Bruce Hanford, two men stood up as he entered and looked at him like a pair of hungry lions. The more important-looking one said, "Thank you for coming, David."

First name terms already. A good sign. Or dismissive? Carefully he replied, "I'm happy to be here."

He sat down in the appointed chair and J. Bruce leaned forward and said, "You were fifteen years at Baker's, I see."

"I'm looking for a challenge," David said. He'd read an article in *Time* that listed *challenge* as an imposing word that worked well in interviews. *Excitement* was out because it suggested crime. But *something to get one's teeth into* was a winner.

The other man introduced himself as, "Henry Rivaldo, Personnel."

J. Bruce asked, "How does it look to you?"

David smiled at him and began to talk about the market as though he hadn't been out of work for one single day and had never for a moment lost confidence in his own ability to predict the winners and losers in the money race.

"The situation in Saudi is affecting oil prices again. I'm investing in the new Tar sands project myself. Computers, no way to go but up. I'm wary of gold at the moment. As for transport, it's all in the air. I know it's contrary to predictions, but I don't believe that passenger numbers will fall for some time."

"We can offer you $40,000 plus commission," J. Bruce said.

Rivaldo was staring at David's ankle.

David said, "I was earning $50,000 at Baker's," hoping to price himself out of the market.

J. Bruce looked as if he was about to offer five thousand more when Henry Rivaldo, Personnel, said, "Excuse me but that's not one of those electronic gadgets is it?"

"It's my pedometer. I'm trying to discover how long it would take me to walk or run, sometimes I run, to my home town in England. I work with a trainer not so much to increase my speed as my staying power, making better use of my leg muscles. I'll probably run back to my house from here. It's only three miles."

"You're planning to run over the ocean?"

"I'm working on the distance, not the actual route. Though I suppose I could go on a ship and run all the way on deck." He laughed. They didn't.

"I see." J. Bruce looked at him with greater interest.

Rivaldo said, "Thank you for getting in touch with us."

David knew a deep hole when he saw one.

"Of course," he said. "I'd give this up right away if I came to work here. I know how important time is in a job like this. I might run to and from work but not take off during the day. You wouldn't mind if I wore this round the office?"

He had failed. He tried to tell himself that he'd done his best but knew that it was a lie. *Could do better, David.*

At home, he'd looked at the map he'd tacked to the wall of his den, above the Bristol board. The shortest route to Kelthorpe was across the Arctic. He ran lightly across the frozen tundra lifting his feet high off the ground, on and on till he was way beyond the line of trees. He ran past Chisasibi, Inukjuak, Puvirnituq and when he reached Ivujivik, kindly Eskimos offered him caribou steaks and seal stew and muktuk and lent him snowshoes, fur parkas, their wives. He said no thank you to the latter offer out of chivalry rather than lack of desire and came to the bleak shore of Ungava Bay.

While he waited for Linda to come back downstairs, he took stock. Daily running was an indulgence. He had to make a concentrated effort to reach short lists, shorter lists, a job. Running only at the weekend meant it would take a lot longer to cover the distance but time wasn't important. He picked up the business section of the paper. Gold was up again. Oil in crisis. He read a piece about a company listed on the TSE that he hadn't heard of before. Bio-Nova. The PE ratio was good. *One to watch. Worth betting on. Buy*! Five thousand dollars carefully placed could become eight or ten in a month if the market moved in the right direction. And if that happened and with a few other right investments, he could make as much money as they needed without having to kowtow to men like J. Bruce and the weaselly Rivaldo. In fact, there was nothing to stop him from setting up his own brokerage business and working on the phone from home and never having to set foot in an office ever again. *I suffer from office-phobia.* Any doctor would translate that into *work-shy* and mark him down as an idler trifling his way through life on the shoulders of a hard-working wife. *And besides that I have lost faith in my ability to foretell the financial future. Who am I to advise people on their investments?*

The phone rang and he hoped it would stop before he reached it. It was Maggie wanting to talk about their dad again. It was J. Bruce calling to offer him a job. It was the principal calling to tell him that Greg was pregnant. John O'Brien was going to tell him about another dead-end 'opportunity' in finance. With any luck it would be someone soliciting for charity to whom he could reply, Sorry, I'm unemployed at the moment.

Linda called out, "Can't you get that?"

He lifted the receiver and said softly, "Hello?"

"David?"

"Hello, Mum. It's late over there. It must be one or two o'clock. Why aren't you in bed?"

"It's midnight. I've been thinking about Mohammed and the mountain," she said.

"You know you're welcome here any time."

"Theo said I should wait till the baby's born."

"You can come now and stay till then."

"As a matter of fact I was thinking of other mountains."

"Mum?"

"How's Linda?"

"She's a very busy woman."

"And you?"

"I'm out there looking."

"I can't give you a note, David."

He held the phone away from his ear and heard her say, "Tell my grandson I want to see him before he's an old man."

"I'll call him and he can say hello."

He went to the bottom of the stairs and yelled, "Greg!" but

there was no answer and when he picked the receiver up again, there was only a dial tone.

I can't give you a note, David. His mother had never been an unkind person. Was she turning now against all men since her husband in his last moment had called out another woman's name? Or was she reminding him of those notes she'd given him in school when he wanted to get out of gym? *David's leg is not quite healed. David is recovering from 'flu.* The truth, *David hates gym and will not do it, now or ever,* was not acceptable. After a time, she had told him he must make the best of it. And now she thought he was skiving off and was letting him know that he was not free to shout, *I will not work in an office ever again,* and to spend his time in speculation. In her gruff Yorkshire way, she was telling him to get off his arse and get out there.

Greg was standing on the sidewalk outside Jason's house. The neat square of grass that was their front yard was protected by a small wooden fence not sturdy enough to support him if he sat on it. Like a sentry he walked up and down the length of the fence a few times and then stood still again and waited. He wasn't sure what kind of sound he expected to hear first. Mainly he expected the door to open and Jason to come hurtling through it as if jet-propelled. But before that, Jason's mom, who had always seemed to him a bit of a pathetic ditz and who would shriek if she saw a mouse, would surely let out some kind of weird siren sound. Jason's dad, unlike his own, was a soldier-like man, precise, on time, sharp-eyed. It would be his foot that sent Jason flying from the front door and when that happened he'd pick Jason up and take him to The Blue Cow where they never asked for ID and buy him a beer.

Two weeks ago he couldn't have imagined this scene. But everything had changed. Here they were just beginning grade twelve and the world had turned upside down. There were mysteries. Tilly Jackson had disappeared just before the end of last term and the only explanation the principal had bothered to give them was that he had to go and look after a sick parent. Rumours going round the school ranged from theft to exposing himself to girls in the park and all of them were believed. Jason said the truth was that Tilly had left because they'd given the guy such a hard time in math class, he'd quit teaching forever and gone to help rebuild Vietnam. Jason was always willing to assume guilt. Like now.

No way Jason should get married. They'd talked about it but Greg couldn't see it as a desirable possibility. He couldn't imagine a house or an apartment that was his, a wife and children who depended on him for their breakfast and lunch and dinner. Couldn't imagine a career or even a way of existing beyond school. People kept asking him what he planned to do with his future and getting married never came to mind. At Christmas, Aunt Maggie had asked about his plans yet again and for something to say, he'd answered, "I'm interested in patent law." He'd read an article on it and it sounded so obscure that it might shut everybody up and make them leave him in peace so he could get on with life and find out what he really wanted to do over time. Of course, Uncle Theo, who should have been called Uncle Theory, had latched on to the idea and taken half an hour to tell him it was a wide open field full of exciting avenues, as if a field could have avenues.

The front door opened and closed again. No shrieks, no hurtling Jason. Greg hadn't realized that once he gave the adults in the family a word, two words, *patent law*, that they would attack them like a bunch of hyenas on a deer carcass and find books, the best post-graduate place, the companies he might work for, the patent office itself. And now his mother knew someone who knew someone he should talk to if he was serious about it which he wasn't but he had to go meet the guy anyway, tomorrow. Jesus Christ!

They were overwhelmingly interested as if since he was five they'd been waiting for him to make a decision. What do you want to do when you grow up, Gregory? They were like cannibals wanting to eat up his life having cooked it first. It never occurred to them that he might like to spend time discovering things for himself, drifting a little, sifting through a whole world of possibilities. And now with his dad behaving like a hippie as if he had to make up for an over-driven youth, there wouldn't be any spare money for him to go and lurch round India for a couple of years or go to Europe and meet *Mädchen* and *jeunes filles* and brush up on his language skills. An awful thought came to him: What if he did set off to India and his dad decided to come too?

The door opened. Jason's arm appeared, waving him away. Seconds later, the arm retracted fast as if there was a pulley attached to it. The door closed. The family conference was obviously going to take some time. He decided to wait a few minutes longer. And there was the baby, Aunt Maggie's baby. He pitied it-her-him. It would have these four elderly people peering into its crib, wanting to know at once what its plans were for the future, giving the poor kid advice, hectoring it, putting books in its way. Before it knew where it was, it would be in medical school specializing in something gross like gall bladders or assholes and hating every minute of it. He might have to act as a counterweight to the all the caring, smothering adults and teach the boy/girl a few ways to ignore what they said while seeming to agree. It was the only way to keep them quiet.

He could also teach the child to play baseball and hockey. He pictured the two of them, the three-year-old wobbly on his first skates and himself bending down to prevent the kid from falling. One foot then the other. *Slipperiness is the nature of ice, kid.*

He looked at the windows of the house. No one had closed the drapes. Nothing had been thrown from upstairs. He kicked the fence. One of the slats fell to the ground. Dominoes! They would all collapse and he would be discovered trying to put it together again. *Just another teenage vandal.* He propped up the loose slat and stood back nearer the curb. He'd never really looked at Jason's house as a house before. From the fence to the front door was maybe around three metres. It was an oldish house made of yellow brick. Big front window by the door. Two smaller windows on the floor above. Boring cookie-cutter architecture. And down below a little window in the basement which is where he wanted to be right now. Where he and Jason would be if Jason hadn't got himself into trouble. He wanted to go into the basement and beat on the drums and play his guitar and just make some terrific noise that would shut down whatever argument was going on in the living room above.

Up till a couple of weeks ago, the universe had seemed to be on a pretty steady course. A new school year. Football practice. The part-time job. That was then. Now it was like the sky was falling little piece by little piece. When he was a kid he'd had a kaleidoscope that you shook to make the patterns change. Someone had shaken the world around him.

It had begun to go weird right after Granddad died, as if the old man had held everything together, held up the sky like the giant holding the world on his shoulders. Since then, his parents and Aunt Maggie and Uncle Theo had begun to whisper about a bunch of old photographs which perhaps showed Granddad with another woman or revealed some family secret none of them had previously guessed at. His dad was not only running to the end of the earth but had some secret stuff in a parcel which he hid away when anyone came near. Fear also had crept around his life like a swirl of smoke.

Jason was the only one of their group who went to church. This, he supposed, would make it worse as far as his parents were concerned. They weren't Roman Catholics so there was no confession. Jason said he went because his family did and he liked the language and the prayers. But if his parents had hoped religion would keep their boy safe from sin, they would now know that it had failed. Was Jason's dad at this moment shouting at him, "Did you not think of Jesus?"

Among other things happening in this strange time was sex. It had seeped into their lives like some kind of poisonous gas in an air duct. Jason had done it with this blonde in the bathroom at his sister's twenty-first birthday party. And had gone out with her a few times after. And now she was pregnant. He could picture Jason and the blonde doing it standing up and wished that he couldn't. The picture was vivid and disturbing.

He also wished he hadn't seen his parents in bed like that. He'd only gone into their room because he thought they were out and he wanted to look for whatever it was his dad kept hiding out of sight. Some mysterious package which might provide a clue to what was going on. And there they were. Parents did it, he knew that. But in the abstract. The fact that they did push their old bodies together was something he didn't want to know about and definitely did not want to see. It was impossible to unsee something you'd seen unless you could manage to arrange five minutes of amnesia to wipe out that particular picture. He'd seen his mother one time before, long ago, lying down with a man but wasn't sure whether or not that was some childish nightmare. There were pine trees in that picture, grass, hot sun, the kind of sun kids drew with sharp lines around a yellow ball.

He was hesitant now to go home without calling first. While they were eating their chow mein yesterday, he'd suggested to his parents that they hang a sign on their door when they wanted privacy. They'd gone as red as beets so he tried to pretend it had never happened. Was it a childhood trauma that could later be blamed for stealing and drugs? At any rate it kind of gave him a free pass. He'd only told Jason and Sherrell about it and both of them had gone 'Yuck!' and been no help at all, except to look at him with sympathy although Jason needed all the sympathy they had between them right now.

And there were tears. In the last couple of weeks, it had become a wet time.

Aunt Maggie was pregnant so maybe it was natural for her to cry and she was probably crying for joy, but from what he was hearing it was more like for sorrow and what would that do for the kid in there if it knew? But why had his dad been crying the other day, sitting outside the duplex on Quantico, sniffling into a Kleenex? Riding by, Greg hadn't liked to stop and ask what was the matter. When he got home, he wished he had. But he thought it might embarrass the old man to be seen like that. Probably he was crying because Granddad had died, but why cry in the street for everyone to see?

And Jason had wept real tears at the idea of being tied to Chloe Jobson for the rest of his life. He figured he'd still be working at the donut shop when he was forty, struggling to support her and their five kids. He would die young never having achieved one single, solitary thing. All because of three quick fucks. It was a dire warning and Greg was glad he'd told Sherrell he was seeing someone else even if that someone else was himself. From now on, it was to be a lonely monk-like life. So be it. His parents had each other. Yuck again! Jason, his best friend since grade five, would disappear into a heap of diapers and laundry and every time he tried to make a break for it, a hand would reach out and drag him back into the house.

He set off to walk home. If he was to be a solitary, he would look to neither side but keep on going without seeking any more friends, and certainly no more girls. Then people would think he was a fag. No sex with girls for five years. I will not have sex for five years, by which time I'll have a job and she, whoever she is, will also have a job and we'll move in together . . .

He tried to think what could possibly be the absolute opposite of patent law. What kind of work could he do to surprise the family and the world? He didn't think he was cut out for a criminal life so it had to be something honest and not incredibly costly. The first three years at university were covered. After that he'd be on his own. Until it got so complicated that it seemed to make no sense, he'd enjoyed chemistry. History was something to read about on the side. His English essays were passable but not brilliant. *Midsummer Night's Dream* was the most boring play in the world and he couldn't see himself going in for theatre work. In any case his mother was not a great example. Directing this stupid musical was making her into a twitchy crabby person living on a hairline. Fortunately she was out a good deal. Being a journalist had seemed like a good thing a couple of years ago. But who'd want to be like Uncle Theo? There was charity work, re-building poor countries, feeding the starving, helping the diseased and eventually being given a medal by the United Nations. But his parents would be gone before recognition came his way and he wanted to surprise them before they went ga-ga. Besides, the pictures on TV showed it to be slow and sad work and he wasn't sure he could stand to hold those babies with their bony arms and bulging bellies. Better to make tons of money and send it to them.

Last year, on the class trip, camping in Algonquin, he'd seen showers of meteors and learnt to recognize certain stars. Astronomy was something that would allow him to spend years lying on his back and staring at the sky. He could begin to do it secretly in his spare time. He would mention it to no one. But to himself he could say, I am about to become a stargazer. I will discover planets and they will be called Nova Parkesonia. He felt more cheerful. Instinct told him that this was it. Walking along this dull street, rush hour traffic belting up both sides, his future had been revealed to him. Tomorrow, the library. Next week, the Observatory. Stealth was the word. The rewards for years of dedication would be fame and books and a beard and his parents saying, "We always knew he was a genius."

He was nearly home. He could delay the return by going to a movie. The last one he'd seen with Sherrell had led to an argument about whether women should fight in wars. She'd spilled popcorn over him and got butter on his new jeans. He wanted to see *Animal Farm* but it was no fun going alone.

When he thought about it, even though he'd hated the sight of them in bed, it was better that his parents were together. There'd been times he'd heard shouting and thought they might go their separate ways and he'd have to choose between them. Live like half his friends: Couldn't do my homework, the books are at my dad's place. I'm with my mom Wednesday to Saturday. Those guys survived but their lives were cut in half. He'd just have to survive the present weirdness.

A girl came out of the corner store and walked ahead of him. She had amazing red curls that came down to her waist and swung as she walked. He wanted to get hold of her hair and tell her it was lovely. But in three more strides he was at his own house and there was Aunt Maggie walking up the front path and who knew what the girl's face was like. He just hoped his parents had their clothes on.

His mother was in the kitchen fully dressed, banging plates about.

"What's wrong?" he asked.

"Nothing."

"I'm not a child," he said, meaning I have seen you having sex and it was awful but I'll get over it and therefore you need keep nothing from me.

"It's this thing about Dr. Morgenthaler," she said.

"Mm?"

"It's in the papers again today. They're prosecuting him for wanting to set up safe, clean places where women can have an abortion. It shouldn't even be a matter of discussion in these times. Women have a right to choose, goddammit. And the last thing a desperate woman needs is to be looking for some shady doctor who'll do it for a price."

"There are doctors like that round here?"

She handed him a sheaf of knives and forks and said, "There'll be four for dinner."

"So what's it to anybody if the guy builds his clinics?"

"It's against the law," she shouted. "And it shouldn't be. Politicians! Lawyers! Men!"

"Sorry, Mom," he said, not sure if he was apologising for being a man, for Jason, or for the entire world.

He went into the dining room and could hear Aunt Maggie and his dad talking softly in the living room, caught up in their own mystery. He took the mats from the sideboard drawer and put one in each place and arranged the knives on the right, forks on the left, salad forks by the larger ones. Napkins on the right. After that, he went to his room to study for tomorrow's test because there was no place else for him to go.

He sat on his bed and leaned back against the pillows and opened the textbook at chapter 23. In the nineteen twenties, the agricultural policies of the Conservative government caused the farmers to march on Parliament Hill and demand to see the Prime Minister. Too much money was being given to industry, tariffs were starving the farmers out of their farms. Good land was going to ruin, herds of cattle were dying off. The Prime Minister, The Right Honourable Gregory Parkes, stood up to loud applause: Mr. Speaker, I cannot believe that in these times when kids are having sex in fields and in bathrooms and basements and cars and on couches and floors and against walls, a man like Dr. Morgenthing who only wants to help my friend Jason who is a genius hockey player who can also play a mean guitar and does not need to be lumbered with a family right now is being persecuted and will have to get married. Shouts from the floor of the House: What about Chloe? What about women's rights? Jason's rights?

"Greg-or-y. Din-ner!"

*

"We hope you can start on Monday, David."

"Monday!" David was shocked.

"Henry checked about the bracelet. I hope you don't mind but we have to know these things of course. And you're just the kind of guy we're looking for. Someone with ideas of his own. We're expanding downwards. Until those offices are ready we can only give you a desk in the main section but . . . "

David hung up.

The phone rang again.

"I'm going to have to fire that receptionist. She's always doing that."

I am causing harm already!

"Please don't. I expect she was distracted. And well—thank you very much. I'm looking forward to working with you."

"Monday at eight. Stephanie will show you round."

Why had it been so easy? The papers, everyone, said it was harder to get a job this year than it had been for decades. They spoke of saturation, of men and women taking courses on how to write computer programmes so that they would be prepared for the new technology. There had to be something wrong with this job. Perhaps he should turn it down out of hand or at least enquire from J. Bruce how many people had applied and how many had been on the short list. Why had they liked him? A man wearing a pedometer who talked about running to England? A man laid off, in fact fired, from his last job? The reference from Baker must have glowed with the guilt of the unjust. He could tell J. Bruce that he didn't want the job, he had larger options in mind. On the other hand, Stephanie was a pleasing name.

When Linda came home, he'd pour a drink and make a ceremony of the announcement. They could lock the boy out and make love again. He opened a bottle of beer and then realized it was only nine o'clock. But on Monday, the day after Sunday, he would be encaged for eight hours in an office with no window to the outside, surrounded by intense people all trying to find a winner. His hand began to shake and he felt cold.

The phone rang again.

"Make that seven, David. We'll have a brief orientation meeting. You won't want to waste any time getting started. The market waiteth for no man."

"Like death."

J. Bruce laughed a hangman's laugh and hung up.

Started on what? It hadn't exactly been explained. The same thing he'd been doing before? Assessing companies, writing reports, giving advice to those who asked? He took the beer to the bedroom, turned on the TV, propped the pillows up on the bed and sat back against them. He was an invalid. Invalid. Validate me somebody, please! On the screen a woman was telling her husband that she was about to leave him. Unless he found a job, this could be his future; watching the daytime soap operas as a substitute for living.

Should he have persuaded Linda to stay in England? Could she, could he, have lived happily in a little town with him running a branch of Barclays, the bank manager respected by everyone? Linda working in the local gift shop and doing charity work? At least Greg would have grown up knowing that an ass was a donkey.

Linda came rushing in.

"I forgot Harold's shirt for tonight. For God's sake! Is this what you do all day? Couldn't you at least do something useful! The whole place needs cleaning. The grass needs cutting. You don't want to work, do you? This suits you just fine. Well let me tell you something, I'm not going to put up with this. I can't stop now. We'll talk about it tonight. And meanwhile. Oh God. What do I care!"

She rushed out. He spilt beer on the duvet as he tried to get up and follow her to shout, I have a job. But it was too late. He could hear the car engine. The engine of the car he'd promised to teach Greg to drive.

"I start on Monday," he yelled in vain.

He dialed her office number to leave a message of triumph and apology but the only answer was the intermittent engaged signal.

He tipped the rest of the beer down the sink and went to the basement. The path to Elsewhere would grow very slowly now. When he started work he would run through the park at weekends, mulling over stock prices and company management.

Now, during his last three days of freedom he wanted to think about the photographs. He couldn't accept the idea that his father had been selected one time only to go to Germany near the end of the war as an observer. If that was all, why the secrecy when the horror was known throughout the world? There had to be more. There was another much larger secret. The men Dad knew in London might well be dead. He turned the pages of the old notebook, and found the draft of an article in his father's hand dated only two months before he died. He picked out phrases here and there '. . . the almost universal assumption that in any conflict between rebels and authority, it is the authority that will cave in . . . ' 'We live in a world in which disruption is too easy . . . ' He turned back to a page dated, April 1942. 'The war has not cleared people's minds. Charlatans, from astrologers to Utopia-mongers, command a large hearing and support the mad theory that though Hitler is the enemy of the human race, the people who support him are not to blame.' ' . . . the new paganism of the Nazis . . . ' There was much more written in decisive terms on the current state of the world. They were the thoughts of a man who knew which side he was on, political statements written clear and they had nothing at all to do with wool.

The mention of 'paganism' reminded him of the dark, hollow Gothic church Nana and Grandpa had taken him to on Sunday mornings. His mother would often come too, and Maggie when she was old enough. But his father had left his Baptist religion behind in Belfast and despised the high Church of England service. *Too much of a pantomime.* So on Sunday mornings, he stayed at home to wash the breakfast dishes and to keep the Swiss woman company. To keep the Swiss woman company! David knew now why she was always 'the Swiss Woman' to him. But when he was a boy, he'd seen her simply as a lodger, someone who worked with his dad, a foreign presence in the house, to be tolerated.

David closed the notebook and put it back into the drawer. The man who'd written on those pages was someone he'd lived with for eighteen years and had known all his life. He had never expressed these thoughts aloud. At least not to his son. Then to whom? To the woman who had imitated his handwriting and translated the poems of Emile Verhaeren? To that someone he knew in London who knew him? And in London now, it was early afternoon.

Maggie was lying on the bed naked. She'd had a shower and couldn't decide what to wear. Soon all her clothes would be too tight and she'd have to let them out or go to those awful maternity stores to buy loose skirts and kangaroo pouch pants. Smocks! She stroked her stomach and could feel no change in its contours. It was all a mistake. But it wasn't a mistake. The doctor had told her it was true. Inside this belly, there was a tiny independent life. What a strange arrangement it was. If human procreation was ever described to aliens from other worlds what would they think about such a primitive set-up? The man and the woman perform this acrobatic act and then, nine months later, a fully formed earthling emerges. During the gestation period there is vomiting, fretting, sleeplessness, great expense—and worry.

The factors that can cause deformity in a baby: Alcohol. Tobacco. Drugs. Pollution. My office is not polluted. What is made in the factory ninety miles away leaves minute traces of PCBs in the water. My office is clean. What about babies in the area round the factory? Am I responsible?

We're going to need my salary. How much money does a baby require?

The magazine article about depression which Theo had left on the table offered easy advice. Lists were good. Short-term objectives were essential. Achievable goals!

Things to do: Choose what to wear today. Decide whether or not to go back to work. Look for another job. Who would employ a pregnant woman? Who needed to know before it showed? Plan a short trip to the lake with Theo.

Three weeks ago she'd been planning to leave him and go to Europe, take her savings and travel across the continent by rail, stopping in foreign towns, unknown, invisible. She had wanted to watch the world from a seat at an outdoor café. Now she had no desire to go further than the end of the street. Sitting in row 29, between trips to the toilet, she'd wished the plane to keep going forever. She came to the end of *The Accidental Man* and felt sad. Ludwig had returned home to his parents and probable confinement. Gracie and Garth had become 'beautiful people' from another era, a different novel.

They'd been very understanding at the office when she told them she needed more time off, but for how long? Corrine would be encroaching on her space, making excuses to pick up that thread or this, pointing out errors that were made and blaming the absent Maggie Parkes for her own deficiencies. But even pursuing such thoughts didn't make her eager to put on a skirt and jacket and reach for her briefcase and stride into the office saying, I'll take over now, thank you.

She touched her breasts. There was no sign of them being any larger yet. Soon, they would be filled with milk that would spill onto the front of her shirt and leave a large stain. In meetings, men would stare and feel disgusted or lecherous according to the kind of men they were. Theo had removed the large canvas from the wall opposite the bed. She had particularly liked the voluptuous painting by Hilary Klein of a naked man and woman entwined. Only the woman's face showed and, her head back, she was obviously at the moment of orgasm. It was now in the closet facing the wall as if seeing that even in embryo would lead the child straight down the road to prostitution. He'd replaced it with Rembrandt's "Madonna and Child."

The clock by the bed was ticking the moments away. She tried to calculate how many minutes there were to the projected due date. Looking back to the July 1st weekend, she recalled that they had spent hours in bed, getting up to drink wine and eat sandwiches. Six months and three weeks. Twenty-seven weeks. A hundred and eighty-two days. One thousand, four hundred and forty minutes a day. Her mother had gone through this process twice. You were born on the day the king abdicated, her father had told her more than once. But he always implied that it was a good thing, the abdication of the eighth Edward. His brother Albert was a better, steadier man, a family man. A Good King. So apparently her birth was auspicious; a star in the sky. And Albert became George overnight.

It was warm out. There was a smell of smoke wafting through the window. On the radio, a man said that Mr. Trudeau was planning to meet President Ford in Washington. She turned and moved the dial till she found music. Perhaps she would spend a hundred and eighty-two days lying here listening to Bob Dylan. She wondered if the baby could feel her hand there stroking round and round in a comfortable circular way.

And did the baby know of the invasion? Would she grow up scarred because of her mother's trip to the Dent Fair with Ron Hobson? You go, Frieda had said the week after the funeral. And she had. Gone with him gladly. He was a Yorkshireman with all that harsh and wonderful scenery and life in his voice and in his arms. That bold look, the broad *a*'s and blunt *u*'s, had quite literally charmed her pants off. For God's sake she was romanticizing a moment of lust and nostalgia! She truly hadn't known she was pregnant when Ron drove her over the moors to the Fair. Who was she kidding! Jet lag never lasted that long. She'd been gradually becoming aware of the fact, and recalling the shrieking passion of that July weekend, and the carelessness of it. And yet she let Ron take her in the little hotel and Theo need never know.

Theo, when he wasn't writing, walked about as if he was the pregnant one. His stomach seemed to be swelling and he muttered names to himself and talked about the advantage of a crib on a rest that would swing to and fro. He wanted to buy a large English baby carriage. She had said they would need a bigger house with an entrance hall to keep it in, not to mention a nanny in a uniform to wheel it about. They had argued. She had begun to cry and he had said, Don't cry. She had cried more in the last week than she could remember in her whole life. Maybe now she'd cried all the tears she ever would. She turned up the corners of her mouth in the facsimile of a smile.

She fingered her pubic hair and stretched her legs and considered what was wrong with her brother. Had he, had she, gone in for the wrong kind of work? Had they left their own country and become displaced in mind as well as body? He'd been persuaded to come to Canada by Linda, who wanted to return to her home country. Tired of being told she sounded like an American, cold in their Yorkshire house, Linda had issued David with an ultimatum. Besotted, he'd pulled up his roots and moved across the Atlantic. Maggie tried to imagine them having sex but could only think it must be an orderly affair done by numbers.

It was through Linda that she and Theo had met. Had Linda planned and directed their lives? First the invitation to her and her parents to come to Canada and spend a couple of weeks at the Grewson cottage. They'd spent the first few days crowded into David and Linda's Don Mills house and then been driven to

Huntsville in the station wagon, five of them and little Greg. Next day, Linda had said, 'Theo is an old college friend. He might drop in.' He had dropped in.

It was two years later in the office in Leeds that Maggie had looked up from her typewriter and seen him there. 'Remember me? The cottage on Lake Scugog. Linda told me where you worked.'

She had to admit that till now, till a few weeks ago anyway, she and Theo had been reservedly happy. At first they'd been like two people walking on air, hand in hand in a magic world of their own. He'd stayed on after his conference, walked on the moors with her, gone to York. In Scarborough, they'd spent a weekend in a hotel that seemed about to crumble down the cliffs into the sea. They had talked and laughed and told each other their secrets. He was, she understood in that weekend, a man who would always be reliable.

And so she had moved to Toronto to live with him and be his love, and had quickly come to like the city, the lake, the people she met, her job.

When Theo had told her how his sad childhood was redeemed by a foster parent who read to him from *Tanglewood Tales* and *Treasure Island* and *Peter Pan*, she'd responded with a kind of motherly affection. And she'd never asked him what Linda was like in bed. He only said it was a brief affair long before Linda had met David. Maggie said she didn't want to know. But she did want to know. She wanted to know whether Linda cried out when she came and why, after they broke up, all Theo would say was that she was too dramatic for him. ·

Would this baby, supposing it arrived whole and grew into a child, be satisfied with her and Theo or wish it had been born to better, richer, younger parents? She went on rubbing her skin. It was too soon to feel movement in there. She shifted on the bed.

Oh, she thought. And put her hand down by her side. This won't do. Oh! What am I doing!

Theo, the lost boy, came in holding a newspaper.

"There's a sale of nursery furniture on at . . . " He looked over at the bed and stared at her for a moment.

He began to undo his shirt buttons.

"Darling. Is it all right to—you know?"

"Oh Theo," she said. "Oh!"

"My name is David Robert Parkes. My father . . . "

"I'm sorry. You'll have to be specific."

"I am being specific. I'm enquiring about civilians who went to the labour camps in Germany when the war ended."

"Which war?"

"The 1939 to 1945 war in Europe. The Second World War!"

"Please hold on."

David had figured that if anyone knew why his father was in Germany in that place at that time, it would be someone in Whitehall. It had taken four calls and half an hour to find this number and it was the third time he'd stated what he wanted and then been told to hold on.

"Hello," he said to the void.

There was no answer. He waited. The kettle was boiling upstairs in the kitchen but fortunately it knew how to turn itself off.

"Yes?" The enquiry came from an impatient male voice. "This is Captain Haverson speaking."

David told his story again, this time more aggressively.

"It is obvious," he said, "that my father, Robert F. Parkes, was in this particular camp in April 1945 when it was liberated by the Americans. I would like to know . . . "

He wasn't allowed to finish.

"That's nothing to do with us, sir. You need to call Maryland. They'll tell you everything you need to know."

"It was the same bloody war," David said.

"You might try this number."

David copied down the figures and stared at them. So it was on this continent, a short flight away, that he would find the answer to his question: What did my dad do in the war?

"Thank you," he said but the Captain had hung up—no doubt he had many similar unhelpful duties to perform. Useless bastard!

Linda was sorry she'd yelled at David. She had tried to call him several times during the morning but the line was engaged. Perhaps, desperately, he was calling every contact he had in the city. She had to be patient with him, she knew that. But with her own day crowded, minute by minute, the sight of him sitting there, the picture of ease, had been too much. The guy needed space, he needed sympathy, not a wife who was too busy to listen to him. The sight of those photographs had brought back all the memory of the bleak household atmosphere of her childhood. She couldn't bear to think that her own house, their own house, could become like that too and that Greg in later years would look back on his home with horror.

She sat at her desk, looking across at a calendar that showed a picture of the planned extension to the emergency wing and the fact that September was into its third week. That meant, with *A Perfect World* opening on Tuesday, the two-and-a-half week run, the conference at the end of the month, the days and evenings were going to be full. Her next two weeks of vacation time were marked off in October. Then she would take David to the cottage, leave Greg with Theo and Maggie, and they would relax, get close again. There were three new novels including a long John Irving that she wanted to read. The sun would shine and they'd take turns to cook.

The sun was shining on the city outside her grimy window. There was a dull roar from the traffic on University Avenue, and overhead the thumping beat of a helicopter about to land on the roof of the hospital across the road. An accident victim was being brought in, or a child in desperate straits. In Emergency, in the OR, matters of life and death were being acted upon. At home, David was sitting back against the pillows drinking beer. She wanted to go home, be there with him and talk to him about the uncertainty of life and the importance of harmony.

The pictures on the wall of her office were copies of Emily Carr's deep forests and Lawren Harris's pine trees. There was a wilderness out there, there were places to hike and canoe and get lost in. David had loved cottage country from the first. Every July when they went to Muskoka, she could see him relax and become playful. Once they'd tried to make love in a canoe and had fallen laughing into the lake and she'd seen that as an augury of their future: Whatever happened they would survive and come up smiling and wend their way into elderliness together. Their lives were at a midpoint now. Their child was nearly grown. They'd gone back to England after that summer vacation when she'd brought him to meet her parents. At the airport her mother had whispered, Make sure you move back here. It'll be best for your children.

She'd fallen in love with David when they met in England because he offered optimism and a cheerful home. He knew how to have fun and to laugh at little things. He'd taken her to the zoo in Regents Park and proposed in front the Siberian tiger. Now she wanted him to be depressed because he had no job! She'd even been glad to find him crying on the wall outside Theo and Maggie's place because mourning was natural. If she was patient, he would return to normal in a month, maybe two. As long as he and Maggie could leave the past alone. She could understand why it upset them. But there probably was no more to the 'mystery' of the photographs than that their father, because he could speak German, had been asked as a civilian to view and confirm what the soldiers had discovered. She had to convince him that it was nothing more than that.

Wendy put her head round the door, "There's someone to see you, Ms. Grewson."

"It's only quarter to."

The woman who walked into her office was small and stocky and cheerful. She looked as if she'd stepped onto the set of *A Perfect World* to sing about sunshine and trees and love.

"I represent the Hospital Workers Union," she said. "We have a grievance."

"That isn't my department."

"Oh, but I think it is. The hours we work are a disgrace and our pay is an outrage. We insist on longer hours and less pay and we'll sew our own overalls. You're doing too much for us and what's that doing to the hospital budget?"

"Who are you?"

"I wish you could see your face. It's me. I met you last year at the Wellness Conference in San Fran."

"Yes." The name surfaced slowly. "Angelina?"

"Close. Marion! Having some trouble?"

"We sorted it out last week."

"At home."

"I beg your pardon."

"You're looking at me as if Mary Poppins just flew in on a broomstick. That evening in the Chinese place. Dinner. We were sitting next to each other. And I was coming here to a meeting of Administrators so I thought I'd stop by and say hello and p'raps we can have a drink somewhere."

"I'd like that," Linda said because with all that was going round in her head, she couldn't find the words to say, *I'm too busy. I don't like you. Go away.*

"What I said just now, it's because when I came in, there was a kind of distressed aura round you. Round your head. I'm a bit psychic. I see colours. It's very useful in my job. I think you should come and have a drink with me. I might be able to help."

Linda felt anger rising and tried to take a deep breath.

"Your three o'clock is here, Ms. Grewson."

"Thank you, Wendy."

"I'm staying at the Renaissance. I'll be in the bar after five," Marion said, and left.

David had got through to the Military Archive Department in Maryland with remarkable speed. Only one transfer and now he was waiting to speak to a Major Bellini who would be with him shortly. After five minutes, he was tempted to hang up and forget the whole thing. Eight minutes and he began to mutter into the phone. *Speak to me, Baby.*

"Good afternoon. Major Bellini here."

"My name is David Parkes."

There was no immediate response, then, "Yes?"

"I have photographs of one of the camps in Germany that was liberated by the American Army. My father who was a civilian— just too old to serve—is in one of those photographs with some of your soldiers."

"Ah yes. Well Mr. Parkes, that was a long time ago. We kept no records. And no compensation was given to those people."

"Compensation?"

"Money."

"I'm not looking for money for God's sake!" David felt his voice rising and couldn't help it. "That's not what this is about. I want to know why my father was there at all."

"There was a war going on," the Major said gently as if he was speaking to an idiot. "Goodbye, sir."

No records had been kept? Who was the guy kidding! David took the words in and considered them. He understood that the search wasn't going to be made easy. He would have to go further. The obstacles ahead of him were like a mass of barbed wire, a wall with broken glass on top. Something the fat man had said, the Olympic trainer, was like a spike in his mind. And in a way, it all went back to the school reports that said he could do better. He had to get out there and find a past for his father and a future for himself.

*

Linda's real three o'clock appointment was an intern who had a plan to speed up treatment in the ER. He'd been passed on to her because no one else wanted to tell him that he watched too much television or that he was sleep deprived and that there was no way they could adopt the kind of conveyor belt system he had in mind.

"Sit down, Dr. Tressell," she said.

He was thirtyish but looked forty. Raccoon rings round his eyes and two-day stubble gave him the appearance of a convict. He sat down with unease as if he had piles due to the irregular hours forced on him by the ER schedule.

"You've read my plan," he said.

She picked up the pages and wondered what she would think on being wheeled into an emergency room if she saw him looking down at her.

"As you know," she said, "some of the others have read it and we're going to discuss it. It's not something that can be implemented overnight."

"Overnight! It's been tossed around for three weeks now." He turned away like a sulky boy.

"Explain it to me in your words."

"At the moment, they come in, the patients, in various degrees of urgency. You've got heart attacks, severed limbs, wasp stings, hypochondriacs. Now we treat the most urgent first and the easy ones wait for hours. We should stream them and have one doctor to take all the simple cases and get them out of there as fast as possible to free up the space. That's to start with." He looked at her closely. "I could let you have some Valium."

Linda wasn't sure she'd heard him but he was still staring.
"I don't need Valium."

"There's a vein twitching under your eye. And it's a pity because you have really nice eyes. That's an unusual colour. Is something bothering you?"

She was afraid, afraid that this second attack of sympathy in such a short time was going to make her cry. She wanted to tell him to come round to her side of the desk so that he could hold her in his arms and she could weep her tears into his white coat and they would both get fired and she too could sit up in bed drinking beer in the morning.

"My father-in-law just died," she answered in a shaky voice.

"You must have been very fond of him."

"Why don't you come back on Monday morning and we can go over this in more detail."

"I sleep mornings. The only chance I get. What about the end of the day?"

She nodded her head and he went out, looking back at her from the door.

I've become neurotic, she thought, and everyone who meets me can tell. I'm a walking nervous wreck. She called David and told him to have dinner without her. It was a short rehearsal. She'd be home by 9:30. She had to meet a woman who'd just come into town.

David stopped by the duplex to see how Maggie was. Theo answered the door and looked at him as if he was a stranger. He showed him into the dining room and returned to his study without saying a word. Maggie was sitting at the table with their father's old postcards spread out in front of her. Some of them were view side up and others were picture down, showing the message on the back in their Dad's writing. She hadn't heard him come in and, for a moment, he stood there watching as she turned a postcard over slowly and stared at it as if she was surprised by what she saw. Laid out, the pictures made a patchwork quilt of pre-war Europe: Sepia pictures of Budapest, Vienna, Berlin, Reichenberg, Belgrade, Prague.

She turned and saw him and said, "Look at this."

Their father had written their surname and 'England' in Cyrillic letters and, on the other side, *Dear Frieda, See how good I am at Serbian.*

"Surely the Serbians had sheep, David. I always imagined the place to be covered in sheep."

"Maybe with their winters they needed more clothes than their sheep had wool."

"It was also crawling with spies."

He looked at all the cities she had spread out before her. Every one of them had a role in the literature of espionage.

"He had to be spying all those years."

"I expect they just asked him to bring back information."

"I don't know," she said, turning over another card slowly like a fortune-teller at a fair. "I don't know what to think."

He wanted to tell her to think about the baby and Theo and leave him to discover the truth. Instead he sat beside her and read some of the messages their father had written before he and Maggie were born.

I have just reached Budapest after a very long journey and feel a long way from home.

Just missed the 4 p.m. train to Dresden which means I shan't get there till late.

"He always cut things too fine when he was travelling," Maggie said. "Remember that time he went to pick up his tickets and the travel agent was closed for lunch?"

But David was wondering who or what had made his father miss the Dresden train. What trail was he following? Who had spoken to him and offered him information? Or was it simply 'Dora' who beckoned to him and lured him off the dual, dutiful paths of home and country? And was 'Dora' a woman or the code name of a burly man who sat in a secret office above an innocent-looking shop on a dark street?

Maggie was moving the cards again, making a long line of scenes. Many of the cards were tattered at the edges from handling, from age. She was moving across Europe. Brussels, Verviers, Frankfurt, Nuremburg, Munich, Vienna, Zagreb, Belgrade, Bucharest. Then she built a return journey which might or might not have been the way he travelled. Bratislava, Prague, Bayreuth, Dresden, Berlin and across to Antwerp to board a boat to England.

"Do you realize he started doing this when he was twenty-three?" she said. "He was only a few years older than Greg."

David couldn't imagine his son in five years time setting off across town to sell pencils, let alone across Europe charged with selling tens of thousands of pounds of raw wool. In his twenties, his father had been at home in Europe with all its variety of languages and currencies. He'd moved from place to place, speaking to Germans and Belgians and Slavs, crossing borders, understanding francs and marks and zlotys. What an enviable, unconfined life. Anyone could endure a few months in the office when the start date of a long adventurous journey was marked on the calendar. In those days, flight was out of the question for most businessmen, but now it would be considered eccentric to say to your boss, *I only travel by bus and train and boat. I'll be back in a month.*

He picked up a black and white picture of an alpine village: snow-capped mountains, forests in the foreground and what looked like a medieval castle on a hill. On the back his father had written, *Dear Frieda, Didn't get here till last night but got your wonderful long letter today which was a tonic. Isn't it astonishing how childish folk can be? Do take care of yourself and our son. I hear there's a lot of flu about.*

"Kufstein in Austria," Maggie said, taking the card from him and putting it between Budapest and Prague in her new arrangement. "Mum should know about those photographs."

"That's what I came to say," he said. "You don't want to be telling her about it on the phone. Next time one of us goes over, will be soon enough."

"One of us?"

"I have to run," David said. "You're feeling better?"

"I'm okay." She spoke without looking up.

"And you know, you need to put these away and think about little Theo."

She didn't answer. He kissed her on the head and went out. From now on, running would only be a weekend pastime. He had other things to do. As he ran along the sidewalk he decided to stop in at the school on his way home and watch Linda's rehearsal, to cheer her on.

"Lift your feet up!"

He hadn't noticed that the man from the café was cycling very slowly alongside him. He picked up speed.

"Guy I trained, could've got the gold but wouldn't lift his feet."

David ran through the entrance to the park and paid no attention.

"Your body needs to be forward a bit," Boomer said. "And you need to make your mind up about the effort. When a guy your age takes up running, it has to be about something else. Running to or running from. Which is it with you?"

They all knew their moves now. Linda took her notebook to a seat three rows back, sat down and breathed deeply and told herself to relax. The actors had made the adjustment from the church hall to the high school auditorium. The composer was happy. The writer had problems but it was too late now to change anything. After the dress rehearsal tomorrow, there was only time for a quick run through on Tuesday afternoon for those who could get off work. At the end of today, she would make her speech about the wonderful work they had done and how much she'd enjoyed working with them. The word round the community was promising. Tuesday was sold out. David had a job. And in her mind, she'd filed the dark words Marion had spoken to her in the bar under 'nonsense.' *Leave him before he leaves you!* What could a stranger know? She smiled.

"House lights," Glenda called out and the hall became dark.

The spot lit Dottie as she came forward on the stage to sing, "'I'm so glad you could come.'"

Linda made a note to tell her to move slightly to the left and allow Harry more space for his entrance. Where was Harry? Moments passed. Dottie sang her intro again. There was a crash offstage.

"It's only the mirror," Glenda said.

"What happened?" Linda asked.

"Harry and Jeffrey."

The two actors came forward.

"I'm sorry," Jeffrey said.

"He pushed me," Harry said.

"It was an accident," Jeffrey said.

"Oh right! And now the mirror's broken. It's unlucky," Harry shouted.

"No it isn't," Linda assured him, assured them all. "In the theatre all those superstitions are reversed. You all know that. It's a good sign. We're going to have a great show. Now let's get on. Clear up the broken glass, please, Glenda."

She didn't know where she found that piece of misinformation but they appeared to have bought into it. The lights went down again and Dottie came forward. At that moment, Linda heard footsteps behind her. She turned to see the writer rushing out. Dottie stopped singing.

"An appointment he'd forgotten," Linda said, wondering how

many lies she was going to have to tell to get through the day. "Go straight to Harry's entrance, please."

*

"What a morning," Boomer said. "What a great day."

"You're right," David replied. He decided to be tolerant. It wasn't for long and the guy seemed to have kindly intentions. He leaned against a tree and stretched his leg muscles.

"My man could've got the gold," Boomer was saying. "All he needed was that extra bit of power in his feet. And I'm saying this to you in confidence. The guy who did win, you know who, had something in his breakfast cereal that wasn't raisins. As it was my guy came fourth and it was soon after that they brought in the proper drug-testing. He was definitely robbed."

David looked at the man. He had to be sixty. His hair was grey and badly cut and he was wearing a tracksuit that had a tear in the leg. What made the fellow want to keep after him? Did he have other 'clients?' Maybe it was an act of charity, encouraging middle-aged men to stay healthy.

"You going to run or not?" Boomer demanded.

"Yes, I am," David said, considering his larger plan. "I am certainly going to run."

"Nice to hear you sounding as though you mean it. You were an indefinite guy when I saw you in the coffee shop. Blurred round the edges. Now I'm starting to see ambition. Purpose."

David was pleased, pleased that his determination showed at least to this amiable stranger. He started slowly. When he lifted his feet off the ground, he was almost airborne. He breathed in and out and felt his lungs expanding. He could run now for twenty minutes with a pleasant rhythm and without getting short of breath. His body was a good machine that he could control. He wished he'd taken up running twenty years ago. He'd invited Greg to come too but the boy was either studying or at work and said he hadn't time. A few leaves drifted down. It felt like a betrayal of his family, his friends, his father, everything he knew, to realize that the happiest times of his life right now were these hours he spent running. He was sorry that it wouldn't be for much longer.

Boomer rode ahead, turning occasionally to shout, "Faster!"

This is living, this is what it's about, David thought. Even though he was concentrating on his feet, he was able to take in the bird songs and note the trees he was passing. Project: Buy a tape recorder and discover which bird made which sound. Blue jays simply squawked but he could hear the soft twitters and chirps of smaller birds and wanted to know all their names. Somewhere in the house, there was a book called *Canadian Birds*.

Boomer turned back towards him to say, "You slowing down again?"

David yelled, "Stop!"

It was too late.

Boomer helped the man up and brushed him off. David pushed the bike to the side of the path.

"The sign says no cycling," the man said angrily.

"I'm sorry," Boomer said, "but you weren't looking where you were going."

"Neither were you," the other replied, and collapsed onto the ground.

"Watch out!" a group of joggers shouted.

The man shuffled his body, snake-like, over to the grass and remained prone. David could see his plan. He was going to fake an injury and sue Boomer who didn't look well-off and he, David, would be called to pay and also to act as witness.

He looked down at the man and said, "There's a phone box over there. Would you like me to call an ambulance?"

"No," the man said. "I'm lying here because . . . well I don't think you'd understand."

Boomer leaned his bicycle against a tree and lay down beside him.

"Try me," he said.

They were both staring up at the sky as if they could see something miraculous. A hawk, a daytime star or a cloud shaped like a camel. David lay down on the other side of the victim. The grass was warm and only slightly damp.

"I can't see anything," he said.

"It's a matter of perception," the stranger stated.

They were all silent for a moment. David was looking at patches of sky through a pattern of maple leaves. There was a little cirrus cloud but nothing large enough to form even a squirrel. A seagull flew by screeching.

"So tell us what you perceive."

A light flashed in their faces. A woman holding a camera smiled down at them pleasantly and moved on.

"Why do you cycle where it says no cycling?"

"I'm Boomer. He's—what's your name, running man?"

"David."

"Jim," the victim said.

"I don't think this grass is doing much for my arthritis, Jim," Boomer said. "How about we go sit over there."

David wanted to run. He decided to sit on the bench with the other two for a moment and then leave.

Jim said, "Thank you. It wasn't your fault. I wasn't looking where I was going." He put his head on his hands and sighed.

Boomer put an arm round his shoulders and said in a motherly way, "Now then, what's this all about?"

"Nobody wants to hear the truth these days."

"You've made somebody angry?"

"She won't listen. People would rather live on lies. But when the truth is forced on them, they can cope with it. They rise to it. They become better human beings because they learn to know that truth is courage is love is life."

Boomer echoed, "'Truth is courage is love is life.'"

"Wait a minute," David said, "if I understand what you're saying, then it's better to tell your mother, your wife, some awful true thing even if it could ruin a relationship forever."

"What kind of relationship is built on lies?"

"Are you married?"

"No. But that's beside the point."

"Do you have many friends?"

"Leave him alone, he's upset," Boomer said. "What he's saying, David, is that inner courage is what matters. I've told all my boys that. You can buy the best shoes, get the best trainer, take whatever substance you like, but it's what you've got in there," he punched David on the chest, "that counts."

"Lies are necessary to living with others. We all need our life myths," David insisted.

"That's a cynical outlook."

"I'm only saying that all of us have to believe in ourselves a bit and if you go knocking down other people's images of who they are, you're doing more harm than if you tell a few lies."

"So you're married and you lie to your wife?" Jim asked.

"My father lied," David answered, and felt his voice become childish. "I just discovered that I didn't know who he was. I thought I did. And he died before I could find out."

"Well there you are! You see. If he'd told you the truth, whatever it was, you would've felt better."

"He was a spy. He was sworn to secrecy."

"You're making that up."

"I am not. My dad did do something important in the war."

"What's bothering you is something to do with your own ego by the sound of it."

"It is not. And what do you know anyway?"

"I'm a student of character."

"Oh really!"

Boomer said, "Now guys, this is getting to sound like one of those dumb TV shows where everybody says things they're sorry for and they end up in a fight. Let's just say you're both right, and get on with our day. David has three more miles to run. Have you tried running, sir? It could ease your stress."

David jumped up and slipped on the damp grass. He fell backwards onto the path and for the second time in a few weeks just stopped himself from shouting *Eureka*. "My dad was a hero," he shouted to the sky, to the trees, to all the ignorant people and the poor and the rich, and to all the boys at school and to an echo that came from nowhere.

Boomer was dabbing at his head. David pushed his hand away and stood up.

He knew what he was going to do. *A family tragedy*! That would be his excuse to J. Bruce Hanford. *I'm taking a trip.* Linda would understand that. He only wanted a few weeks in Europe. Somewhere over there was the key to his father's life, and the weird guy was absolutely right: Truth was everything.

"Thank you," he said to the other two. And then, feeling the need to sleep, he lay down on the earth again. A fine stream of contentment flowed through him in the way, he thought, that milk must flow through a cow.

Frieda felt glorious. *Happy and glorious,* just as they'd sung for the reluctant king who'd died too soon. His daughter had already reigned twice as long as her father and would perhaps be queen longer than the first Elizabeth. But that was England and now she was here in a foreign city once ruled by emperors. A spring of joy had opened in her soul, something she hadn't expected ever to happen again. One minute, it seemed, she was sitting in Bob's chair crying over a picture of Salzburg, and the next, she was perched on a seat in an outdoor café on the Imbergstraße. It was like being whisked over the Channel on a magic carpet. And the lie she had told to Val next door had turned out to be a prophecy after all. She smiled at the people walking along the street and hoped that they were happy and that their children were kind.

Two days after the cream cake event, Linda had phoned to say that David had hurt himself in a fall but that it was nothing serious and Frieda was not to worry. She had worried. Then David himself rang to tell her he was fine. Three days later he'd knocked on the door and said, "Here I am, Mum." And she had replied, "I knew you'd come."

Once he'd noticed the blurred brochure it hadn't taken him long to make arrangements for them both to fly to Austria. She could tell he had another purpose in coming to the continent besides a wish to please her, but she didn't care. He'd only said that he had business to take care of in Germany and would put her on a plane back to Manchester in ten days time.

"I'd like to walk up the Kapuzinerberg this afternoon," she said.

"'Life is for ascending,'" he answered.

"This is so wonderful, dear." She reached across to wipe chocolate off her son's cheek with her serviette.

"Vienna tomorrow," he said.

Now that he'd made two flights, David knew he could fly anywhere, any time. Once aboard the plane, he had simply closed his eyes and let aerodynamics and the pilot do the rest. He put the last piece of pastry in his mouth and watched his mother, delighting in her delight. At the same time he reproached himself for not taking her on this trip long ago. His mother had only asked once whether he was being extravagant. He'd told her he was spending the interest from his investments. Sitting here against a backdrop of mountains, he wasn't concerned about money or about the salary he should have been earning by going to work for J. Bruce Hanford. The luxury of time settled around him.

He had another twenty-five years of work left in him. Time enough to restore his bank balance and plan for old age. Right now he was with his mother and he vowed to bring her on a journey like this every year from henceforth.

He'd given himself two months to search and research the events of spring 1945. And while he looked, anything might happen. His mind was open to every kind of eventuality. When he returned home —and he would return home—bearing gifts for Greg and Linda and Maggie and Theo and his unborn nephew, he would be able to tell them why and where Robert F. Parkes had been standing on that day beside an American soldier.

His mother was looking at him seriously and she said, as if she was reading another part of his mind, "Linda never seemed quite right for you, David."

He smiled at her and said again, "Vienna tomorrow."

PART 3

Getting There

Greg looked across at the CN Tower and weighed its merits as an achievement. Compared to the pyramids or to Roman aqueducts, given the tools and knowledge of men in those ancient times, the Tower was no big deal. The Egyptians had no helicopters to help set the crowning stones in place at Giza. The Greeks designed the Acropolis without computers. But the Tower stood as modern man's testament to his desire to reach ever upwards, to be higher, better; to be noticed. Down below, a haze hung thickly over the lake. It was hot out there and would get hotter. Here in the office, his linen jacket was barely warm enough. Behind him, on the desk, the phone stopped ringing. It was probably Bertie. She was young and would eventually learn that it was better not to probe too deeply into things.

Not a hero, him. Greg was beginning to wish he hadn't repeated Granny's words to his cousin. Bertie might have left the whole thing alone then, and not kept on trying to dig up their grandfather's past. They'd been in the kitchen last Christmas, doing the dishes, talking about parents. "The last time I heard my dad's voice," he'd said, he had been passing by the living room and overheard his dad and Aunt Maggie talking. It was twenty years ago but the scene was as vivid as yesterday to him. His dad was standing by the window, and Aunt Maggie was half-sitting, half-lying on the sofa, the way pregnant women do. His dad was saying, "I tried to tell Mum about the photographs, Maggie. About what he might have been. But she could hardly talk about him after what she thought he'd done. She kind of mumbled, 'Not a hero, him . . . not a hero . . . chased women . . . that Dora.'"

There'd been tears in his father's voice as he spoke. Tears in his own eyes when he told Bertie. Because very soon after that, David Parkes had gone to Europe and never returned.

For years, Aunt Maggie had believed her brother had gone underground to be a spy like their father. Uncle Theo, after his fruitless search, thought it was a matter of amnesia and lost identity and that he would turn up eventually. For weeks after his dad had been declared missing, people kept turning up at the house to comfort his mother and to offer advice to him. Dr. Tressell was there most weekends. And the fat guy who called himself Boomer and said he was his dad's best friend had stopped him on his way to school and offered to train him for the New York Marathon. The Grewson grandparents had abandoned their retirement home in Florida and stayed for weeks muttering imprecations against their son-in-law. They saw his disappearance as something he had brought on himself, even if he had been murdered and robbed and tossed into a canal. Had he not been fired from his job? Did that happen to men who were reliable? No! There was hidden sin, a hidden lover, an absconding with funds. As evidence, there was the picture in the newspaper. Do cameras lie? After the third angry scene, his mother sent her parents back to their place in the swamp and a quiet sadness settled over the house.

Well-known cruising area for homosexuals, the newspapers said at the time, showing a photograph of the three men lying on the ground. That picture had been taken by a hateful prurient snoop and, at seventeen, Greg had learnt the meaning of the word *infer*. Nothing more needed to be said. No denials were allowed. Suddenly his dad was a fairy and all the kids at school knew it. Or thought they knew it. And even Jason, caught up with his own problems, was no support. Grade twelve was a year he was still trying to forget.

Diane O'Brien, his parents' friend, died while he was still at university and the widower had come round indecently soon to propose to his mother. She had laughed and cried and said no. But it might have been a safe haven for her. Company for both. *This is my step-father, John O'Brien, M.L.A.*

He envied people who called themselves 'single-minded.' Their brains were dedicated to whatever they were up to at the moment. His own mind was a beehive. His grandfather's legacy was Bertie's obsession. His father's strange disappearance should have been his. And to some extent it was but there was also the matter of his relationship with Marni, his mother's idea that his current job was a stepping stone to something great, his guilt at what others saw as a lack of ambition, and his desire to one day trek through the Brazilian rainforest.

Work never entirely erased all these buzzing thoughts from his brain. Sex did for the time it lasted and he could be proud of that, the time he could make it last, with Marni or without. He tried not to think about the 'without.' He wanted to be a faithful man and was. It was only when he went out of town to look at some invention too large to be moved, or to meet an inventor too old or weak to travel, and had a hotel room to himself, that he spent time in his own fantasy land. He always asked Marni to come with him on those trips but she was too busy. And so, in a way, it was her fault if he committed small sins.

He heard voices and disturbance in the reception area. Doreen came into his office. Today she was wearing a blue knee-length skirt and a green top with short sleeves. Her earrings jangled as she walked.

"Mr. Parkes?"

"Yes, Doreen?"

"The men about the—you know."

"Show them in."

His father would have enjoyed this visitation. His mother would see it as a performance piece: The entrance of the madmen. The truly obsessed. The ones who knew they could make the world a better place if only the world would wake up and pay attention to their latest invention: A perpetual motion machine. A device to harness energy from plants. A water powered television set. Robot prison guards. Microphone implants for the deaf.

I know I could earn more money elsewhere, he'd said to Marni just last night. But I live in a world of wonder and among people who do things for the love of it. Crazy people, she'd said. And he'd made his usual defense, If it's crazy to do something they hope will make the world a better place then they are quite mad, most of them. Sometimes they're hoping for the riches of Eldorado, but often all they want, truly, is to enhance, improve, the conditions of our lives. I know that's what politicians are supposed to do but these men and women are sincere. And besides that, every now and then, an ordinary looking person will come into the office with something that turns out to be a winner.

This morning's inventors entered slowly carrying a green garbage bag between them. They set it down on his desk with great care as if it might explode. The shorter man stared at the bag perhaps willing the invention to crawl out of the bag on its own to prove its worth. The tall one stared at Greg. He was smartly dressed in a pinstripe suit and white shirt and dark tie. He held out his hand.

"I've read your paper, Professor Alcock," Greg said, shaking the man's hand.

"I'm Alcock," the other man said, "he's Bronstein. Like Trotsky."

"Let's have a look."

The two men took hold of the corners of the garbage bag and drew it back slowly to reveal their treasure. Silvery strands of wire wound round on one another irregularly to make a lop-sided hollow sphere. Inside, like a trapped bird, a solid black ball was suspended on a piece of thread.

"It's beautiful," Greg said.

"And it works like this." Bronstein began to move the sphere very gently with one hand. The ball swung more to one side than the other and then picked up a rhythm of its own. The inventors watched it intently, glancing at Greg now and then like parents of a child prodigy.

"So you're saying . . . ?"

They began to speak alternately like a comedian and his straight man.

"We're saying that this small toy you see here, a few times larger, the size in fact of a car."

"A small car."

"Is an amazing air purifier. A super cleansing device. How much are we hearing now about pollution? How much about people getting sick from toxic fumes? One of these set down beside a factory that spews out disgusting stuff will cleanse the air of pollutants for a two kilometer range."

"It's attractive. No one will mind having it in his backyard."

"No tower, no vanes. Just a pleasing modern sculpture. And the air is moved around so. Even a slight breeze will set it in motion. And it can be fitted with any kind of scent you want."

"Think of an industrial area which reeks of waste. Put one of these nearby, add a purifying agent into the ball, air comes in stinking there, comes out here smelling of violets."

"I'm not a believer," Alcock said, stroking the silver strands of the sphere, "in that old saying that what is too good to be true, isn't true. In some matters, what is too good is also true."

All the people who came to him seeking a viaticum to the patent office held to that same creed. Left to himself, he would have given them all a huge grant to develop their devices for as long as it took but there was the committee, there were limited funds, and his boss had no faith in magic.

"Now you know it isn't just up to me," he said.

"Ach," Bronstein growled, "don't give us that old tale. We know that you have only to speak to him." He nodded his head in the direction of Lipson's office. "He pays attention to you."

"There's still the committee."

"We will see them one by one."

"You don't have to do that. I'll make sure they see it."

"Meanwhile," Alcock said waving his arms to suggest noxious clouds, "children are being poisoned to death."

"On summer days in this city, old people cannot go outside."

"Everybody is coughing."

"We shall become extinct."

"In a few years, this city will be a wasteland, humans will have fled, buildings will crumble, ugly things will wash up on the lakeshore. There will be a fence round it, warning people to enter at their peril."

Greg sat back and admired the object. He imagined a series of huge metal balls set up around the city's edges, sunlight glinting off them perhaps causing planes to fly off course. It would be a city of the future with light beams shooting skywards into the purer air, attracting flying saucers and deflecting all harm.

The two inventors kept their eyes on him. He was well aware that his next move was critical. A nod of his head, a wave of his hand could encourage or dismiss them. To give them hope was to deceive them. To tell them at once that their fine sphere was impractical was to unleash sorrow followed by bitterness followed sometimes by aggression.

"The assessment will take three weeks."

Both men leaned towards his desk as if he'd made a move on a precious child. They looked at each other and at him. Bronstein looked at his watch.

"Three weeks today at ten a.m."

"Not a minute later."

From the doorway, Alcock shouted, "Anyone who turns this down is a stupid and murderous idiot."

"And an ignorant asshole," Bronstein added.

The room seemed empty after they'd gone as if a whole crowd of people had pushed their way out into the corridor. Doreen looked in. He shook his head. She turned the corners of her mouth down and went back to her desk. Greg tapped the sphere and watched the ball swing on its thread. It was a pleasing, not quite regular movement. The professors might have been better employed inventing something that prevented the pollution rather than something that simply swirled the muck about. Those who'd tried to do that had come up against politicians who shouted, 'It's too costly,' and union leaders who saw only closed factories and unemployment. *Gott im Himmel,* he said to himself. His grandfather had taught him several useful phrases on that long summer visit years before. He gently pushed the sphere again.

Lipson came in. "New desk toy?"

"No, Fred."

"Alcock?"

"And Bronstein."

"What?"

"It's an air purifier."

"Small."

"Multiply by a thousand."

"Big!"

"They want them placed round the edge of the city to make it cleaner and healthier."

"Backyard gripers?"

"They perceive them to be elegant, artistic objects that people will be glad to have near their property."

"Cost?"

"A lot."

"Hm." He went back to his lair.

If Lipson had ever spoken a sentence of more than four words no one who knew him could remember it. He got through life without adjectives, few verbs and no similes. He told no stories, embroidered no anecdotes. Greg and Marni had laughed together imagining his love-making: Foreplay: Want? Act: Wordless grunting. Post-sex: Light, please.

Greg got down to work. His task was to sort out the wheat from the chaff. He had to contact three experts who were known to be without bias and prepare a report on the garbage atomizer designed by three students from Waterloo. He was still trying to get in touch with the woman who had left her model of a silent lawnmower with him five weeks ago and hadn't returned. She'd said, and he remembered her well because she looked like a soft-edged Madonna, that she'd be back in on the 13th. He let himself consider what might have happened to her. She was with her lover in a hotel room and neither of them had got out of bed. Room service left trays at the door . . .

The phone rang.

He picked up the handset and said, "Hi, Bertie."

"It's me," Marni said. "Is she calling you all the time? What's going on? She should go back to school or get a job. She shouldn't be bothering you at work."

"She just wants to tell me something. I'll talk to her later. What are you wearing?"

"Your whole family has obsessive genes. I've got a meeting at Osgoode Hall this afternoon. Do you want to meet for a drink, maybe dinner? I'm wearing the navy blue."

"Time and place?"

"The Four Seasons. Six-thirty."

He hung up and pictured her in the navy bra and pants. Why couldn't she come straight home and have a glass of wine and hop into bed with him? She had something to tell him! The timbre of her voice had been serious even when she told him about her underwear. She was pregnant? She was seeing someone? He would have known. She had to go to New York for six months? And who was she to talk obsession? Her work, every case, was a do or die affair that took up all her thinking space and left too little for him.

She was right though about Bertie. The child was obsessed. She'd gone through her grandfather's notebook, contacted the Imperial War Museum and had been given the name of a camp over the phone and an address in the States. The brief letter she received from an official in Washington had only told her that, yes, civilians had been asked to go to the camps and the army had been grateful for their presence.

Like her father she had an evangelical approach to information. If one person knew, all should know. It was also a dictatorial approach: Thou shalt know! Like it or not. And it was, after all, her story now.

She'd begun by having the tiny photographs enlarged and insisted on giving him copies. *He was your grandfather. You have to be interested.*

His grandfather was a kind man who'd stayed with them for a whole summer when Greg was about five. The old man had taught him some German words and shown him how to play dominoes. After he'd died, the world had shaken on its axis and Granny had gone on a coach trip with his dad through the Austrian Tyrol. A coach trip! Like his mother who was on her retirement trip somewhere in British Columbia. Was this what there was to look forward to down the line? Travelling around with busloads of old folk, staring at scenery, involved in nothing and, like Granny, having a heart attack while walking up a hill far from home? He shuddered and pushed the little silver sphere again to keep the ball rolling and turned to the report on the garbage atomizer: This miracle machine will solve the problems of world-wide rubbish and do away with rat-infested dumps. Total pulverization guaranteed. No droplets or specks would get out into the atmosphere. Greg wasn't sure the inventors had thought this all the way through.

We have to go to Germany. That's what Bertie had said two days ago. *I've done all the groundwork. Now we have to see the place where they took him and we'll understand.*

Greg had tried to avoid too much understanding. He knew that much about himself. He'd chosen to work with the unachievable, the incomprehensible, in a world where success was rare but wonderful. He admired possibility. His mother knew too much and his father had known too little. Greg had chosen the middle, happy course. He took the atlas down from its place among the reference books. It stood there beside *Forms of Energy for the 21ˢᵗ century, A History of Ingenuity, The War of the Worlds, An Encyclopedia of Electricity, Patents and Insurance, Fraud and Delusion.* Above it on the shelf for smaller books were copies of Uncle Theo's works which Marni refused to have in the house. She said he was a master of woolly-thinking philosophy, misleading the masses.

Germany was green in the north and brown where it joined onto Switzerland and Luxembourg. He'd looked in the index and there was no mention of the place Bertie had insisted was there: Durmittelberg. Moving his finger down from Hamburg, and then across from Belgium to Czechoslovakia which was now two countries, he found no such name. Had they erased it post-war? Filled in the caves? What was there to see? He knew that, for Bertie, it wasn't so much about seeing as experiencing. So why didn't she set off with an alpenstock and a backpack by herself and leave the family alone? He imagined her hiking up a mountain path wearing brief leather shorts and a green hat with a feather in it.

Marni wouldn't go on such a trip. It's a family affair, she would say. One glance at the photographs had been enough for her. Not that I mean we should forget, she'd said. She was always reasonable. *The world moves on, Greg, we have to live in the here and now.* She was right. And she was also wrong.

*

"This is the highest paved pass in North America," Elise said into her microphone.

The passengers leaned to the right to look at the forest below and the bus lurched sideways as the edge of the road gave way due to erosion after prolonged heavy rainfall. It rolled over and over as the passengers screamed and prayed. The great metal tube crashed against pines and birches, flattened ferns and came to rest at last on the valley bottom. Wild creatures ran to hide. Screeching thoughts of children, wills, chocolate, fairground rides, sex, war, unlocked doors, locked secrets, missed chances, messages to loved ones left unsaid, cannoned round the inside of the fallen vehicle. For hours the bus lay there, the moans of the injured the last sounds heard by the dying. Elise, always the guide, tried to point out the rare orchids pressed flat against the windows in a final effort to educate her charges. Roger, the driver, was lying unconscious against the door and none of the thirty elderly women and five elderly men was strong enough to move him. They would never be found. Tall pines closed over the scene and only their tire tracks could lead to rescue. Tomorrow? Next week? A hundred years hence?

Linda sighed. None of these people deserved to die on the forest floor just because she, at the moment, saw the remainder of her life as a desert with no oasis in sight. She allowed the bus to roll back up the steep side of the valley, righted the trees and the plants and left the animals to their usual hunt-and-devour pursuits. The birds sat back on their branches and the bus hummed again with low key conversation.

Large corporations gave their retired executives a cruise round the world or at least three weeks in Hawaii. When she returned to the apartment after the farewell party at the hospital and opened the envelope, she'd found a plane ticket to Calgary and a voucher for this bus trip through the Rockies. They had taken for granted that once out of their employ, she would have nothing at all to do and the dates would be convenient.

"When we reach Radium . . . ," Elise was saying.

Last night at dinner, sitting with four of the other women and one man, Linda let them think she was a widow to save having to explain David's disappearance. When she admitted that she had no grandchildren, they lost interest in her. Over their coffee and pie, the others began to hand round pictures of little Ezra, little Jamie, little Bobbie, *All so cute you could just eat them up.* Cannibal grandparents! She did her best to admire the curls of little Danny and the obvious intelligence of two-year-old Brett.

Marni was too taken up with her career to want a child and Greg was too easygoing to make his own wishes clear and say, *If you don't want children, Sweetheart, I'll find a woman who does.* Linda wanted to show these people a picture of Greg and say, This is my beloved son and I am proud of him. When my husband left home—she had never in all these years been able to say *left me*—my son bought food and made meals and stayed around when I know he would rather have been out with his friends.

She'd kept on admiring the pictures of assorted grandchildren, wondering that there could be so many among so few.

The forest on either side of the road was so dense that there could scarcely be room for a deer to walk between the trees. A human being would get totally lost in moments. The woods were truly 'dark and deep,' and sinister too and there were many more miles to go. She still dreamed sometimes of David wandering in such a place, trying desperately to get out, perhaps calling her name. All the scenes of re-appearance she had conjured up for him over time, and her greeting when he stood at last on the doorstep, were faded images now. He was not coming back. She had no need to feel guilty about Tressell or John O'Brien or the man at the administrators' conference in Chicago.

George in the seat next to her had fallen asleep and his head lolled onto her shoulder. George was also travelling alone. His wife had died a year ago and he would never get over it unless perhaps. . . . She shrugged him off and he woke up with a resentful grunt. Maybe his dream had taken him back to the time when a woman who loved him let him sleep with his head on her breast.

"When we reach Radium," Elise repeated in a louder voice to reach the deaf members of the group, "we'll stop first at the hotel."

Linda looked round at her fellow passengers and decided that when they reached Radium, she would say goodbye to them, plead family problems, make her own way back to Calgary and pay the penalty to change her flight. If life in retirement was to be boring, she wanted to create her own kind of dullness and did not want to pass her time as part of a herd.

She began to feel more cheerful. First of all when she got back, she would work out her finances and figure out what kind of journey she could afford to make through the next few years.

Cousin Greg was not a serious man. His work, her father said, was play. But even though he was eighteen years older, he was her generation. The two of them were the only offspring born to the brother and the sister who were the children of Robert and Frieda Parkes. She envied her friends who had a galaxy of siblings and cousins. And 'friend' was a singular word in her case. Aside from Katie, there was no one she had ever tried to explain her ideas to. At school they, *they* mainly being Mr. Owen who didn't return her affection, said she was wise beyond her years as if that was a huge problem which could only lead to trouble. Boys had found her clever and even the geeks left her alone. Older guys were attracted to her but they were too caught up in 'getting on.' They talked about the office, the boss, the rising price of gas. The two she'd taken home had found more in common with her dad than with her. Eric was the exception.

But as of yesterday Eric was history and she had to remind him to get out of Aunt Linda's place by Friday. It had been a mistake getting the key from Greg, promising to water the African violets and the hanging plant. The way Eric had assumed, really assumed, that they would play house all and every day and had moved half his stuff in, had ruined the whole thing. He quite obviously had no sense of the transient or, come to that, responsibility.

Snooping round there, she'd found the notebook belonging to grandfather Parkes, and read his writings. His views were old-fashioned but the old man was cleverer than all of them and had led a greatly mysterious life. Added to that was the strange story of Greg's dad who had gone off in that weird way and never come back. They said it was the shock of Granny's death there in Austria that had made Uncle David stay behind after her funeral and travel around, sending postcards from German cities. But only her dad had gone in search of him and what could he do in two weeks in a vast place like Europe? She'd heard them talk about the little that was done by their embassy in Berlin. But what had Aunt Linda done, or Greg, or her parents? It was as if they'd built themselves a nice igloo and climbed inside. Maybe not an igloo. More as if they'd built a railway track through life and were not going to ever get off and do anything different. She'd read two of her father's books and trying to get him onto another track was like butting her head against a cushion. As for her mother, all that remained of the young exciting person she must have once been was a woman with a kind of good energy and glimmers of humour and light.

She wanted the old folks now, before it was too late, to become bold, enter into adventure. Unlike a whole lot of people, they did have a family mystery to solve. In fact, two.

All her thinking life, she'd heard comments among the rest of the family about her grandfather: We'll never know what he was doing there. What made him go? Did they have something on him? One day, she'd shouted, exasperated, Why don't you try to find out? All of them were in the room then, and they'd turned to look at her as if she had said *Fuck*. And then she realized that they preferred to live with the unknown. Greg said his dad had gone in search of the truth and never returned. Her mother talked about a Swiss woman who was involved in the matter but whenever Bertie mentioned her, her mother's lips tightened, little lines round her mouth appeared and the atmosphere went acid.

As for the tragically disappeared Uncle David—for a few years, the others had seemed to expect him to turn up every Thanksgiving, Christmas, birthday. By the time she was ten, they hardly mentioned him and it was a long time now since Aunt Linda's eyes had filled with tears at the mention of him. But her dad said that Linda saw the loss of her husband as a failure and that was why she used to cry. Bertie thought it more likely that she was just plain lonely and starved of sex. Which reminded her again to get Eric out of there soon.

The ale was sharp to taste. Next year, she'd change to wine. Surely Robert Frederick Parkes had liked wine. A man who'd traveled as he did must have drunk Tokay in Hungary and Riesling in Germany. Ambrosia in Switzerland? She considered ordering a ploughman's lunch but wasn't sure it was what he would have enjoyed. Like an Inuit child, she'd been given the name of the family member who had died just before she was born and she was glad of it. It connected her to a grandfather she'd never seen except in pictures. There was something shamanistic and spiritual about carrying on his name, even with a feminine ending. If she had been an Inuk then her mother would have had to call her 'Dad' and give her a present on this day, except that Inuit most likely didn't carry the names across genders.

She'd begun to celebrate his birthday years ago. At first it was simply a glass of lemonade and a cake taken from the kitchen and eaten in her room with a recital of a few lines of poetry. It had to be done on the sly because even then she'd known they wouldn't understand. For the past two years, she'd come to this fake British pub by herself and drunk a glass of dark ale for him.

She got her paperback copy of *The Island of the Day Before* out of her pocket and began to read, trying to block out the boring music and the loud voices of the men at the bar.

"All on your own?"

She hadn't noticed the guy come towards her carrying a bottle of Big Rock.

"I'm expecting a friend."

"Maybe we could talk till he comes."

He sat down and looked set to stay and bother her with questions about her life all leading up to a chance for a fuck.

"She."

"She what?"

"My friend."

"You mean?"

"Yes," she answered and gave him what she hoped was an aggressive grin. *Two witch's eyes above a cherub's mouth,* Eric had said in his poetry phase. But Katie said her eyes were an enviable green and told her which eye-shadow to use to enhance them. At any rate, the man still sat there looking at her till she began to move her foot towards his leg.

"Ah. Right." He sipped at his beer and after a moment saw someone he had to talk to and went back to the bar. Both men looked over at her and shook their heads. She walked out into the street. It was a hot, polluted day and she tried not to breathe too deeply.

Greg opened the dictionary at 'let' and came upon 'letch' a craving, longing. And then there was 'lethargy.' 'Falling into carelessness and (as I may call it), a lethargy of thought.' Dryden. And that didn't mean Ken. The old poet no doubt would have had no time for a man who spent his time playing games. *Letch* scored forty-five points. But *lethargy* stayed in his head. He let the computer win by default and moved the mouse to open Marni's e-mail. There was nothing today from the man who signed himself KA.

She was late. Held up. By a client, a mugger, a highwayman? Pressed against the wall by a naked lover in a motel room?

We should have children, he thought. Bertie would stop bothering him and he wouldn't have time to play solitary games or imagine wild scenarios. And Marni would wait for him to come home from the office. The sky out there was purple and yellow and orange, the sun setting now earlier and earlier. He wished he could paint, get those pale greens and blues onto a canvas and contrast them with the darker colours.

He heard Marni come in and felt her hands on his eyes, closing off the view.

"Surprise," she said.

Surely not after last night when on the way home from the restaurant, she'd let him put his hand between her legs and later they'd rolled on the floor in the hall till he'd managed to carry her across to the bedroom. He was still tired.

He held on to the table and leaned back to let his head rest on her breasts but she moved away so that he turned and the chair tilted backwards and he was on a bed looking up at Marni and a stranger. His head ached and the stranger looked like his father. *Hello, Dad. You've been gone quite a while.* His 'father' was wearing a white coat and a stethoscope dangled round his neck. No great damage, he was saying. But we'll keep him overnight to be on the safe side. What is the safe side? Right or left? East or West? Jays or Penguins?

"Thank you," Marni said to the stranger. Then she looked at Greg in a way that made him close his eyes. He truly didn't want to hear what he'd done wrong. He only wanted to be on the safe side.

"You're an idiot," she whispered to him. And he knew that no side was safe.

Theo said, "What have you signed up for?"

It was such a dumb question and Bertie wanted to scream at him, *Nothing! I'm opting out. I'm going to solve the family mystery that all of you would rather just talk about till you die. This will be my education. And yours.*

But she didn't shout. She knew her parents were old. She had all the responsibility of being a late child. She had to bear with their simple ideas. And her father's face with its surrounding fringe of soft grey hair was like that of a teddy bear. He couldn't help his ignorance, his fussiness, his increasing deafness.

"I'm ok, Dad," she said. "How's the piece going?"

"You're deflecting, which means you're not going to answer me."

"Let's sit down," she said.

He sat down, pleased to be with her. He smiled so softly, so benignly, his beard made him seem even older than he was, and she sometimes thought he looked like God. He reached for her hand and said, "So Bertie," as if they might speak as lovers.

"I want to have a family party," she said.

"Any time. We're a small family."

"Everybody together, nobody having to rush away. And Greg must be here too."

"This is important to you."

"It's important to all of us."

"You haven't got a dire announcement to make?"

"I'm not going to marry Eric, I'm not a lesbian and Professor Michaelson hasn't got me pregnant."

"Now Bertie. I didn't even think . . . " he shuddered.

"I bet one of those things crossed your mind just then. I saw it in your face."

"We should've had six children."

"Dad!"

"You've watched us too closely. Parents should be a little unknown. Up there on a pedestal."

"Too late."

"So?"

"Sunday brunch."

"I hate that word. Why not lupper? Why not binner?"

"Dad!"

She shook her head and went to the kitchen. Her mother was mixing paper and water in the large bowl.

"Sunday brunch, sweetie?" she said.

"I'll do everything," Bertie replied. "What's that?"

"Masks. The new woman in kindergarten has no idea."

"A week on Sunday when Aunt Linda's back."

"I can't imagine her on a bus trip."

"How are you going to colour that goop?"

"Food colouring," her mother replied.

Linda wished she'd left the car at the airport. There was a damp unpromising feel to the air. It would be hot later but autumn was creeping into the city like a play that comes into town on 'tennis shoes.' She'd known she would lose the day by travelling on the redeye but there was a seat available and no penalty to pay and she had, after all, no engagements; no one knew she was back, not even Greg. She waved and a taxi crawled towards her. She gave the driver her address and then sat back to contemplate her future.

Driving down 427, she looked at the metal and concrete growth on either side of the road, man's blight, man's infection, a mushroom bed of low expedient buildings. And then the lake, the early sailors out because in a few weeks their boats would have to be hauled in. The sky was clearing. It was going to be a lovely day. Coffee first, then a walk to clear her head and buy a few groceries. And after that to set out the ideas that had crowded into her head while she travelled through the night. She'd ripped open her sick bag to jot down the thoughts and when she'd covered both sides, she reached for her sleeping neighbour's and wrote all over that too.

She would have to delay work on *A Perfect World*. She understood why Boris Shaw had bequeathed it to her: It was unfinished business. The show had not gone on. The script had landed in her mailbox months after his death and lain like a brick on her desk for over a year. His handwritten notes in the margin had faded slightly but were still legible. She knew that it was something she had to do to appease his spirit. Dottie had died since. Harold was too old to hoof it about the stage. She had only meant to postpone the opening for a week but in that week, David, acting strangely, had made up his mind to fly, Jeffrey contracted shingles and the auditorium roof developed a leak. Then there were the dark days after Granny Parkes' death and they grew darker after David had been gone for weeks beyond his promised date of return. His last message was a postcard from Dresden signed, *All my love, David*. The card he'd sent to Maggie, postmarked only two days after hers, said, *I have found Dora. Back next week.* After that there had been nothing. Nothing at all. Only a bleak emptiness in her mind which echoed with alternate cries of despair and reproach.

The play she was going to write now, set in a bus, could be written in various ways: Tersely as Shepard, complex as Stoppard, kindly as Wilder. But it would be hers, her own style, owing nothing to anyone. A title had sprung to mind at once. It would simply be called *The Omnibus*. A character like Elise, the guide, might introduce the passengers while expressing the frustrations in her own life. If Elise and the driver were sleeping together and decided to make up the route as they went along . . . . Or perhaps there was a Pina Bausch element; the characters sitting in two rows of chairs and coming forward to tell their stories which would interconnect. To make for a smaller cast, it could be a custom-arranged trip in a large van or small school bus. And there would have to be drama, action. *Murder on the Rocky Mountain Explorer* had been done. *The Ship of Fools. The Bridge of San Luis Rey.* Everything had been done before. A travelling group of individuals separated from all the things that kept them sane was a well-used device. But she could make it new and different. She wanted to get right to the computer without even changing and having a shower. It was all there in her head, ready to be sorted out and set down. Coffee would keep her awake. She would go on till it was done and she could write *Fin*. The characters' voices were rattling round in her head, vying to be heard. There was a man on the bus who was running away from the law, and a woman who . . .

She paid the cab driver who seemed weary and didn't offer to lift her bags even as far as the entrance to the building. Making two trips, she got her luggage to the elevator and pushed the button. It was good to be home. There would be letters and messages that she could ignore. For days she would be alone in the city. No one need know she was there. If Greg turned up to water the plants, so much the better. After his first surprise, she could sit down and talk to him about his future, the possibility of children, the truth of his relationship with Marina who called herself Marni and tell him that she had found her retirement occupation and only wanted a computer with more memory.

She put her key in the lock with that same satisfaction she remembered from years ago when they had returned to the house from the lake at the end of the season. Summer over, peaceful fall here at last and with it a return to real life. By Christmas, *The Omnibus* would be in rough draft. Actors she knew would come and read it, she would make chili and cornbread and serve wine. She wanted a glass of wine now, at 7.30 in the morning, to celebrate her new life. Maybe, after all, the administrators at the hospital had designed the trip to force her to think. A cruise would have softened her mind and led to a desire for luxury. She tripped over what felt like cloth. She set down her bags and drew back the drapes. In the dim morning light, she saw a man's shirt lying over the back of the couch. She had tripped over an empty backpack. There were socks on the coffee table and a wallet and change.

She stopped. She'd had this dream many times. Why would it be true now? And how had he discovered where she now lived? The phone book of course! She was tempted to rush straight into the bedroom and shout, Where have you been you bastard! And follow that with a list of recriminations two decades long. She sat still for a moment on the chair by the window and considered her next action. She tried to settle her mind by recalling that afternoon twenty years ago when she had lain in his arms content and loving.

Quietly, she began to take off her clothes.

First of all the cut glass jug had to be filled with orange juice. Bertie had bought a mesh bag full of oranges and that morning she'd cut them all in half and held them over the spike of the juicer while she listened to the hymns on the radio. Quiche was outdated. She'd read that in a magazine in the doctor's office. Now was a time for frittatas, for shirred eggs and soufflés. All right, we'll have them all here if you cook, her mother had said, probably hoping she'd forget the whole thing. She took ten eggs from the fridge and set them on the counter so that they wouldn't be dead cold when she wanted to use them.

Greg and Marni and Linda weren't due for over an hour. Linda had sounded strange on the phone but then she often did. Her father was sitting in the sunroom reading *The New York Times*. Her mother was tapping at the computer in the den writing her newsletter for the retired teachers' association.

Since this was a family affair, she'd decided to use grandma's linen tablecloth. It was one of their few heirlooms, ecru with a drawn-thread design in the corners. There were five napkins to match. She would do without one. Knives and forks, small knives for apples or pears or mangoes. Side plates. Large cups and saucers. She stood back to admire the table for a moment. Elegance was easy.

In the kitchen, she took the three fat tomatoes she'd bought and sliced them across. A bed of lettuce! They had to be arranged on a 'bed' of washed and shredded lettuce. She'd forgotten to wash the tomatoes but they were a cleansing kind of fruit. No one was about to die from dirty tomatoes.

If she broke the eggs into the bowl now, she'd have time to sit in her room and consider exactly what she was going to say to her only close relatives. Being the young one in the group, she was often patronized by them and sometimes pandered to. Her least favourite was Aunt Linda who had always seemed to be sharp and bitter as if she wished she belonged to a better family and one day would find it and leave. She had, though, bought her great presents that were still treasures; her black bear, the huge box of paints, *Tanglewood Tales*. Linda was good at gifts. Marni, more her age, was too absorbed with her career and with Greg. Bertie hoped that if she found a partner, she would be more attentive and less possessive.

There should be in a civilized feast of this kind, a background of pleasing sounds. They were not going to like Björk or Three Fat Men on a Bicycle. Her Dad liked jazz. It was Sunday. They could listen to the Beatles. To hear them talk, the four Brits had caused a kind of religious frenzy in their day. But God it was slow stuff now. She couldn't see what the fuss was about. Eric said they were a milestone on the road to Rock. Not a word from him for a week. She had expected at least one pleading phone call begging her to reconsider. Thank heavens anyway, that he'd been gone from the apartment before Linda returned so sneakily early.

The phone rang. They weren't coming. Their car had broken down. Linda had got out of bed and said, What does that stupid child want now? But it was Katie wanting to talk about her own love life. Bertie looked at her watch. There was time.

Greg, driving his mother to Aunt Maggie's, cursed the Sunday drivers who came out of their caves on this one day of the week and took off like bats to visit relatives, go to church, and refresh their pathetic driving skills. His mother was looking out of the window at the trees as if she wanted to avoid talking to him.

This summons to a family meeting was a bit of a surprise. Bertie, as a child, had usually got her way by going from one adult to another and keeping her plans to herself. Her start in life under a dark cloud of depression had its effect. As a little girl she had been a combination of bright sunny delight and sly secrecy.

His mother had given no explanation for her early return. The look on her face was unfathomable. Had she met someone on the trip and gotten broody, even at her age? Some cowboy in big boots and a hat twice as big as his head?

He said, "Marni would've liked to come. She has to read up about a case."

"She works hard. It can't be easy for her."

And that too was unusual. Normally his mother would have said something like, *Well she might have made an effort*. Had his mother now gone completely over to Marni's side, abandoning him? She did look at him sometimes as if he'd inherited a bad gene from his father. She could hardly say to her friends, my son could have been a trial lawyer. She might, though, like to see, in the company ads and in large letters on the office window, Parkes alongside Lipson and Inhofs. Greg had thought of getting a pot of gold paint and putting his name up himself. Inhofs was dead and Lipson might never notice.

"You haven't said much about the trip."

"It was fine."

"Bertie was insistent about this brunch."

"I expect she has some plan."

Greg was looking forward to the morning. These were the people to whom he belonged. They were all strange in their way. But in their way too, they loved him. For no reason whatever, tears came into his eyes. It wasn't only the brunch, the girl, the deep tiredness from last night's lovemaking, the reminder that his father had deserted him and his mother, or the knowledge that Uncle Theo, when he least wanted to leave Maggie, had gone to look for his brother-in-law and found the trail cold. He had a sense that things were about to change and he didn't know whether for better or worse. He sniffed. His mother handed him a Kleenex.

"Hay fever," he said.

"How's your head?" she replied.

"I'm fine. It's lucky I kind of slipped forward and held onto the table. Marni stopped the computer from falling on me."

As they drew up to the duplex, Greg recalled how he'd seen his father sitting on that very wall, crying. That was the beginning of the weirdness of a fall that only got weirder and worse. The wall hadn't crumbled in the twenty years that had passed. And Theo and Maggie, even though his books brought in a steady income, hadn't moved to a bigger place.

"Come in. Come in."

Maggie looked at Linda's long skirt and sweater and said, "You look years younger. The bus trip did you good."

Greg thought his mother looked as though her mind had been emptied of all ideas, like the actor in the movie they'd seen last week when the aliens had occupied his brain. Marni beside him had dropped the popcorn and shrieked because the butter had stained her slacks. He went into the kitchen to find his cousin. She told him to go back to the others so that she could concentrate on the food.

Theo was talking about the waves of dirty air that drifted over the lake from Buffalo. Maggie listening to him, or appearing to listen, still reminded Greg of Our Lady of Sorrows. That time she'd stayed with them while Theo was in Europe, she and his mother had spent evenings together talking softly. Coming in from school, he'd hear them murmuring, crying, sometimes letting out a kind of hysterical laugh.

"It's ready," Bertie called.

They moved into the dining room and took their places round the table. Greg noticed the extra place and apologized for Marni's absence. Bertie glanced round at them all as though she was a conjuror who had performed the first part of her trick. Now to put the two halves of the woman back together. She had put the scrambled eggs on a large platter and surrounded them with half slices of whole wheat toast. The tomatoes, now dressed with olive oil and basil and wine vinegar, were in a glass dish in the centre of the table.

"Help yourselves," she commanded.

"This looks great," Greg said.

Theo asked, "Did you see *The Times* this morning?"

No one else had. He went on, "This big oil spill in Alaska. It's killing thousands of seabirds."

Bertie said, "And fish. Eric is probably up there, helping to clean it up. It's his thing."

Greg noticed that his mother's hand shook and she spilt some of her coffee. When he got home, he'd see what he could find out about strokes on the internet. He foresaw difficulties if she had to move in with them. A wheelchair, a ramp, a small van with a back door and a sticker that read, *Please do not park too close*. It could all be done. Marni would understand. Marni would probably understand. Most likely she would understand.

To liven things up, he said, "A guy came into the office last week with a gadget for removing the bones from small fish. A kind of magnet."

"So," Theo said, "people keep inventing things. The human mind is amazing. Most of the ideas that are brought to you are totally impractical and yet. . . ."

"Once in a while, a man or woman invents something that will change the way we do what we do. Take the paper clip for instance. We're always on the lookout for the next paper clip."

"It's a dream world."

"Two guys came in last week with a great idea for an industrial air purifier."

"Now *that* I can see."

"I'll take the cloth home and wash it," Linda said. So far she had hardly spoken a word, only glanced at Bertie now and then in a secretive kind of way.

"No," Maggie insisted. She felt insulted, as if she couldn't wash it herself, but Linda knew and she knew that she would just as likely wipe the stain off and fold the cloth up and put it back in the drawer.

"We'll send it to the laundry," Theo said.

"Let Mom do it, she needs something to do now she's retired," Greg put in.

His mother bared her teeth at him as if he was a foundling.

Bertie was looking at them all, one by one. Maggie recalled that face from Mothers' Day mornings when the tray was set down on the bed and she had to look at the hard egg, the scorched toast and say, 'This is lovely, darling,' and then eat every bit while the little girl watched. How many mothers, she wondered, were constipated for a week following their special day?

She said, "You cooked the eggs in the microwave?"

"They're perfect," Greg said.

"They were undercooked," Bertie stated. "Fortunately we don't have salmonella problems with eggs in this country."

"Once they've been nuked, they're fine," Theo said.

"Weird word for you to use, Uncle Theo."

"I'll soak it first," Linda said with a gentle, faraway smile.

"You're not taking the cloth," Maggie insisted.

"It was my fault."

"Well perhaps it'll be your fault if the sky falls on us."

"There are croissants," Bertie said and went to the kitchen.

"Couldn't eat another thing."

"I could eat two," Greg said. "And I'll take two back for Marni."

"Hey," Theo said, "leave one for the old man."

Bertie brought in the croissants and set the basket down on the table with a bang. She didn't look at all like her grandfather but there were ways about her that reminded Maggie of him, especially of those moments on her last visit when he appeared to be full of something he wanted to say and then died before he could. If he'd spoken, if only she'd got him on his own, told him she'd overheard him talking on the phone that morning, everything might have been made clear. And Bertie would be at university writing an English essay instead of pursuing an old man's ghost.

They all helped themselves to a croissant. Bertie poured more coffee and offered them butter and jam. Maggie was proud of her daughter, mystified and proud. The child may be father to the man but the girl isn't necessarily mother to the woman, she thought. Whatever that meant. She smiled to herself as she remembered her fear before their daughter was born that the child would resemble Theo. Or worse, that she would look like the invader, Ron. But Bertie, slim and small with an oval face, hair neatly pulled back, was there in the old photographs of Theo's mother. She had seen him lately looking at those pictures and then at his daughter with a kind of reverence.

Bertie banged her knife on the table making another stain on the cloth, causing Linda to wince and Theo to spew crumbs onto the table.

"You all know," Bertie began, "about Grandpa and the photographs."

I should be doing this Maggie thought with a resentment she tried to douse with a large gulp of coffee. She wondered for the thousandth time whether it had been wise to give the child her own father's name. She'd done it out of love, out of guilt for not understanding him, for never asking the right questions. She knew that Bertie had some mystic feeling for her grandfather and it had intensified after her exchange trip to Iqaluit. The child had discovered more than she could cope with up there in the far north and had come back blaming the government, the people in the lower part of the country and even, for no good reason, herself, for the plight of the Inuit. *Those people's lives have been ruined.* A new anger had taken hold of her, a social awareness that was fine and at the same time hard to live with.

"I think we should go to Germany and see the place for ourselves," Bertie said.

"If we were going to follow in your grandfather's footsteps," Theo said, "we'd have to travel all over Europe. And who is going to pay for it?"

"Just Germany," Bertie said. "We believe he was some kind of spy for the government when he was travelling before the war, and that someone in the army called him to go to that camp, the place in the photograph. We know he came back shocked and just horrified and all that. I think we have to go for him—a sort of memorial—and stand in the place where he was and see that it's become all right."

"They've probably filled the caves in."

"They might not let us go there."

"It'll be a tedious journey."

"I've got a client coming in with something that could be really big."

"I don't think I can get away just now."

"Can you hear yourselves?" Bertie shouted. "You sound like a bunch of old people who've given up ever doing anything new. You're rats on treadmills. You've forgotten life. You've built little spaces for yourselves to be safe in. And who made the world safe for you? What have any of you done to deserve to be safe? What have you done to earn the right to your little conservative, bland ordinary lives? You've hung up the 'Do not disturb sign,' and you're happy to stay inside and never look out and see what goes on. Or what went on. Have you ever thought why he did what he did? He's the only hero in this family of slugs and I think we should honour him. It's not very much to ask is it? We're a little family, a little tiny group. If Greg and I don't have children, this is it. This lot round this table is all of us, and that's pretty depressing. I can see why it doesn't matter much to you, Dad, or you, Aunt Linda, but you're connected. You have to think about what happened to Uncle David. Why he decided to run, and what made Granddad what he was. Would it hurt to make this little trip to Europe and see the place? I don't want to go back to school. I told them I might come back in January." She looked round the table at their faces and saw surprise, a little bit of fear, middle age in Greg, elderliness in the others. A total lack of adventure hung over the room like a wet drape.

"I suppose I'll have to go by myself," she said. And then, to annoy her mother, she added, "I'll clear up and then you can take the cloth, Aunt Linda."

She went round the table and picked up their plates piling them one on top of another, not taking the cutlery off so that she was holding a tottering uneven pyramid, and went into the kitchen. The others waited for a crash. Maggie was about to apologize as she might have done for a mouthy thirteen-year-old but instead she said, "More coffee anyone?"

Linda spoke gently, "She's quite right. There comes a time in life when you do or you don't. You move on, or you don't. Strange things can happen which drive you to reflect on the essence of time. The slipperiness of time. The meaning of guilt. The beauty of the young, the rightness of the young."

Greg knew then that his mother had crossed a line. He wasn't sure what line or what it meant but the few days on that bus had changed her entirely as if she'd been on a trip to a magic mountain or had descended briefly into the underworld and returned with a different mindset.

"I just don't think it's feasible," his uncle said.

His shoulder had begun to hurt on the plane from London. The only young male among them, Greg had lifted all their cases on and off luggage racks, onto security conveyor belts, into taxis. He was a mute in this country where the language was a mystery. He wanted to be back in his office waiting for the next surprise, an invention so far out, so unimaginable, that he could enjoy considering its possibilities for a whole month. He had joined this expedition for the simple reason that he didn't want Bertie to despise him. Marni was angry with him and he should have cared more about that but he didn't. His mother had started out from Toronto in that same beatific frame of mind that had come on her after the coach trip. But now she was edgy and crabby and obviously hadn't yet forgiven herself for agreeing to be part of this caravan. Maggie and Theo were indulgent, kindly, and tired.

He knew that the three older ones were wishing they hadn't gone on so much about the expense. They would have liked the comfort of a chain hotel, reliable, the same in New York as in Toronto as in Tokyo. Bertie had picked out 'economy' lodgings all the way. And here in Frankfurt, they seemed to have hit the ultimate in cheap. His room was so small that the bed occupied ninety per cent of it and getting dressed required careful planning. He was sure that the words on the notice over the washbasin in the corner meant, Please don't pee in this sink, but he wasn't prepared to go down the hall to the bathroom and anyway, who would know?

He could hear Theo and Maggie arguing in the room next door. In his younger days he would have put a glass to the wall and listened in. Now he just wished they'd shut up but didn't feel he could tell them to. He moved his shoulder backwards and forwards and counted his deutschmarks. How much would he need to tip a porter to carry eight suitcases and Theo's laptop?

And they were all here at the whim of a twenty-year-old girl. What had her search to do with any of them except that her determination was the driver and she'd put them all to shame? That was it. In dark moments he thought she might want to push them into the cave, if the caves were still there, and abandon them so that she could start a new life as an orphan, relative-free. But she had gone after this unlikely grail as if, until she had found what she was seeking, her life was at a standstill. As if there could be no love life, no learning, no other journey until this one was completed. He desperately wanted to protect Bertie from disappointment. But that might require some magic invention from a different Alcock and Bronstein. An inventor who was concerned with the life of one person rather than the whole universe had not yet crossed his office threshold.

A loud knock on his door startled him.

"Come on, Greg, we're off."

Maggie looked at her daughter walking ahead of them. From the back she looked sturdy, boy-like. She had a long stride, her hair was cut short, the peak of her baseball cap was facing the wrong way. The jeans were expensive, the shirt a throwaway. What will become of her if at this age she can inspire (if that was the word), cajole/ drive/ harass this group into such a foolhardy expedition? By the time she was thirty, she would be running a company, be president of a university perhaps. Though that was hardly likely if she had no intention of taking a degree. Theo worried that she was headed for a life of dilettantism. Or that, like Greg, she'd settle for a life below her capabilities and be satisfied with being less than she could be.

"Daydreaming?" Theo said.

"Still catching up on sleep."

"In Toronto it's . . . "

"Don't do that. I'm trying to live in this time. As it is here, now, in Frankfurt."

"She could have arranged to have the van brought to the hotel."

"They probably wouldn't risk their property down that street."

"On the way back we'll stay at the Ritz. Or its equivalent. If she'll allow it."

"How did we come to have this dictator child?"

"We were too weak."

"I'm sorry about that."

"Good God, Maggie, I wasn't blaming you or thinking of then. That wasn't your fault. Your father died. And David went away. Besides, depression happens, especially in older mothers."

"It must have had an effect."

"You know damn well that she's fine, and we're as proud of her as two peacocks."

"Do you think it's far?" Maggie asked. "And I'm a peahen."

Linda had caught up to them and said, "A forced march before breakfast. Your girl does think of some things. I could even eat a Knackwurst or any kind of Wurst."

"That might be what we get."

"We could have waited for her to drive it back to the hotel."

Linda's logic hit them. In the middle of the sidewalk, they stayed still and laughed. Bertie was drawing them on like a pied piper and not letting them rest. Yes indeed, they could have waited for her and Greg to drive the vehicle back. They'd have to go back to the hotel for their luggage anyway. What were they doing on this cool German morning straggling along in slow pursuit? But they knew. They were protecting her, not letting the family child out of their sight. And they had other reasons. Theo thought she might need his credit card, a senior guarantor. Maggie was there because she was there. Linda didn't want to be alone in that strange hotel.

Greg had called Marni the night before and she'd said, Come back now, today, or it's over. I love you, he'd shouted back but the only response was a raucous *'Ich liebe dich auch,'* from a woman passing through the lobby. And now, trotting along beside Bertie, he had time to wonder if it was true. Was Marni his one true love? She had seemed so. But maybe somewhere in the world there was a woman who would keep him from solitary sins, who would absorb his entire being, sex would be complete, they would be each other's equals in every way. She would admire him and he would appreciate her.

"I'm surprised," he said to Bertie, "that no one has invented a divining rod to help people pick out their true love, the one who is meant for them."

"Do you think there's only one?"

"Hey! You're too young to think like that."

"It's a serious question."

"Dad!" Theo heard her from a long way off as he had always done, as he had twenty years ago when the sound that came from her was only a cry without form. He hurried along leaving the two women to follow in his wake.

Caves, Linda thought as she walked along beside her sister-in-law, picturing a long dark tunnel driven deep into the earth, we're here about caves. At least there'd be none of that Malabar nonsense. Young women now have sex instead of hysterics. More use for marijuana than smelling salts, not that that was a good thing. She'd come along to spend time with her son and because there was a chance of adventure but mainly because she didn't want to be left out. She had seen the future on the awful bus trip and it wasn't pretty. She had made up her mind to take everything that was offered. And that included the boy in the bed. Watch out world! Linda Grewson is into her second life. And after that there might be a third, a fourth. But here she was a fifth wheel if ever there was one.

The new computer had arrived with room in its memory for a hundred plays. The one she planned to write now was about a late sexual awakening, renewed desire and it had nothing to do with old people on a bus. And not a lot to do with the boy who had got up early and left only a note that said, 'See you.' There would be a scene describing a woman's grief after her husband says, *I have to follow my father's footsteps,* and sets out to Europe on a cargo ship. She began a monologue with, *I am neither wife nor widow* but threw out that line because it sounded stilted.

She said to Maggie, "How are things?" and prepared to listen.

"You didn't enjoy the bus trip?" Maggie asked, putting the ball right back in her court.

"David said your parents used to do that."

"What?"

"Build up a wall of questions which neither of them ever answered. It's a kind of defense mechanism, I guess. You don't want anyone to know what you're doing, thinking, feeling. It's a bit pathetic."

"They survived."

"But look at what he didn't ever tell her."

"He was bound by the Official Secrets Act."

"Your whole damn family is, if you ask me. I'm not going one step further till you tell me how you are, you and Theo."

Maggie walked on two steps and then turned.

"You're a bossy woman, Linda. It comes of directing plays all the time. Theo and I are getting on with our lives. We haven't had sex in eleven months and three days. But we get along. After all we're here, aren't we, and we're together."

"I was only asking."

"Because you want to know? Like that woman in David Copperfield."

"Rosa Dartle."

"She wasn't a pleasant person."

"I've never aspired to pleasant."

"What then?"

Bertie and Theo and Greg were out of sight. The two women hurried along. "Now we're lost because of your prying. How'll we find them?" Maggie said.

"They went down that road. Come on."

Linda began to trot and Maggie tried to keep up but was soon out of breath. When she turned the corner there was no sign of the others and Linda was far ahead. Her right foot hurt. The sensible shoe was crushing her arthritic big toe and all she wanted to do was sit in a comfortable chair somewhere and finish the Lindsay Davis novel she'd been enjoying so much on the plane while Theo annoyingly tapped the keyboard of his laptop. He only did it to let the world around him know that he was important.

She was alone, limping along a street that was foreign. The houses on either side had no front yards. Their doors opened right off the sidewalk and the shuttered windows were at a level for even a small peeping Tom to peer through. As she had no idea where the car rental place was, she decided to turn back. The others had to return to the hotel with the van and would find her there, drinking coffee and perhaps having a halting conversation with one of the local inhabitants. *Guten Morgen*, she practiced to herself. *Ich habe eine Tochter.* And they would reply?

*

"You know she has no sense of direction," Theo said.

"She knows the name of the hotel," Linda replied. She was not about to be taken to task by Theo who had become more pompous with age and should have been looking after his wife himself.

"She'll be all right," Greg said.

"I'm going to drive round and look for her," Bertie stated.

"We'll both go. You guys stay here and wait."

Linda watched the two of them set off. Greg looked so much like David that at times she felt he was a reincarnation. He had the same relaxed attitude to work, the same annoying way of doing the right thing before anyone else had realized what that was. The wrong thing he'd done was to marry another lawyer who would take over the importance in the household and give him the leeway to go through life on cruise control.

"I want a grandchild," she said, speaking aloud without intending to.

Theo took her arm and said, "Let's go and have coffee. I wouldn't mind one of those rolls as well. I'm hungry. I think she'll be all right. I've lost her before, you know."

Linda looked at him and wasn't sure whether he was speaking metaphorically or physically. At any rate, she knew that she should be the one offering reassurance, and she went with him to the café at the back of the hotel.

The river Main was wide. Maggie sat on a bench and watched a pleasure boat go slowly by. What a leisurely way to travel. It was painted bright red and blue and black. There were people on the deck and a voice could be heard describing the points of interest. *On that bench sits a lost tourist who will never find her family if she doesn't make an effort.* The others would be back at the hotel and must be wondering where she was. She looked at her watch. It was dark in Toronto: All over the city people were sleeping. The older kids, some of them young prostitutes, were making downtown their own. Drunks were reeling out of bars and trying to drive home. Homeless men and women who hadn't found a bed in the shelters or didn't want one, had stacked their belongings and found a corner on the street. The night workers had taken over to clean up the subway, get the streetcars ready for another day, staff the hospitals. Which is where she would end up if she didn't get back to the others. She'd be found here unable to speak more than a few phrases of the language and taken in as a mad, wandering halfwit. *Sprechen Sie Englisch?* The only German words she knew aside from the obvious phrases had filtered through her mind from those evenings when her dad read to her and David from *Struwwelpeter*. It was all there, coded. *He who runs may read.*

A smaller boat passed slowly by and a man on the deck waved to her. She waved back. A wanderer. In the first years, she'd seen David in all kinds of places. She had often wished him a new life, a different life. She liked to think of him living on a sunny island in the South Seas with a woman who loved him. There were several children in that picture and all of them were brown.

The early chill of the morning was giving way to warmth from the sun. She lay down on the bench for a moment to let the sun warm her body. She floated gladly in a space that was cut out from her usual life. No one in this city knew her. She knew no one. A fresh life could be started here. She could go to an employment agency and say, I am sixty years old and have taken leave from my job/senses. I am willing to take up a post in marketing. Or perhaps you need someone to teach advanced English to diplomats. For years I worked for Harpeck Industries, a company that made synthetic fabric. And then, after my daughter was born, I went back to work half time. A few years later, when I saw she wasn't being taught to read properly, I woke up and got a teacher's certificate. And I have taught grades K through 4 ever since. So you see, *meine Herren*, I am eminently qualified . . .

She heard footsteps and sat up quickly. She'd lingered long enough. Theo would be getting frantic. She put her sensible shoe back on and set off back the way she thought she had come. The hotel had to be over there in the populated part of the city. Her foot felt better for the rest. And her mind too. There was just so much closeness a person could take and going about in a group of five like nursery kids holding onto a rope was tiresome. She headed towards a church spire that she didn't remember from before but that was probably because she hadn't raised her eyes. It was Sunday morning, and she walked along less painfully singing to herself, 'Jesus loves me, this I know,' and the words brought back a memory of safe times when there was no more on her mind than the next day at school, her homework, and whether the aircraft overhead were 'ours' or 'theirs' and were they going to keep on going or to drop their bombs on Kelthorpe.

The coffee was bitter. Theo dipped a piece of the hard roll into his cup and wished he was at home. Opposite him, Linda was trying to read the *Frankfurter Allgemeine*, making out words and putting them together to make some sense and saying the phrases out loud.

Their destination was the place that Bertie called Durmittelburg. She'd copied the old map and marked where she thought the camp was with an arrow pointing towards Dresden and another to Frankfurt. It meant little because all the surrounding area on the map was white. She'd put in the names of the other camps and beside them, the dates of liberation. If you could call it liberation, Theo thought. Some of the prisoners died from eating the first real food they'd had for days and weeks. Some of them died of joy when the day they'd dreamed of for so long had arrived. The sight of friendly soldiers was more than they could stand. He thought about that for a while, 'they died of joy.' It's the waiting that counts. But in their case, the waiting had been terrible. They had been dispossessed of all that made them who they were. Only the spirit could keep them human.

He knew he should have done more research himself before they set out on this trip but the publisher was demanding final revisions to *Men and Women at Play*. He wanted to write another chapter based on those adult board games that involve several kinds of risk.

"*Das ist ein* . . . " Linda read out.

Three skinheads looked in at the window and tapped on the glass. Theo dropped the whole roll into his cup.

"Do you think Maggie's ok?" he asked.

"Look, I'm sorry. I'm sorry I got ahead of her. She was rude to me. I was fed up."

"There's no need for this defensiveness, Lindy. I was looking for a bit of reassurance that's all. I came on this trip because . . ."

"You couldn't let your precious daughter out of your sight."

"Because I was afraid the horror, the realization of what happened here might send Maggie over the top again."

"But it's been twenty years."

"Eighteen and a half."

"Theo. You watch her every minute! How does she stand it? Right now she's probably in a café somewhere having a much better breakfast than we are. Maggie knows how to look after herself."

He grunted. He couldn't think of anything to say. He was afraid. He feared for Maggie's sanity, for his daughter's happiness, for his future as an old and possibly demented man. After all, his loved ones had deserted him when he was an infant. It could happen again now.

He caught himself thinking of a story he used to read to Bertie. The book was a battered copy of *Tales From Old Ireland*, a gift to Maggie from her Belfast grandparents. The inscription in fine handwriting read, 'To dear wee Margaret with love from Granny and Granddad Parkes.' Bertie had laughed when he put on a phony Irish accent and told the tale in a woman's voice. She wasn't scared of the conjured demon, the horse that lived under water. On November Day, the pooka came up out of the lake to grant three wishes to anyone who would get on his back. But like all those stories, there was a price to pay. The careless wisher, getting greedy, might make one wish too many and be destroyed. On the other hand, if the rider of the pooka were careful and restrained in his demands but let the creature see the water, it would carry him down to be torn to pieces at the bottom of the lake. And right now he felt afraid to make a third wish. He had wished for a healthy, lovely child, he had wished for his wife to come out of her depression. Those, his major wishes, had been granted. The little desires for rewards and citations about his work could hardly count and in any case had often been refused. So he did feel that he rightfully had one major wish left but didn't want to use it up too soon or to ask for the one thing that might lead to destruction.

"You're smiling."

"At myself. At translating an imaginary demon into something that might mean God. Wishes to prayers. A story I used to read to Bertie."

"Maggie will turn up. The kids'll find her."

Theo took a piece of cheese and nibbled round the edges.

"In your last book, Theo . . . "

"I wish you'd say latest or ninth. 'Last' sounds like the end."

"You began writing when Maggie was depressed."

"It's not strange, Linda. I think a lot of writers write out of impotence. Not that kind. More a feeling of absolute helplessness. I did everything I could to help her. I thought I had. And I was afraid that I was missing the one thing that would make her better. The key. I knew it was probably something completely ordinary but I had no idea what it was and I didn't know where to look. So I tried to work it out. My latest book, you were saying?"

"Your books are out of my range usually but I tried to read the last one and you wrote that a person's relationship with nature was the clue to his whole makeup. Did you mean that?"

"You had to read it in context. But yes. I mean, consider the bird watcher or the intense cultivator. Why is the first prepared to spend cold hours waiting to hear a particular tweet or catch sight of a blue feather? Or think of the gardener who makes his plans in winter and buys seeds and nurtures them. And what does it tell you about someone if they say they love trees or flowers but can't tell you the names of any but the most ordinary?"

"They might simply like being in the forest."

"There you are. That's a clue. Happy ignorance. Why are you thinking about this now?"

"I'm writing a play."

"And you're trying to distract me. Thank you."

"She will turn up."

Linda had grown sharper-featured with age. There had always been a kind of thrusting look to her but now it was more beaky, a pecking bird seeking the best seeds. She was an interesting woman he'd always admired but hardly knew. Their affair had barely lasted a month. And then they'd had one intimate moment all those years ago. Unintentional, simply an enjoyable naked fuck when they were both wet from swimming in the lake. No one had seen them. They never spoke of it. But for a moment he'd felt like Apollo picking a wet nymph from the river to mate with. Had she been deprived of sex after David left? He'd never liked to ask. She was slim still and the pink shirt she was wearing . . . he recalled Bertie telling him that in Inuit families it was forbidden to speak to in-laws of the opposite sex. The reason was easy enough to fathom.

He sat back in his chair, amazed at himself. His wife was wandering loose in this alien city and suddenly he wanted to get his hands on his sister-in-law's breasts. He was nearly seventy and yet the urge, though less frequent, remained the same as at seventeen: desperate. And she was looking at him as if she could read his mind.

Maggie smiled. The man sailing slowly by on the river, waving as he went, reminded her of the evening long ago when Theo had taken her to see *Lohengrin*. It was a few months after Bertie was born, and he thought it would cheer her up. It did. The people around her had shushed her when she laughed aloud as the hero had begun to drift away in a white swan. The whole story had seemed ridiculous but watching the tenor pour his heart out to his love as the swan changed into a man and a dove came from the flies to save the situation, was too much. Theo had patted her arm, glad to hear her laugh but embarrassed too. The man floating by just now had not been singing but had seemed to be looking directly at her. David and Bertie would have got on well together. What was he like? the child had asked. He was gentle. He had a lot of fears—of flying, of being enclosed, of being still. And so he had gone to follow in his father's footsteps. And the very last postcard, the one mailed from Frankfurt in 1982, had said, *I have found 'Dora.' Love, David.* The promise to be 'back soon' had not been fulfilled.

Maggie was near the church she'd seen from a distance. A sign pointed to *Nicholaikirche*. It was the one with the Glockenspiel, mentioned in the guidebook. She would have liked to look round it but what she needed was a sign that pointed to a small cheap hotel whose name she couldn't remember. She must know it. She had to know it. She'd been driven up to it in an airport bus and had first stood in the street looking around with dismay at its narrowness and the discouraging front of the building. She'd gone inside and waited while Greg checked them all in. An odd group they must have looked as he handed keys to his mother and cousin, his aunt and uncle. He would take the single, he said. The dark little lobby smelled of cheese and might have smelt worse.

They'd ordered in pizza the day before they left Toronto and listened while Bertie explained the route and the stops. In London, the bed and breakfast near the Cumberland had been called Nightingale House. The hotel they were to stay at in Berlin on Thursday was called the OberHof. This one, the one where by now the other four might be getting a little frantic, was called—what? It was the name of a tree and it meant? Laburnum! That was it! If she could remember what that was in German she'd be able to ask the next passerby where the hotel was. She had imagined a little stone patio at the back with laburnum trees casting a nice shade over small tables and people drinking wine.

She walked on looking for someone who might be bilingual in German and English, and tried to frame her question so that it didn't sound ridiculous.

Was ist der Name . . . ? And tree? What was the word for tree? *Arbre. Arbor. Tannenbaum. Bäume.* And the word for yellow? A tree with yellow drooping blossom, *bitte.*

Greg and Bertie set off from the hotel driving west. After ten minutes, they came to a river and turned back. Greg knew that his aunt would have had more sense than to cross a bridge that she hadn't crossed before she got lost. Bertie wasn't so sure.

"It's a handicap," she said. "I read about it. It's a bit like dyslexia only they have no sense of direction whatever. And maps don't help because they can't make them out."

"As long as she remembers the name of the hotel."

Greg wound down his window. There wasn't much traffic about yet and the air was fresh, the sun not yet over the tops of the buildings. He looked at his young cousin. She was worried now. Her mother had thrown a monkey wrench into her plan. This was the important day, the day they would drive to the mountains. They were meant to start early. They'd set out early together to fetch the car so that they might stretch their legs before the long drive. She'd wanted to be on the road by 8:30. An hour of the morning had gone and there was no sign of Maggie. He reached for Bertie's hand.

"Watch out," she said, staring at a bike that was coming towards them too quickly. He moved back to his own side of the road. "This isn't England."

There was the bitterness of memory in her voice. There'd been other times like this when Maggie had not necessarily got lost but had in some way delayed or disrupted her daughter's plans. Never on purpose. But Theo who wrote about the subconscious would have known what name to give to these episodes.

"I think we might stop and have coffee," he said. "She might be anywhere and will surely turn up. It's not as though this is a jungle. It's a city. There'll be people who speak English. A helpful policeman."

The girl was almost in tears. He looked at her hair, her profile, her shoulders hunched under the soft shirt. He drew up in front of a little café and got out of the van. Slowly she got out of the other side. He put his arm round her and she turned to him and let him hold her. A couple walking by said something that might have meant, Go for it, guys.

In the café, they ordered coffee and it came piled high with cream. Sitting there with this grown up version of the little girl he'd condescended to in his adolescence and twenties, Greg felt a stirring of lust and tried to quell it by putting his face down into the cream.

"You've got a moustache," Bertie said when he looked up. And she smiled.

"Your parents took good care of your teeth," he said while all he wanted to do was smear cream on her breasts and lick it off very slowly. He felt as though even in thought he had desecrated a holy symbol and was ashamed.

"I'd have liked it best if it had been just you and me," she said.

"Yes," he replied. He felt dizzy. It was the strong sweet coffee.

The cream. Any minute now, he was going to fall to the floor and make strange sounds.

"We would've been on the way by now. We could've driven through the night. I'm fond of them all but they are getting a bit doddery. Except your mother. She's very sharp for her age."

"Have you got a steady boyfriend?" he asked.

"Not since Eric."

"What happened?"

"He was too old."

"How old?"

"Twenty-eight. And you know we should be thinking about my mother."

"I am," he said, wondering how such ordinary people as Theo and Maggie could have given birth to this amazing girl.

Theo was not wishing that Maggie had disappeared forever. He loved her. He knew that because when she came into a room, or gave him a kiss in the morning, he was pulled towards her as if she were a magnet and he was a fragment of metal. But right now, if she, the kids, the whole German nation would just go on hold for a couple of hours, he could make love to Linda, release her from that tight director's mode, and have a glorious morning. I am a beast, he said to himself. To her he said, "You complained that the window in your room was stuck last night."

"It doesn't matter, we're moving on."

"I'll look at it all the same," he said.

He reached for her hand. To his surprise, she put her hand in his and it was a soft, pliable sort of hand.

Maggie thought of advice given to people who had become separated from their group while in a strange place. Stay where you are and they will find you. It seemed a passive sort of thing to do, to sit and wait, and not altogether useful in a large city. The others would need luck or some kind of homing device to come to where she was and if they used their common sense, they would be the ones who stayed where they were until she found them. She turned the corner and found herself in a kind of square that she did recall. There was an island of trees in the centre and a newspaper shop on one corner. The airport bus had come through here just before it stopped to let them off. Four streets led from the angles of the square. If she went a little way down each one in turn, she was bound to find the hotel that was called, in English, laburnum.

"You're lovely," Greg said.

"No I'm not."

"You're beautiful."

Bertie could see what had happened to her cousin. He was away from his wife and in a completely strange place. He'd travelled in Canada and had been to New York twice and once, briefly, to London, that was all. The enchantment of elsewhereness had fallen over him like a net. He was staring at her with fish-eyes and she knew that had there been a bed handy, he would have been making for it and trying to pull her along too. He wasn't unhandsome. Katie said he was cuddly and had potential. His eyes were the same pale blue as her mother's and, so she'd been told, her grandfather's. His mouth was not too wide and fortunately he didn't have that jutting lower lip that made some men, when they got older, look like camels. His brown hair was thick and cut a little too short but that could be changed.

"We're looking for my mother, Greg," she said.

"So we are," he replied as if his mind was on the moon. "Let's go back to the hotel and wait in your room. We can watch the road from the window."

243

*

This is not my trip, Maggie thought as she walked down past a
nice-looking café. I don't want to be in this German city. I know
where the camp was. I've looked at the place a thousand times
on the map, I've seen the photographs and imagined the horror
of those lives. None of what happened there was my fault or my
father's fault. The therapist's usual question hung around in her
mind from years ago and popped up at odd moments: *And how
do you feel about that?* She stood still to gather in a sense of
this soft Sunday morning feeling, as the streets began to fill
with traffic and people, that here she was at last in Germany
for the second time in her life. Her plan of two decades ago
fulfilled at last. *Here I am. But I am not alone. I could be alone.
When the others return home, I will stay on and wander
wherever I like.*

"*Achtung!*"

She had bumped into a man who was now staring at her
angrily. He said something that she thought must mean, Can I
help you?

"Laburnum," she said. "A tree. A hotel."

He pushed her aside and muttered something like "*Passen Sie
doch auf!*"

The street widened into an *Allee* with stores on either side. Her
foot was hurting again. If she bought some softer shoes, or even
sandals, she'd walk better. The smell of coffee was drawing her
on. In a café there would be tourists. But the store she was
standing beside sold books. She went inside.

"*Ich bin* lost," she said to the young man behind the counter.

"*Ich* also," he said.

"You're English?"

"From Manchester."

"Tell me how you say laburnum in German, please."

She could see he thought her crazy so she explained, "It's the name of the hotel. My family's waiting for me. I can't find my way."

He pulled a dictionary from under the counter and as he turned the pages, he said, "I hoped you were a customer. No one bought anything yesterday."

"I'm sorry."

"'*Goldregen*,'" he said. "It means golden rain."

"Of course," she said. "My father told me that years ago. I'd forgotten. I have to find it. They'll be calling the police. The hospitals."

"It's just down the street," he said, "on the other side. I wish you'd buy a book. The English section is over there."

"I'm going to need something to read on the way back."

"What were you reading on the way here?"

"Oh!"

"What's wrong?"

Maggie sat down on the comfortable chair by the shelves. The day was already full of strangeness; the man on the boat could have been David and now she was looking at a copy of the storybook Dad had read to them so long ago.

"*Struwwelpeter*?" the young man said.

"It's still in print."

"Never out. I like this one."

The young man began to read the cruel rhyme about the boy who sucked his thumb. Maggie could tell that his accent was wrong and he read very slowly. But she closed her eyes and when she heard him say *Klipp und Klapp*, she began to laugh.

"Have you had breakfast?"

"No," she said.

"There's a café in your hotel. I'll go to the door with you so you don't get lost again."

He told her that he'd come to Germany to learn the language but it was difficult and he wasn't sure he would ever master the tenses, and that his name was Ian Campbell.

At the door of the *Goldregen,* she sighed with relief. She felt cheerful again because now she was in the right place. She was having a better time and the others, when they turned up, would be pleased to see her safe and sound.

"I'll bring them all back to say thank you," she told the young man. "We'll all buy something."

She walked into the dark foyer and through to the café ready to apologize. The tables were empty. They were probably all out scouring the city for her. The only thing to do was to go to the room, tidy up and bring the bags down. Then when they returned she could tell them she'd been waiting for ages.

Her father was driving. Greg was sitting beside him reading the map. Bertie was in the back between Maggie and Linda. They'd been on the road for two hours and no one had spoken except Greg who now and then told Theo to keep straight on. The scenery flashed past on either side of the autobahn. First houses and then green spaces; they were heading towards forests. Her aunt and her mother were holding Kleenexes to their noses. This was going to be one jolly ride. She was glad she'd let Greg embrace her in a way that wasn't quite cousinly. Affection seemed to be in short supply. She and Greg had returned to the hotel and been delighted to see Maggie there safe and sound. But there was a tension between the three older folk that could be cut with a spoon and no one was explaining anything. She'd asked her dad what was wrong and he just said, Nothing. But it would have been obvious to the deafest, blindest person that something had happened to make them all look like sick owls.

"I thought we'd stop at Grünhausen for lunch," she said.

Aunt Linda said, "Fine."

"Did anyone have breakfast?"

"No," her mother said.

Bertie dug into her bag and found a Power Bar and handed it to her. "You must have walked miles, Mom."

"Not far enough, obviously."

That was the longest sentence spoken by any of the others for the past half hour. No clues were being given for its decipherment. She could tell that Greg had some idea of what had happened and when she got him alone again she would make him tell. Here they were on a serious expedition to a place where appalling things had happened and her parents and aunt were behaving as though their trivial little miseries were more important than history, her grandfather, and the deaths of millions of people.

She decided to concentrate on the scenery and to hope that some thing or animal or traffic problem would divert them. In her head she wrote a letter to Katie. *I am beginning to think I should've come by myself. The responsibility for these people is too much. They are behaving like selfish morons and today I can't get a word out of them. Can I somehow ditch them and go off on my own? I would take Greg with me but he seems to have a different agenda. We lost Mother so we drove about and when we got back to the hotel, he said he'd go up to see if she was back while I checked the café. And then he came down looking as if he'd found an alligator in the room or something. Then my mother came down dragging her suitcase, bumping it on every step. And my dad was silent which as you know is very unlike him.*

Theo was afraid. Fifteen minutes of pleasure and cries of, "I've been wanting to do this for ages," from both of them, and the pooka had taken him down into the water. He did feel that for Linda it wouldn't have mattered if it had been him or anyone else at all. They were about to get dressed when the door opened and there was Greg and, suddenly, behind him, Maggie. What happened next was peculiar. Greg had said, "Uncle Theo!" and then pushed past him to get hold of a suitcase and left. Maggie, on the other hand, sat down on the bed and stared at the two bodies in front of her as if she'd never seen anyone naked before. He and Linda were struck dumb and petrified. He didn't want to get dressed with Maggie watching, as if he'd become a stranger to his wife. It seemed like an hour till Linda gathered up her clothes and turned away to put them on. Maggie continued to stare while he put his shorts on and pulled his pants over them and dragged on his shirt and tucked it in. He knew he had to speak but there were no right words. Then Maggie said, "Bertie needn't know about this," and turned and went out.

He wanted a shower. He wanted to say to Maggie, *We were enchanted. It was a momentary illusion.* All the books he'd written, books meant to help people deal with children and with each other, had nothing to offer. The first paragraph of a piece for the Journal came into his mind: *Travelling with your family can lead to problems unless you set out certain boundaries.* To Linda, he'd cried angrily, Why didn't you lock the door?

He said now, "We should perhaps come back this way and spend a couple of days. There's the Goethe museum, the Opera House, and the zoo is one of the best in Europe. Besides that, the Holy Roman Emperors were elected in the city hall. Goethe, dressed as a waiter, smuggled himself into the banquet celebrating the coronation of Joseph the second."

Greg was trying to read the map. He wanted to stuff a Kleenex into his uncle's mouth but didn't because at least some talking was better than the heavy silence of the previous hundred kilometers. When they stopped, he would take Bertie to one side and tell her that everything was all right. The old folk had had a little quarrel. Nothing to worry about. He couldn't believe how dumb his mother was and with Uncle Theo who was a large and not very attractive old man. And then again, he could believe. What would've happened if the room had been empty and he'd persuaded Bertie to come with him and he had made love to her? Or if Bertie had gone with him up the stairs and seen what he saw? What was wrong with them all? Had someone sprinkled them all with magic dust?

The sight of his mother's naked body for the second, maybe third, time in his life made him shudder. Why had they not been brought up as Naturists, to go about admiring bodies of all shapes and sizes, firm and sagging, hairy and smooth? But Naturism had nothing to do with the fact that they had obviously been having sex. His mother aged sixty-five and Uncle Theo, sixty-eight, were screwing each other while Aunt Maggie was wandering lost about the streets and they should have been worried out of their minds. Meanwhile he and Bertie . . . this was a truly ill-fated expedition.

"I saw a man out there who looked very like your father, Greg," Aunt Maggie said, obviously willing to speak to him but not to the others.

"We should turn round and go back. Get a flight home and forget all this," he said.

"He was on a barge."

"On the river?"

"He waved and if I'd asked him to stop he would have and I wish I had and could have gone off with him."

"If you're thinking about this morning," Theo said.

"I'll never stop thinking about this morning."

"We should talk about it rationally."

"It all looked pretty obvious."

"I don't know what you're all going on about but you're behaving like a bunch of sulky kids," Bertie said.

"Stop the car!"

"We're on the autobahn. It's forbidden to stop except for emergencies."

"For heaven's sake."

"Dad. Do something."

They were talking over each other like hyenas. And then there was a sound familiar to Greg from drunken undergrad evenings long ago. He turned to look. Aunt Maggie was throwing up into Theo's hat. Theo drove on to the next lay-by and pulled over. No one spoke. Maggie wiped her face and put the hat into the garbage can. Theo watched as if his life had gone in there with it.

Bertie was crying. Linda put an arm round her. Theo moved to Maggie who moved away from him. Greg got his camera out of his pocket and pointed it at them and said, "Smile!"

Bertie dove at him and took the camera and threw it into the garbage can. She hoped it had fallen into the hat and that Greg would reach in and put his hand in the vomit. She still didn't know what they'd been up to but there was only one thing that could have made them behave this way and she could hardly believe it. She looked at her father and at Aunt Linda. They were guilty. Two old and ravaged people! They had come on the trip with no true idea about its purpose, no sense of her feelings and not one crumb of reverence for an old man's memory. All they cared about were their petty gratifications. Little bits of groping and sex. While they were all staring at her, she gathered her strength into her arms and pushed her aunt to the ground then leapt into the van, closed the doors and pulled out onto the autobahn. There was a great screech behind her as a car she hadn't noticed moved into the next lane. She had a sense of fists being shaken at her but didn't care.

She'd never driven anything as big as this VW van; in fact she despised people who drove big cars and polluted the atmosphere but she was sitting high off the road, could see well ahead and it was a great day. The sky wasn't bright blue as it would be on such a day in Ontario. The light was soft so that she didn't need sunglasses. She was simply going to keep up with the traffic ahead. She could see the heads of two children in the back seat of the blue car in front and drew back a little. Six car lengths, the instructor had said. Keep a safe distance. Leave room to brake if necessary. Behind her an impatient driver honked his horn and then overtook her and came between her and the blue car. She hoped the guy would stay far enough back.

For miles and miles, she drove with a great feeling of freedom. She would be in the area of Durmittelburg at this rate by midafternoon and surely there would be signs. Then, alone and in her own way, she could think about all that had gone on in that place and about that one day when her grandfather had answered the phone and been asked, probably in code, to go out to the airfield at Yeadon where a plane would be waiting.

She reached across for the map and then remembered that she'd last seen it in her father's hand when they were all standing by the roadside. By the roadside! Abandoned. A group of wanderers. The picture of a family group: Her mother dabbing at her face with a Kleenex. Her father shifty and upset. Aunt Linda totally without her usual chin-up, girl guide leader we-can-do-this-girls, drive. And Greg, peering into the garbage bin, staring down after his lost camera and afraid to fish for it. They had the map. She had their passports and money and credit cards. Their passports and money and credit cards! And they were standing by the side of a foreign road with scarcely a word of the language between them. She also had her dad's precious laptop with all his stored thoughts in it. He would be howling. He would also be afraid that she would have an accident.

She began to watch out for the next turnoff, driving with care. It was there just ahead. Gladly she got off the autobahn and turned to go back towards Frankfurt. By going under the bridge she was on a road parallel to the highway but quieter and slower. If she got back onto the autobahn, she would be on the wrong side of the road and would go sailing past them. But at least they might see her and she could wave to let them know she was coming to pick them up. Then she could turn at the next off-ramp, go back under the road and find them. They had to be still there. She'd only been driving for half an hour and who would stop to pick up such a pathetic group.

The *Polizei* would come by and demand to see some ID. For all the family's rotten behaviour, they didn't deserve to be taken to a detention centre without a cent to call the embassy, if there was one in Frankfurt. She picked up speed.

Theo was sitting on the verge plucking at blades of grass. He could not believe that the daughter he had loved and nurtured from her inception would drive off and leave him there. The others maybe but not her beloved father. It was all his fault for giving way to his lust—the only word for it. And why suddenly had desire overcome him in such a way? And Linda of all people! If he'd had his laptop he would have written everything down and worked it out later. But first he had to get beyond this ridiculous moment, back home to the house he loved. What then? Maggie would leave him. Greg and Bertie would despise him. Linda? Who could tell what Linda would do? She was a woman of sudden moves. Right now she was leaning against the garbage can with Greg, telling him not to worry, he could wash his hands later and the camera had cost three hundred dollars and he must grit his teeth and pull it out.

Maggie was picking dusty little flowers like some elderly Ophelia about to weave a garland and then throw herself into the river of cars.

He stood up. "Listen," he shouted. "Bertie will come back for us. Understandably, she's angry."

Linda turned to him, "Understandably she's driven away with all our stuff and left us by this goddam road with no money, no ID, nothing! I'm not seeing understandably."

"Given this morning, mother," Greg said, not looking at her.

Maggie stopped picking flowers and yelled, "You have ruined her plans."

Linda opened her mouth to reply but no words came. She sat on the grass and looked down the road the way Bertie had gone.

"She has a lot of spirit," Theo said.

Greg felt that his uncle was taking a dig at him. Bertie the go-ahead girl with 'spirit' had driven off and left them stranded. He the slow, plodding nephew could only mourn for his camera. He began to laugh. He couldn't help it. He wished he'd leapt into the van with his cousin and driven off to Budapest, to Rome, to Moscow. He would though have thrown out the bags belonging to the others. As it was, they had nothing to show who they were. No chance of checking into a hotel. And now, here was a police van pulling onto the lay-by beside them. Unfortunately only his mother had much of the language and she was already at the police car window talking about *ein Mädchen* and *ein Auto* and pointing down the road angrily in a way that was sure to get Bertie into trouble. He went to stand beside her, smiling at the policemen hoping to make them understand that this older woman was exaggerating and that everything was, aside from the fact that they were standing here without any belongings or any transport, fine.

Bertie knew she had somehow taken a wrong turn. The parallel road had ceased to be parallel just at the time when she'd hoped to find her way back onto the main highway. She was now still going in the same direction but had entered a wasteland of industrial buildings and scrubby patches of ground. *Vorsicht!* was written in large letters on a board stuck to the fence. She'd stopped relating the story to Katie as she went along. That story had a simple happy ending, a reunion in which mutual forgiveness was the theme. But she was lost. The others could by now have been picked up, perhaps singly, and by nightfall would be scattered all over Europe without papers or money. Now in the middle of this German Sunday, she had to find a person, any person, who could help her.

She saw a man and a woman walking slowly along the road and pulled up beside them.

"*Guten Morgen,*" she said.

"*Guten Morgen,*" they replied.

"*Ich will . . . ich werde . . . ich habe,*" she said and wished she'd paid less attention to verbs and more to truly useful words. In hope, she began again in English.

"I need to get back to the autobahn," she said. "Autobahn?"

The man smiled and pointed towards the way she had come. Bertie pointed the other way. The man kept his arm out to the left. The woman smiled and nodded to emphasize his gesture. Bertie tried, wordlessly, to explain that she wanted to go in the other direction.

"*Nein,*" the man insisted and kept on pointing the other way.

"*Danke schön,*" Bertie said. Perhaps he was right. No need to panic, though she could feel panic rising along with a need to cry. Go back. Get on the autobahn where she had left it and return to her family who must by now be very upset. No problem really.

She turned the van round and began to backtrack. In a short time she could hear the rushing sound of traffic. It wasn't far to the bridge. Mom! Dad! Greg! She called their names as if they might possibly hear. *I am coming.*

It couldn't be far to the place where she'd marooned them like outcasts on an island in the middle of nowhere. In years to come they would talk about the day Bertie left them beside the highway and how they had cheered when she returned to them. And how they had all gone for a drink and ended up in a beer hall laughing and singing.

There was a siren sound behind her getting louder and louder.

It was a different kind of siren from the ones at home. It must be for the motorcyclist up ahead. She accelerated to get past him and make room for the police car. The siren persisted. The police were pulling her over, flashing their lights, causing the traffic to slow to a standstill.

"So!" The policeman, seven feet tall in his boots and helmet, was looking at her as at some strange animal. He made a sign for her to step out of the van. And then he got inside the back and began to rummage in the handbags and the luggage.

He called out to the other man who had his hand on her wrist and said a lot of words. She heard *'tief'* and knew what it meant.

"*Nein*," she cried to the one still in the van. "*Ich bin . . . Ich werde . . . Ich habe einen Vater, eine Mutter.*"

"*Ja ja ja*," the one holding on to her said. "I also."

"She will come back this way," Theo said. "Already, she's turned and is trying to get back to us. I know her."

"She'll be on the other side whizzing past," Linda said.

"The cops said they'd send someone to pick us up."

"Probably armed guards who'll pile us into a closed van and drive us to a prison to languish forever."

"This isn't a joking matter, Maggie."

"I think," Maggie said, "that I should be allowed to laugh. I think I should be allowed to do whatever I like. My daughter did exactly the right thing. We all except, as far as I know, Greg, have behaved badly this morning. If I'd taken more care not to get lost . . ."

"Don't blame yourself for all this."

"Let me finish. I'm not blaming myself for all this, but the fact that I got lost began it. That didn't give you license to hop into bed when our children could have turned up any time and did. You're just lucky it wasn't Bertie who found you."

"She guessed," Greg said. "You couldn't have acted and

pretended nothing had happened. Oh no, you had to behave like people caught in the act, which you were."

"It was over before it began," Linda said.

"Is that her. Is that her on the other side?"

They watched the grey van go rushing by. Ten minutes later, it pulled up onto the grass beside them. Two policeman got out followed by Bertie. Linda rushed towards her but Greg pulled her back. He put his arms round Bertie and she put her head on his shoulder and he stroked her lovely hair.

"They're awful," he whispered to her, "but we can't desert them."

Theo grabbed Linda and propelled her towards the cop to explain that this was indeed his child and they were glad to see her and wanted no more trouble. He stood with his hand on her arm to make sure from what little he could understand, that she didn't make accusations and have his daughter committed to jail.

"Smile," he said to her. "Smile! Talk softly."

Maggie gave Bertie the flowers she'd picked and said, "Thank you for coming back."

Another police car drew up. They were a spectacle now causing the autobahn traffic to slow down. It was like a movie scene. Greg wished he had his camera but there was no way he was going to risk putting his hand into the vomit. The cops were smiling: An American family. Indulgent parents. What could be expected? The younger one took a good look at Bertie and perhaps wished he could have taken her with him. But he said something that probably meant, Have a nice day. The cops watched the family climb into the Volkswagen van, and then they zoomed off down the autobahn with their lights flashing.

There was a kind of communal sigh between the five of them. Greg put the van into gear and they set off in the same direction as before. Theo was in the back seat reaching for his precious laptop. Linda had climbed into the front passenger seat. Bertie sat between her parents. Greg considered all the permutations of seating five people, each one of whom had an issue with at least one of the others, in two rows. His preference would have been to have Bertie beside him and let the other three fight it out in the back. But the way they were arranged now made for silence, if not real peace.

It hadn't been a pleasant morning. The one shining moment, sitting in that café with Bertie, cream on his nose, lost in fantasy, stood out in relief. To say it had gone downhill from there was an understatement. The vision of the naked ones was something he wanted to forget. The bleat of Aunt Maggie behind him would remain in his head as the cry of a wounded being. Through the past eighteen years or so, when she'd recovered from her depression and begun to teach and live and love, she'd been a quiet stable presence in the family. He just wished she could have been more joyful throughout Bertie's first months. His mother and Theo—his mother and Theo!—had long conversations about post-partum misery in those days. Perhaps it had been a comfort to his mother after his dad's departure to know she wasn't alone. Sitting in the living room drinking coffee, the baby playing round their feet, they'd talked about the psychological effects of childbirth and his mom would suggest ways of bringing Aunt Maggie back to normal. That problem did exist. Only a couple of years ago a woman had thrown herself and her baby off the subway platform. Those cloudy months had left him with a fear of getting any woman pregnant. Not just the pain of giving birth but the darkness that could settle into a woman's mind and drive her to destruction. Come on, he said to himself. He knew very well that there was another fear behind all that: Fear of taking on a new life, of disturbing the *status quo*.

The silence in the van was like a weight of wet earth. He said, "There's a cow in the field on the left."

For a moment no one spoke and then his mother responded, "There's a cow in the field on the left and a pig in a sty on the right."

Theo carried on, adding, "Giraffe in the middle of the road."

Aunt Maggie let them go on without a word until the list was ten items long and then she went through it all without forgetting a single creature, and said, "There are adulterers in this car."

"I'll pull off at the next place," Greg said.

He imagined himself lying on a psychiatrist's couch. *When I was five, we were by a lake and I heard animals grunting in the bush and called my dad. He said it was probably porcupines. Granny took me to look at the ducks. When I was thirty-eight . . .* As he drove off the autobahn, he saw the mirage of an inn, the sun glinting off metal on its roof. The village was more of a suburb but there was the stone building he'd seen. The wooden sign hanging above the door had a picture of a foaming stein on it. He ignored bleating suggestions from the others that they drive a little further to find something better. He had a ton of memories of being driven past great hamburger places and washrooms as a child on the 'find something better' theory. There never was anything better than the place they'd just passed. Never!

"I'm thirsty," he said and parked the van in a parking lot full of VWs and Passats.

"So what do we all want," Theo asked with a kind of avuncular jollity which was about as real as a three dollar bill, "besides the restroom?"

"*Das Klosett,*" Bertie said.

Greg and Theo standing side by side in the men's room, glanced at each other.

"Uncle Theo, how much farther?"

"That depends," his uncle replied in an Alice in Wonderland way, "on where we think we're going. I'm surprised at how far we've come."

They washed their hands and Greg decided that he would say no more until they'd had something to eat. They sat at a table under a tree. It could have been idyllic. Greg and Bertie on one side and the old folk on the other, all smiling little smiles. Linda got up and came round the table to sit beside her son.

"So what do we all want?"

"Beer, Dad," Bertie said, "and a sandwich."

"I'll come and help," Linda said.

"I can manage," Theo replied and walked into the inn. Maggie looked at the tree shading their table and pronounced it to be a linden. His mother took several things out of her purse and put them back. Bertie was as still as a statue. Greg wondered if they could continue in this way for the remaining seven days. Ten or fifteen minutes or an hour or a month passed with none of them saying anything except that Bertie remarked on the size of a dragonfly.

Theo returned followed by a waiter carrying a large tray. Beer, sausages, bread . . . and wine for Maggie.

Greg watched their faces lose something of the strain of the morning's events. He chugged the first half of his beer in seconds and reached for one of the fat sausages.

"Knackwurst," Theo said.

A party of young men came out of the inn carrying mugs of beer and sat down at the next table. They were about to have a good time. Greg could see no possibility of a good time for his group until long after they were home again. In the next hotel, if it had a phone in the room, if Bertie hadn't booked them into a hostel, he'd call Marni and tell her to drop everything and meet him in Paris. They'd max out his credit card and live it up and have one great memory to tell their children. Because they would have children.

He felt Bertie's thigh pressing against his and knew that he was her only friend at the moment. He put his hand on her leg. She put her hand on his hand. And then lifted it off and put it on his leg. The others, still caught up in their own tangle, paid no attention to the little game. He turned and smiled at Bertie to see if she'd cheered up.

Maggie said, "I want to make some things clear."

"Not now," Theo said, his mouth greasy from the sausage.

Maggie stood up. The young people at the next table thought she was going to make a congratulatory speech and raised their glasses and yelled, "*Prost!*"

Maggie nodded at them and went on softly. "I've been thinking. I've been thinking all the while we've been on this trip. Twenty years ago, after I came back from England I was angry and sad. David was confused. My dad, the man we thought we'd known, had held something back from us all our lives so we felt as if we didn't know who he was. He was a stranger."

"But, love," Theo said.

Maggie sat down and talked towards him. "Listen to me. We don't know why David was involved with those men in the park and whether it had anything to do with him never coming back. But we do know that my dad, Granddad to these two, had another life. Whether he spied for England during all those years he was on business abroad we aren't sure. We felt deceived, right? "

"Well I don't see . . . "

"Linda, you didn't have to come on this trip but you did and it's changed things, but it was good of you to come in the first place. It's too late now for me to say I wish you hadn't, so just let me speak, ok? I know now that we should just have accepted the fact that he was our father, he did what he could for us, and left it at that. People should be able to have more than one life.

"I want you all to consider why you came on this long and expensive journey. What did you hope to get out of it?"

"Mom?"

"Bertie here had pure motives," her mother said, "and we've

been doing our best to ruin things for her. I hope she'll forgive us."

They were all quiet. Greg remembered weird encounter groups at college.

Maggie looked at them all sipping their beer, not looking back at her. It would be Theo who spoke next. Greg could almost hear the cogs in his uncle's mind turning.

"Sometimes we use words too easily," Theo said.

Linda was snuffling, "I've been lonely," she said.

Greg put his arm round her and whispered, "You've had me."

She hit him on the side of the head with her purse. Of its own accord, his arm drew back to return the blow. He held it still and looked at her face. Had she wanted to clobber him since he was six? Or did she blame him for his dad going off like that? He touched his ear hoping for blood and wanting to howl in outrage but the brass buckle had missed him.

The group at the other table shouted, "*Prost!*" again.

Maggie put her hands up to make the family listen.

"I came," she said, "because I felt as if my life was dwindling away. Retirement and life without Bertie at home didn't exactly fill me with delight. I wasn't sure I could expect delight. But I have had that. The kids I've taught have now and then delighted me. Bertie of course. And Theo. But I didn't care in fact if this was the last thing I ever did. If the plane fell out of the sky or if the car crashed—not that I wanted harm to come to any of you. Probably that's why I got lost but no convenient thug came out and attacked me. They probably weren't out of bed yet. I feared, you see, that the depression would come back and ruin the rest of our lives together, mine and Theo's. And he didn't deserve that. But I see now . . . I see that I was building a false future."

"No! No! No!" Theo shouted.

Linda began, "It was only . . . "

"You're doing it again." Maggie went on, "You're assuming that you know what I'm talking about."

Bertie had gone to the other table and was practicing her German with the drinkers. Greg wanted to follow her but had to hear what his aunt was saying.

"All of us have an idea of happiness. But it changes over time. It has to."

"What has this to do with the purpose of this trip?" Linda asked.

"We came because an old man left us a few pictures and a secret. We came to lay ghosts to rest but we can't. They're not our ghosts."

Greg couldn't ever remember his aunt saying so many words at one time. In the talking stakes she always lost out to Theo and Linda and, as soon as her daughter could talk, to Bertie too.

And she hadn't finished. "We're not looking for his secret. We're looking for ours. Greg, Linda, Theo? What are you looking for?"

Linda stopped crying and said, "Love."

Maggie smiled at her in a way that was almost cruel. "Perhaps you've found it."

Theo said, "Get Bertie over here, Greg. We have to make some decisions."

"She's having a good time."

Maggie caught Bertie's eye and waved her hand and Bertie said something to the fellow next to her and came back to them.

"We've been pronouncing it wrong," she said. "The camp was in a place called Mittelbau Dora. Karlheinz wrote it down. It's where they made the V2 rockets. There's a museum there now."

"Let me see," her mother said and took the scrap of paper. She stared at it for some time. "Dora! That's what he wanted to tell her."

Maggie got up and walked towards the inn. Of all the dumb, mistaken things in life. Her mother had died thinking that 'Dora' was his real love, someone he had kept on loving all of his life. So in his final moments, her mother had hated the man she'd lived with for fifty years. Her last words to him, if he heard them, had been words of accusation. Perhaps on her own deathbed, Frieda Parkes had muttered a kind of absolution: Forgiveness was necessary for the innocent as well as the guilty. And she herself, what had she blamed her father for? When he was dead, when she really knew he was dead and his ashes had been scattered on the moors behind the house, she had a strong unreasonable feeling of disappointment that he had never once bought her something expensive and shiny. Of all things in that moment, she wanted a necklace or a bracelet that she could show to her friends and say, My father gave me this. What a ridiculous thing to think! And dear David, in that final message from Germany, was telling her he had found not a woman, but a place. She knew that Theo was watching her. She turned to him and smiled.

"Do we want to go on?" he asked.

"I absolutely knew you'd say that," Bertie said. "Of course we have to go on. You've all been thinking that Granddad was a cheat. But he was a good man. A man who did brave things. You should have known that from the photograph. You're pusillanimous. The least we can do to make it up to him is go and see the place."

Linda leaned over to Greg and whispered, "Do you think she's still a virgin?"

"Mother!"

"I was only asking."

"Linda? Are we to continue?" Theo asked.

"Questions! Do we know why we're here? Do we want to go on? What's life all about! Quite frankly I like it when Bertie's telling us what to do. I can't believe I'm saying that but I am. Half an hour ago I wanted to go home. I wanted to leave you all here and just go back to my apartment and turn on my computer and write a play which no one will produce. Now, I've decided that the drama is all here. I'll go along with anything. It depends on Maggie."

Greg said, "I mean I'm happy to drive but I think we need to sort a few things out."

"If you mean our lives . . . " his mother replied.

"I tell you what, Dad. We'll get there and see the museum. After that we'll go back to Dresden and then you can all go home or look around or whatever."

Theo took Maggie's hand and said, "Sit with me, please."

It was the voice of a contrite man, an elderly and contrite man. Greg felt sorry for him and would, if he'd been Maggie, have forgiven him then and there.

The two of them got into the front seat and Maggie took the wheel while Theo scanned the map. In the back seat, the other three, with Greg in the middle, dozed. It was nearly four o'clock and they were still a long way from their destination.

When Greg woke up it was twilight and he heard his mother saying, " . . . and I've lost two men in my life, three really if you count losing a son to another woman, though I'm glad to say I've never been possessive in that way. I haven't looked forward to this part of my life. I suppose it was a kind of despair that made me do it."

"Mom," he cried.

"What?"

"What are you saying?"

"I'm telling Bertie why I'm writing a play. And anyway she knows. While you've been asleep various scenes have taken place."

"Bertie?"

"I might always wish I'd kept driving and not come back for you all but I'm going to stay on and meet up with Karlheinz and the others on Tuesday."

Theo was in the driver's seat though Greg couldn't recall them having stopped to change over.

Maggie said, "If you've driven past it, there's a turn about sixteen kilometers from here."

Theo turned to say to Bertie, "You can't. You don't know him. You don't know anything about him. You can't speak the language. This is a foreign country."

"He's a philosophy student."

"So he says."

Maggie screamed, "Watch out, Theo!"

"Fortunately we didn't hit anything else."

Bertie heard her aunt's voice through a haze. She was sitting on grass. Not far away, someone was leaning over a body, wiping its face, and speaking words of love. She herself was propped up against a tree or a person, something solid. A hand was holding hers. There was a rushing, roaring noise like a river or waterfall.

"Are we there?" she asked. The hand that had been holding hers moved to her breast. *I never thought it would be like this.* Bertie was afraid to say it aloud. She'd brought them all this way to look at an overgrown meadow, a piece of ground. She could see that none of them was inspired. They scattered and wandered around, lightweight figures wafted about in a breeze. Aunt Linda's long grey skirt was blown against her legs and she was looking at the ground as if for bones.

The woman weeping over her dead knight was holding one arm against her body.

"Dad?" Bertie said and stood up but sat straight down again.

"It's ok. It's all right, sweetie. He'll be fine."

It was Cousin Greg who was holding her in his arms. She leaned back against him and closed her eyes to let these curious images sink in. Her mother's voice was telling a tale without

meaning, of a long-lost brother, of limping men, of railway trains
and love in alpine meadows.

And then strangers were standing among them, talking, taking
charge.

It was nearly dark. Maggie could see the shapes of trees. Her arm
hurt. Theo was breathing and trying to talk. Paramedics were
attending to him. Bertie was being cared for. At last, Maggie could
give a moment to the images that were crowding into her head,
even in the midst of disaster. As a young man, her father had sent
a message home. On the back of a postcard in 1927 he had
written, *I sold 2,600 lbs. today to Darfen. Am now free for the
evening and going for a walk with my French friend. A good trip
so far. Love to you, Darling, Robert.* The picture on that postcard
was of the opera house in Bayreuth. In his thirties, he had sat
beside them and read stories, '*Weh! Jetzt geht es klipp und klapp,*'
to his children who, not understanding a word, loved the sound
of his voice. And in his forties, he had come to this place, to be
shown the horror of what men could do to men.

And now, here he was, walking slowly towards her, a
sprightlier version of the man who had limped towards her on
Kelthorpe railway station.

"David," she said.

Bertie heard foreign words mixed with English and someone said,
"They're all here." Did he mean the ghosts of a million prisoners
or these few familiar people? She allowed herself to be put onto
a stretcher and said, "Thank you," because in a foreign country,
it was best to be polite.

"Then?" Theo said. His voice was still harsh.

"How are you feeling today?" Maggie asked.

"I'm fine. What about your arm?"

"It'll just take time, they said."

"We'll be home tomorrow. Maggie, I do love you, you know that."

"Don't talk so much, Theo. Greg's coming to pick us up soon."

"It was good of him to wait."

"Linda wanted to get back. To write her play, she said. I think she felt the shock more than she let on."

The pause that followed lay between them like a dead dog.

"It's all right, Theo," she said. "It was nothing of importance."

"You're saying that because I nearly got you all killed."

"Are you going to write a book about guilt?"

"I might. Maggie, did you really think it was David there, where we crashed?"

"It was wishful thinking. He was just another tourist looking for the museum. I expected David to be there. It was him I came to look for. I realize that. We'll never know what happened to him."

"We can always invent what we don't know, dear Maggie."

"Yes," she replied, and saw her brother as a hero, as young as he had been when he went away, lost in a brave rescue attempt at sea. Tomorrow, alternatively, she might imagine him caught up in a netherworld of secret agents working to prevent another war. "That's true."

After a moment, Theo asked, "Bertie's really ok?"

"A slight concussion. I told you yesterday. They checked her over and she's fine."

"But she's gone."

"She waited till she knew you were all right."

"I just hope . . . "

"She'll be fine. She hasn't gone off with the same kind of madness I did all those years ago. Young women have more sense now. She'll learn the language. She'll study. She'll come back to us."

"A visitor. A transient. On her way to somewhere else."

The doctor came into the room and looked at Theo.

"You are pleased to get out of here, Herr Krause?"

"I'm anxious to go home."

"Anxious? Try not to be anxious. Be calm. Stay still."

"Thank you for everything, doctor," Maggie said. "You've been very kind."

"One more thing, Herr Krause. Not to drive for three months."

"But."

"A life of quietness for a few weeks. Not too much speech. And see your own physician on your return."

The doctor nodded at them and went out, a busy man with many other calls on his time.

"Well." Theo stood up and then sat on the bed again.

"I think," Maggie said, "that we should move to a condo next year."

"Have we become two old crocks?"

"Fossils perhaps."

With her good hand, she put his toothbrush and soap and razor into his toilet bag and helped him on with his jacket.

"So we didn't get all the way there."

"We were at the entrance."

"Maybe we got as far as we were meant to."

A nurse came pushing a wheelchair. She handed Maggie a bottle of pills and said, "Night and morning." She helped Theo on to the chair and set off down the corridor at a fast pace. Maggie, carrying the overnight bag, trotted to keep up.

Greg was waiting for them at the hospital entrance. He took Theo's arm and guided him to the front seat of the taxi.

"Thank you," Theo said.

Greg climbed into the back with Maggie and said, "*Zum Flughafen, bitte,*" to the driver. "You're looking good, Uncle."

"I'm a wreck. I've got a voice like a crocodile and I—well—thank God you're all okay."

"It was an accident."

"No. No it wasn't. I made the wrong wish."

Maggie reached over from the back seat and patted his shoulder.

"Don't do that, Maggie. I'm not out of my mind."

"Will you be all right on the plane?"

"I'll sleep. I have pills. It was kind of you to wait for us, Greg."

"I've learned a few more phrases, seen some of the sights. And it's been a good time to think about Marni and me."

"Your job?"

"Lipson's going crazy. I promised to be there on Monday," Greg said. It wasn't the time to tell them that he and Bertie had gone back to Mittelbau Dora and had seen the tunnel hollowed into the mountain, the place where slaves had been forced to manufacture deadly weapons and had died in the process. That they had gone into the museum and looked at pictures much more terrible than the ones their grandfather had kept. They had faced ghosts and he had cried, and Bertie had comforted him and said, "You have to know." That story was for later, when Theo was feeling stronger. For now, he had to help his aunt and uncle to make the long trip back to Toronto. The taxi stopped outside the departure area and he went to fetch a luggage cart.

Theo woke up and asked, "Will she be all right?"

"Yes," Maggie replied. "I think so."

He sighed.

"She couldn't stay with us forever, Theo."

"What about you, Maggie?"

"You've never been a mystery to me."

"I'm sorry. Can you live with that?"

"We missed Thanksgiving."

They were seated in a row of three, Theo on the aisle so that he had room to stretch his leg, Greg by the window, and Maggie in the middle. She set down the thriller she'd bought from Ian Campbell and looked past Greg at the city tilted below. The ground was coming up to meet them. The trees were bare. The boats were gone from the lake. It was a landscape waiting for winter.

"In spring, I'm going to travel across the country to Vancouver. Maybe drive. Or fly part way," Maggie said. She'd had enough of Europe for now. In the country below them, there were rocks and fossils and dinosaurs and glaciers: A different kind of ancient history.

"You're using the first person singular, " Theo said.

Maggie reached for his hand. After all, she had, twenty years ago, gone to the Dent Fair with Ron Hobson for no better reason than that he had a Yorkshire accent. Smiling, she said, "Come with me, Theo."

"Thank you," he replied.

The wheels touched ground. They were told to remain seated so that a wheelchair could be brought to the ramp. The other passengers stood up anxious for the door to open and release them to whatever life awaited them beyond the airport. Greg smiled. He was home. Marni had promised to meet them. Bertie was learning to live in another culture. His mother was happily occupied. He had not behaved badly after all, and next week strangers would come to his office bringing plans for devices that they hoped would make the world a better place. And maybe one of them would succeed.

ABOUT THE AUTHOR

Rachel Wyatt was born in England and moved to Canada with her family in 1957. She is the author of five novels, two works of short fiction, and has writen over a hundred radio dramas which have been produced by the CBC and BBC. She also writes for television and stage. In 2002 she was awarded the Order of Canada. She lives with her husband, Alan, in Victoria, BC.